Cat Girl's Day Off

KIMBERLY PAULEY

TU BOOKS

an imprint of Lee & Low Books Inc.

NEW YORK

To cat lovers everywhere
(especially the ones who have always wondered
what little Fluffy was *really* thinking)

♥

Copyright © 2012 by Kimberly Pauley
Front cover photograph of girl © Pansfun Images/Stocksy
Back cover photograph of cat © Asurobson/iStock
All rights reserved. No part of this book may be reproduced, transmitted, or stored in an information retrieval system in any form or by any means, electronic, mechanical, photocopying, recording, or otherwise, without written permission from the publisher.
TU BOOKS, an imprint of LEE & LOW BOOKS Inc.,
95 Madison Avenue, New York, NY 10016 | leeandlow.com
Manufactured in the United States of America by
Worzalla Publishing Company
Book design by Einav Aviram
Cover design by Abhi Alwar
Book production by The Kids at Our House
The text is set in Cochin

(HC) 10 9 8 7 6 5 4 3 2 1
(PB) 10 9 8 7 6 5 4 3 2 1
First Edition

Library of Congress Cataloging-in-Publication Data
Pauley, Kimberly, 1973-
Cat Girl's day off / Kimberly Pauley. — 1st ed. p. cm.
Summary: High schooler Natalie Ng has always kept secret her talent for talking with cats, but when she learns--from a cat—that a celebrity has been replaced by an imposter, she and her friends investigate, becoming movie extras to get the scoop.
ISBN 978-1-60060-883-4 (hardcover : alk. paper) | ISBN 978-1-64379-050-3 (paperback)
ISBN 978-1-60060-884-1 (epub) | ISBN 978-1-62014-247-9 (mobi)
[1. Human-animal communication--Fiction. 2. Cats — Fiction. 3. Motion pictures — Production and direction — Fiction. 4. High schools — Fiction. 5. Schools — Fiction. 6. Family life — Illinois — Chicago — Fiction. 7. Chicago (Ill.) — Fiction. 8. Mystery and detective stories.] I. Title.
PZ7.P278385Cat 2012
[Fic]--dc23
2011042997

MIX
Paper from
responsible sources
FSC
www.fsc.org   FSC® C002589

E A S T O N   W E S T ' S   B L O G

Wednesday, September 2, 6:02 A.M.: La, la! You read that right, little poppets! Six frickin' o'clock in the morning! What, you ask, could you possibly be doing up at such a god-awful hour, O Easton love?

There's only one thing that could get me up this early, poppets! And, no, that's not it! Get your minds out of the gutter! I am headed to LAX to wing my way out to the Windy City (that's Chicago, little ones . . . really, you should get out more) to watch a movie being born!

And not just any movie, but THE movie. Or, THE movie of next year (these things take time—think an elephant's gestation cycle, 'kay?) . . . *Freddy's Day Off*! Starring the one and only Ty McKenzie and good-girl-turned-diva Victoria Welling! (Is she really going to be the next big Hollywood starlet to melt down? I'll tell you here first!)

This promises to be a fun movie, since it's a takeoff on one of my personal faves, the classic teen movie *Ferris Bueller's Day*

Off, which was written and directed by the amazing John Hughes! Total homage to the great man, may he rest in peace. Ty's character is a loser nerd (ha, that'll be a stretch for him to pull off! Hey, makeup lady!) who decides to spice up his life by re-creating a day in the life of ultimate slacker Ferris Bueller.

I'm sure you'd like to know how I got an all-access pass to the set, but a girl's got to have her secrets. More soon! ♥

ONE

SUNDAY, SEPTEMBER 6, 5:46 P.M.

"NEVER LISTEN TO A CAT."
—NATALIE NG

I opened the front door to my house and gagged. The smell of something burnt beyond recognition enveloped me like a toxic cloud. Meep, my cat, was sitting by the door as if she had been waiting on me, which she probably had, since no one else paid any attention to her.

Someday, she yowled, *your mom is going to burn the entire house down.* Like I could do anything about it. Then she took off down the hall toward my room without bothering to see if I was going to reply. That's a cat for you—sometimes they just need to complain.

Though Meep had a point. My mom may be one of the ten smartest and Talented people on the planet, but she can't cook. At all. Actually, she can't do anything remotely domestic. I've been washing my own clothes since the time she turned my entire wardrobe pink back in the seventh grade.

I held my nose and went inside, almost running right into

3

my older sister, Viv, as she carried out a charred, smoking pot full of something vile and vaguely orange. Our would-be dinner, I supposed. Mom had been ambitious today.

"I've got it, Mom! Why don't you go work on your research paper? I'll take care of this," Viv yelled over her shoulder toward the kitchen. "Hey, Natalie." She nodded at me. "I didn't make it home in time to stop her. Can you boil some water for noodles? I'm going to throw away the risotto. And the pot."

"Is that what that was?" I tried to avoid looking at the wreckage—it would only make me lose my appetite.

"Yeah. Pumpkin risotto. She didn't stir it. Or cut up the pumpkin."

I let Viv by and went into the kitchen to start a pot of water. Mom had already disappeared into her office. The only days we ever ate a decent meal were when Viv came home from Northwestern and did the cooking. Sunday was supposed to be her day, but Mom often seemed to inconveniently forget and start her own disaster, fueled by weekend ambition or a badly timed cooking show.

Dad was almost as bad a cook as Mom, but at least he had the sense to order out when it was his turn. Mom didn't believe that there was anything she couldn't do and she ignored all failures—at least, her own. Hence the pumpkin risotto. If there were any way to cancel only the Food Network, we could probably save ourselves a fortune in spoiled cookware.

Emmy, my younger sister, came in and opened the window and the back door to air out the house. "It doesn't take a genius, you know," she said with a smirk.

"Ha ha." Not funny at all, considering Emmy has the current highest recorded IQ in the Western Hemisphere. And is twelve. And is two years ahead of me at Shermer High. She'd actually already be in college except Dad wanted to make sure she experienced "normal life." Like there's anything normal about being a twelve-year-old senior in high school, but whatever.

At least Emmy had only one officially recognized Talent (since supergeniusness didn't count), unlike Viv and her trifecta of superness: truth divination, levitation, and X-ray vision. All Class A Talents. It was no wonder Viv had followed in Dad's footsteps and was already working for the Bureau of Extrasensory Regulation and Management (or BERM) part time even though she was just a freshman in college. All Emmy could do was blend into her surroundings like a chameleon. It was Class B, but definitely a cool enough Talent that she'd probably get BERM attention as a covert-ops analyst or something someday, especially when you added in her smarts. She was a shoo-in, so long as they didn't expect a good personality.

Though, that chameleon thing was nearly as annoying as her supergeniusness. Let's face it: a know-it-all, bratty little sister who always won at hide-and-seek was a huge pain in the butt.

5

Of course, all of that completely trumped me and my Class D—as in totally dumb—Talent. I've even met cats that didn't want to talk to other cats. I was ranked right down there with the rest of the idiots with "party trick" Talents. BERM wouldn't want someone like me for anything more than hired entertainment at their annual Christmas celebration, telling the director how much his widdle Buddy-cat loved him.

Viv entered the kitchen like the super-efficient whirlwind she was, and spaghetti sauce was bubbling away in no time at all. Dad wandered in from work a few minutes before dinner was served. Weekends meant nothing to him—he usually worked Saturdays *and* Sundays. And given that he always came in right before dinner, no matter what time it was served, you'd think impeccable timing was his Talent, rather than hypersensitive olfactory perception with a side of chemical conductivity, which sounds really complex . . . and is. I think he was classified as an A Talent since even BERM didn't know what to call him. He worked for them now, so apparently they'd figured out a use for whatever it was he was good at other than sniffing out the chemical components in things.

Viv finally pried Mom out of her office by levitating her laptop into the dining room.

"You could have called me," Mom said as she kissed Dad on his bald spot on her way to her end of the table. He was still standing, but being that Mom's family was Nordic and he was Chinese, she had him by half a head at least. Pity I'd inherited Dad's height instead of hers.

Viv smiled sweetly and didn't mention the three times she had called Mom. Our mother was incredibly focused, but only on "important" things such as her research and Emmy's grades. Maybe it was her laser vision or maybe the fact that the rest of the world (other than Emmy) couldn't keep up with her brain, I don't know. But she simply couldn't seem to retain "extraneous" information. You know, stuff like birthdays and grocery lists.

"Everything smells good," said Dad. Given his olfactory prowess, he was obviously trying to be nice to Mom, since even I could still smell the lingering odor of burned pumpkin. Come to think of it, maybe that's why he always got home right before a meal—so he could miss the full brunt of Mom's disasters. He had an olfactory inhibitor, which he had invented when he was only six (naturally), but he didn't usually wear it at home. He said it made his nose itch. I think he didn't want to insult Mom.

We started eating. All you could hear for a good ten minutes was the clink of silverware and Emmy slurping noodles. It doesn't matter how smart you are when you're twelve. You're still twelve.

"So," said Mom, "what's the plan for school this week after the holiday break?" If Mom had her way, we wouldn't even get Labor Day off. Seriously. If she ruled the world, she probably wouldn't even give us weekends off.

That was our cue. Suck-up Emmy gave her report first, as always, then me, then Viv. Youngest to oldest. It wasn't like I had anything in particular to report anyway, but this was the one area of our lives that Mom meddled in. Constantly. You'd think she was the overachieving Asian parent instead of Dad.

"I've got a trig test this week. Should be a piece of cake," I said. That was a safe topic, since it's my best subject. I'm no supergenius like Emmy, but I could hold my own in trig.

"How about biology?" Mom asked.

"Fine," I said, stabbing a meatball. "Nothing to report." She would ask. I've had issues with Mr. Tollfinger since I refused to dissect a cat. I wasn't about to explain to him why, so I spent a week in detention. Mom told me to suck it up, basically. She didn't even go to bat for me with Principal Johnson. I mean, like I could disembowel someone I could have had a conversation with the day before? I don't think so. Personally, I think she was too ashamed to admit in public that any daughter of hers could have such a lame Talent.

"Are you sure about that?" asked Viv, all sweetness and light.

"*Yes.*" I glared at her. She could just keep her little lie detector Talent to herself, thank you very much.

"I liked Mr. Tollfinger," Viv continued. "He was a great teacher. I don't know why you have such problems with him."

"*Are* you having issues with your teacher, Natalie?" Mom

8

turned her steely gaze back to me. I bet she wished she had Viv's Talent. Laser vision was great in a lab, but it didn't help you weasel the truth out of your kids.

"No," I said again, ignoring Viv smirking around a mouthful of pasta. "Everything is *fine*. No problems at all. We're practically best friends."

"Hmmm. Let's keep it that way, shall we?" she said, and then turned her focus to Viv, who had apparently decided she'd tortured me enough for now. Or maybe she'd figured out that I was about two seconds away from kicking her under the table with my combat boots. Steel toed. So much more than a fashion statement.

It was like I wasn't even at the table anymore. You'd think being invisible was actually my Talent. Actually, that would be cool. That's got to be a Class A or B at least. Though with my luck, I'd probably get, like, half invisibility or it would only work every other Tuesday or something and I'd just be a Class C.

"Genevieve," continued Mom, "how is your job at the BERM treating you? Not interfering with your school work, is it?"

"Everything's good. I heard I might be getting a promotion to field agent, and they'd like me to go full time during summer." Viv took a dainty sip of her water. If I had a water-based Talent like one girl I knew from school, I could have made Viv choke on her drink or given her a wicked case of the burps. Maybe not useful, but definitely satisfying. "And my social psych professor asked if I would be willing to do an in-class demonstration of my lie detection."

Well, isn't that nice. My Talent makes my biology teacher detest me. Viv's gets her the star treatment. I rolled my eyes as Viv shot me another smarmy grin when Mom wasn't looking. My friends were so lucky they didn't have any siblings, especially ones with annoying Talents.

I grabbed two breadsticks from the basket and considered holding them out from my head like antennae, but decided not to bother. No one would notice anyway. Dad was deep into a discussion with Viv about some top secret BERM stuff. They were even whispering. Mom and Emmy were talking quarks or string theory or I don't know what.

If Emmy was Mom's favorite, Viv was Dad's. They spoke the same language. The only one in our family that speaks my language is Meep.

Speaking of the furry little devil in disguise, Meep sauntered into the room, licking her lips. *Nice sauce*, she said. *A little heavy on the garlic, though.* Like most cats, she was never one to let an opportunity pass. Viv must have left the lid off the pot.

"You better not have left a mess," I whispered down to her as she jumped in my lap.

Me? she said. *Of course not.* She grinned a wicked cat grin up at me. I knew what that meant. She'd marked her territory. Somewhere in the pot was at least one cat hair, not to mention cat saliva. Why did cats have to do that? I made a mental note to skip the leftovers.

I stuck one breadstick upright in my spaghetti and took a big bite out of the other one as Meep settled into my lap. *Did you bother telling your mom you got an A+ on your English paper?* I shrugged and kept on chewing. *Or that your art teacher picked your project to display in the case during Parents' Night last week?*

I swallowed my bite and hissed at Meep, "Give it a rest, would you?" She's always on me to be more "involved," like that's something a cat knows anything about. I swear sometimes that she's half dog. She's the only cat I know who's more interested in people (i.e., me) than in other cats.

Besides, Mom and Dad had both gone to Parents' Night, but neither of them had noticed my artwork. They had, of course, been all over Emmy's science project. Well, them and a reporter from the Chicago Tribune. I guess isolating some kind of isotope in a high-school lab is bigger news than an interpretation of some of Leonardo da Vinci's mathematical concepts using a vector-based fractal program. But whatever.

"Dennis," said Mom, "did you know that the school is allowing a movie to be filmed during school hours?" Both of her eyebrows went up and she set down her fork. Bad news. "Emmaline told me that they actually moved her calculus quiz to next week because they are being forced to vacate their classroom and work in the library!"

Ooooooo, said Meep. *What a crisis for poor widdle Emmy! Call the papers! Alert the police! Something must be done!*

I totally snorked the sip of water I was drinking. See,

Meep gets me even if no one else does. I scratched her in her favorite spot by her left ear.

"No," said Dad, barely looking up from his tête-à-tête with Viv. "I wasn't aware of—"

"Well, we'll just see about it," said Mom. "It's absolutely scandalous that they're even considering interfering with our child's education for something so frivolous! Besides, couldn't they have just filmed during Labor Day?"

Great. Mom was on a crusade, though it was obvious that she was worried about only one of our educations. I didn't bother mentioning to her that they already were filming this weekend, or the possibility that Melly, one of my best friends, was probably going to sign up as an extra and there was a good chance I'd be dragged along. That counted as extraneous information anyway, right?

I volunteered for dish duty so I could make a faster exit and check for any telltale Meep mess in the kitchen. Viv actually cleans as she cooks, so it's super easy on her nights. (Have I mentioned how totally flawless she is? I swear she never even gets pimples.) And Emmy thinks she's the smart one. Now it would be her turn when Mom cooked, and she'd be scrubbing for hours.

TWO

"THE CAT IS ABOVE ALL THINGS,
A DRAMATIST."—MARGARET BENSON

I headed over to my friend Oscar's house as soon as I finished washing the dishes, leaving the rest of the family to a rousing game of extreme science trivia. Melly was already camped out in Oscar's bedroom. It was our unofficial headquarters since Oscar's parents didn't mind a little mess and noise. They were both artists. My house was supergeek central (literally) and Melly's dad liked everything to be perfect, as in *perfectly* clean and quiet. He'd been like that since Melly's mom died back in fifth grade, like he had to be both a dad and an übermom too. We came to Oscar's so we could let loose a little.

"Nat! You're finally here! Let the drooling commence!" Oscar hugged me and then spun around in circles with his arms spread wide. "I cannot believe Ty McKenzie and Victoria Welling are going to be at our school this week. *Filming.* I swear, I'm going to faint as soon as I see them." Oscar collapsed theatrically onto his bed, his Hello Kitty pillow clutched to his chest. "Preferably, right into Ty's arms."

I laughed. "I'm pretty sure Ty doesn't swing that way."

Melly, my slightly saner best friend, threw a teddy bear at Oscar. "You better not make a scene," she said. "This is totally my chance to be discovered. You think, Nat?"

I snorted, but she was right. With her light brown hair strategically streaked honey blonde, delicate porcelain complexion, practically anime-sized eyes, and curves in all the right places, Melly was nearly fairy-tale beautiful. If I didn't love her, I'd have to hate her. She was way prettier than that Victoria Welling actress. Not to mention, Melly could actually act. As far as I could tell from Victoria's last movie, she ought to be playing Pinocchio. As in, someone made of wood.

"We *have* to be extras. You guys are going to sign up with me, right?" Melly looked from me to Oscar and back again.

"Of course!" I said, trying to sound enthusiastic. Not that I remotely wanted to be involved with the whole movie thing. Even though my best friends were complete and total attention hogs, I wasn't. My invisibility "talent" worked for me in school just like at home. I was perfectly happy that almost no one at Shermer High even knew my name.

But I wasn't too worried. The chance of me actually getting picked as an extra was pretty slim. Short, flat-chested, half-Chinese chicks with purple streaks in their hair? I've yet to see one of those in a movie that wasn't animated. And come to think of it, even the animated characters usually weren't all that flat chested. Melly, on the other hand, was a shoo-in, and

Oscar could probably talk his way into anything, even with his crazy Asian-dude-with-attitude hair and non-mainstream fashion sense. I was perfectly happy to cheer them on from the sidelines.

Though usually where I found myself was right in the middle of whatever scheme Oscar had cooked up. Some of the kids at school called us the Vienna Finger, with Melly being the cream-colored filling to our Asian yellowness. I never have figured out whether they mean it nicely or not. Of course, they might also be referring to the Halloween that Oscar had made us come to school dressed as a three-part cookie. The theory had been good, but he'd neglected to consider the fact that we wouldn't be attached at the hip. I'd wandered around school all day looking like a piece of cardboard.

Oscar flipped open his laptop and began clicking like a madman. I groaned, but Melly clapped her hands. It was time for the Oscar Report, whether I wanted to listen to it or not. He was more reliable (and sensationalistic) than CNN.

"Quit your bellyaching," said Oscar. "You know you wanna know."

"Not so much," I said, and went to sit down on his desk chair, even though it was covered in clothes. Melly climbed on the bed and leaned over his shoulder. Oscar was certifiably addicted to celebrity dirt and she was his all-too-willing audience. She claimed it would help her with her acting, but I couldn't see how. What would knowing which teen actress was getting drunk or what the stars were wearing on the red carpet do for her career?

"So, who do you want to hear about first?" asked Oscar. He wiggled his eyebrows suggestively. "Victoria or Ty?"

"Can't we talk about something else tonight?" I said, not completely managing to keep the whine out of my voice. "We could complain about our families." Or maybe we could talk about a certain somebody in my trig class. I could use some advice, but definitely just from Melly. She was much luckier in the love department than either Oscar or me. Okay, technically Oscar had had more boyfriends than me too, but his last breakup had been pretty rough.

Oscar looked at me like I was insane. "Victoria and Ty are going to physically be in our high school tomorrow. *Tomorrow.*" He paused for a moment to take a deep breath. "In our school. We have to prepare!"

"But—"

"Come on, Nat, this is really important," Melly said. "I need to know *everything*. You never know what will give you a foot in the door in this business." She was practically batting her eyelashes at me. Oh, for heaven's sake.

"Yeah, you can moan about your mom any time," said Oscar. "She's always good for it. How often do famous people come to *our* school?"

"Oh, all right," I said. They were too worked up about the movie thing anyway, even though they hadn't talked about anything else for weeks. I would be glad when it was all over. Maybe I could figure something out about Ian on my own anyway. At least I was able to talk to him without stammering now. I'd barely been able to look in his direction the first week of trig class, and I sat right next to him. I hadn't been able to take notes on anything Mr. Beck had written on the left side of the white board that whole week.

"Woot! Okay, where was I?" said Oscar.

"Ty," Melly said, grabbing my hand and pulling me over onto the bed.

"Uh-uh," said Oscar, and gave us his evil grin. "Let's save the beefcake for last, shall we? Let's talk Victoria Welling!" He pushed the laptop screen back a little so we could both see it. "According to this article, Victoria has turned into a diva with a capital D, just like Easton West was saying on her site last week. Victoria actually had a five-page list of demands that the directors had to agree to before she signed on to *Freddy's Day Off*. Total prima donna." He pointed at the screen. "I mean, look at this. She actually insisted on having an entire house rented for her in the suburbs so she could 'really feel what it was like to live near Chicago' and prepare for her role. But not just any house. One with"—he peered at the screen—"at least two floors and a finished basement, plus a home security system and minimum seven-foot-tall privacy fence. Oh, and a pool. Who even has a pool here? It's *Chicago*. We have *winter*. It's September and it's already, like, 50 degrees."

Melly pointed to something farther down the screen.

17

"Not to mention getting some special brand of Japanese spring water flown in."

Oscar batted her hand away. "I was getting to that!"

"Maybe she bathes in it," I said. Oscar and Melly both looked at me. "What?" Why did they even care about this stuff? She could drink rainwater from Argentina for all I cared.

"Anyway," said Oscar, "I think Easton came out here to chronicle Victoria's meltdown. That's what she's best at, being there when an actor goes down. She was there when Rory Barnes bit the dust. Remember that? Victoria's probably, like, one step away from shaving her head." He rubbed his hands together. "I cannot wait for school. We're going to have front row seats! This movie is the best thing to happen to us in, like, *ever*."

That was probably the first I'd ever heard Oscar looking forward to school since the eighth grade, when he wanted to show off his first pair of combat boots. "I still don't see why they want to film at Shermer High," I said. "It's such a lame school. Why aren't they filming at one of the schools in the city?" It wasn't like Shermer even had a cool building. It was mostly prison-issue concrete block all the way. Usually, the high schools shown in movies were all brick or some kind of imposing historical building. Not that I'd ever seen one like that in real life, but presumably they existed somewhere. Maybe downtown.

"D'oh!" said Oscar and flipped a big *L* for "loser" at me.

"Haven't you been paying any attention? They have to film it here for authenticity. The story totally wouldn't work if they didn't film it here."

"Authenticity?" We'd watched *Ferris Bueller's Day Off* a few times over the years and I liked it okay, but I didn't see what the connection was.

Oscar looked at Melly. "One of the best teen movies of ALL TIME," he said to her, "and the girl doesn't pay any attention at all."

"What?" Yeesh, it's just a movie. Sometimes, I really didn't get them. It had been a lot easier back in elementary school when Melly had first moved here and Oscar and I had adopted her. We had been united in our hatred of boy bands back then.

"Shermer High is where John Hughes filmed parts of *Ferris Bueller's Day Off*! Didn't you ever notice while you were watching it with us that parts of the school looked really, really familiar?"

"*The Breakfast Club* too!" chimed in Melly. I assumed that was another movie I hadn't paid enough attention to. Was it too much to ask to just watch a movie for entertainment, rather than dissect it for career advancement?

"Sorry I asked," I mumbled.

"Hey, what's this about Easton?" asked Melly, looking at a *News of the Weird* headline. Praise poodles. At least we could get off of my shortcomings in movie knowledge now.

"Omigod! Did I not show you that yet? It's awesome!

Just watch. Funniest thing I've seen in forever!" Oscar launched the video and waved his hand at the screen like a magician. He was in full-on Oscar mode.

I recognized the hotel from walking past it whenever we go to Millennium Park downtown. The York? Something like that. It had these huge marble columns and they always rolled out an actual red carpet on the sidewalk so that visiting famous people wouldn't get their feet dirty or something.

Some tourist must have been taking the video while on an architecture tour of the city because at first, all you could hear was some boring tour guide droning on about the stonework and Grecian columns. Then someone said, "There's a limo! Who is that? Is it someone famous?" and the picture swerved way too fast to finally focus on a limousine at the curb. The doorman stepped forward and opened the car door, and the first thing that came out was a pair of hot-pink stilettos attached to some really long legs. Like, legs for days.

"Easton West," whispered Oscar reverently. Like we couldn't tell from her signature shoes. She was known for three things: her pink shoes (actually, pink everything, but especially the shoes), her ability to out-scoop major newspapers on her blog, and her lavish, jet-setting lifestyle. She'd been heiress-rich even before she became famous.

Easton climbed out of the limo with a fluffy yapper dog tucked under one arm. It was barking its head off. I couldn't blame it. It had been dyed the same shade of bright pink as

Easton's hair and shoes. She should be arrested for animal cruelty.

Then she leaned in the car, giving the videographer a gratuitous shot of her butt, and came back out pulling a leash. On the other end of the leash was a really, really pissed off cat, also dyed bright pink. As soon as Easton yanked it out of the car, it went totally mental. If the cat hadn't had little pink plastic things on every claw, Easton's entire body would have been bloody. She juggled the dog and the cat while everyone stood by and shouted out not so helpful advice. She finally threw both of her pets at the chauffeur and went shrieking into the York. The crowd applauded and the video ended.

"Is that not to die for? I mean, I love Easton, but that's pure awesome," said Oscar. "It's totally going viral."

"Wait," I said, "can you play it again? And turn up the volume?"

"Sure, I could watch that over and over." Oscar hit play again and cranked up the sound. When it got to the part with the cat, I leaned forward.

Help me! screamed the cat. *Helllllppp me! Kill the imposter!*

"Crapola," I said.

"What is it?" asked Melly. "What's the cat saying?"

Melly and Oscar were some of the very few people outside my family who knew my secret. Basically, the only people who knew I could talk to cats were my two best friends, my family, and some poor schmo who filed the registry paperwork over in Washington at the BERM. What a waste of paperwork. What good is being able to talk to cats? I'd really rather we all pretended my Talent didn't exist. After all, the rest of my family had Talent to spare.

"Play it again," I said, and then repeated back for them the rest of what the cat had said.

What's wrong with you people? This isn't Easton West. This is not my person! Save us! Stop barking and bite her, Fergie! Do I have to do everything myself? Stop laughing, you cretins! You there, fat man, drop the camera! Help us! She'll kill us all!

"Not so funny now, huh, Oscar?"

Oscar dropped his laptop and dived off the bed and half-way into his book bag. He came up with his cell phone and punched three numbers. I don't think I'd ever seen him move that fast.

"What are you doing?" I asked.

"What do you think? Calling 911! We have to tell the authorities! Easton West has been murdered!"

"Are you crazy?" I tackled him and grabbed the phone as a voice came on saying, "9-1-1. What is your emergency?"

"So sorry," I said into the phone. "Wrong number." I hung up the phone and glared at Oscar. He glared back at me.

"Hold on, you guys," said Melly, holding one palm out to each of us. Always the mediator. "Nat, are you sure that's what the cat said?" I just looked at her. Why would I make that up? "Okay," she continued. "Then why shouldn't we call the police?"

I took a deep breath. "Okay, for one thing, how do we even know the cat is telling the truth? It's a cat. Cats lie. That's what they do." Sometimes it seemed like every other thing out of Meep's mouth was a lie . . . or a thinly veiled attempt at scoring some tuna. "Two, what are you going to say to the police? That you think some famous blogger has been murdered or abducted because a cat said so?"

"Yeah, but your Talent—" said Oscar.

"Is not something I want broadcasted around." We all knew what had happened to Jonas Smith, the kid who could kiss frogs and turn them different colors. Word about his Talent got out and no one has talked to him since—except to call him Frog Boy. I have no desire to lower my social rank even further into Cat Girl territory.

"But we have to do something!" Oscar grabbed his phone back but held it without dialing. Then it rang. Oscar looked at the caller ID and dropped the phone like it was on fire. "It's the police," he whispered, like they could hear him even though he hadn't answered the phone.

I grabbed the phone and answered it. "Hello?" I said as calmly as I could while motioning at Oscar to shut up and stop whimpering. Melly clamped a hand over his mouth.

A woman's voice came on the line. "Someone dialed 911 from this number and we're calling to confirm that no emergency is in progress. Is everything okay?"

"Sorry, that was us. I mean, me. I, uh, butt dialed by accident. I'm really sorry. It won't happen again."

"Please see that it doesn't." *Click.*

I threw the phone back at Oscar. "Great," I said. "Now the police have your number. If you ever really need 911, you're screwed."

"Whatever," he said, and shook off Melly's hand. She wiped it on his furry purple bedspread. "We're talking about Easton West!" He flopped back on his bed and nearly landed on his laptop. "And you know what? She hasn't put up a new blog post in days, since that one about coming here to Chicago. That's not like her at all! She usually posts at least once a day. I think the cat is right. Something has happened to her."

"Cats are known to exaggerate," I said. "Just like you, Oscar, only they're furrier, and with worse breath. Besides, what're we supposed to do about it? We're teenagers. Even if we did tell someone, they wouldn't believe us."

"What about your parents?" asked Melly.

"What about them?" My Class A Talented, supergenius, overachieving parents with their two super-Talented daughters: Genevieve and Emmaline. My Talent was not something we ever talked about, either in or out of the family. I'd met one of Mom's coworkers once and she hadn't even known there was a third daughter in our family because all Mom talked about were the cool things Emmy and Viv were always doing.

"Couldn't you . . ." Melly trailed off and then smiled apologetically at me. She's met my mom. At least her dad supports her. He even schlepped her around to acting classes in the city. She'd been to every Broadway play that ever opened in town. I sometimes wondered if my parents even remembered my middle name—and they'd given it to me.

"We have to do *something*." Oscar looked about as distraught as I'd ever seen him. Even more than the time his favorite dancer got kicked off of that celebrity dancing show, and he'd lost his TV privileges for a month then because of how crazy he'd driven his parents over the whole thing.

"We'll submit an anonymous tip. How about that?" Melly asked. "Then they can at least check it out, right?" Melly looked so pleased with herself at coming up with a solution that I didn't argue, even though it sounded like a stupid idea to me. Not that I'm an expert on Easton West or anything, but the person in the video looked exactly like her. Either the cat was lying or something weird was going on. I didn't see how the cops could possibly tell.

Melly used her cell phone since she had a blocked number because her dad was both anal and overprotective. She called the main police number instead of 911 and used her best adult voice, the same one that she'd used for the part of the weirdo mother in *The Glass Menagerie* last year. "Yes, I'd like to report some foul play," she said.

Oscar, back in good humor again now that someone was doing something, clucked and flapped his arms like a chicken. "*Fowl* play, get it?" he whispered. Melly and I ignored him.

"I believe that Easton West, the celebrity blogger, has

been"—she faltered a minute and then recovered—"is in danger or has been hurt. I—um—am concerned for her safety." She answered a few more questions, and then it seemed like the police officer was getting a little suspicious. The officer wanted to know how Melly knew Easton, why the blogger was in town, what their relationship was, and all kinds of other things that Melly, of course, didn't know how to answer. The police probably thought it was some kind of weird prank call. Not that I blamed them. I mean, "Hello, police, someone I don't know anything about might possibly be in danger. Can you please go check on it?" How much more vague and stalkery can you get?

Finally, Melly faked a bad connection and hung up the phone.

"I think they bought it," she said.

"Awesome sauce!" said Oscar. "Now that we've got that out of the way, how about we talk Ty?" I didn't have the heart to tell Oscar the possibility of the police believing Melly was worse than my chances of winning an Academy Award.

EASTON WEST'S BLOG

Sunday, September 6, 10:35 P.M.: To whoever it was out there in crazy Internet land who apparently cannot live for a few days without the stellar wisdom of Easton West, I AM FINE. If, in the future, I ever happen to not post something for a few days, how about we restrain ourselves a little and NOT CALL THE POLICE?

I am in Chicago and busy hanging with the ultrafab Victoria Welling. She's my new bestie, and all those rumors about her being a total diva are a complete exaggeration. More soon. I've got all kinds of plans for the city — Millennium Park and that famous Bean sculpture, a Chicago-style hot dog, and drinks at the John Hancock. ♥

THree

"NO ONE OWNS A CAT. HUMANS
MERELY BORROW OUR TIME."—MEEP

I woke up to the sound of my cell phone screeching "Born this Way" by Lady Gaga. Oscar had custom selected that ringtone for himself on my phone. I glanced at the clock and fumbled around for my cell, nearly knocking it off my bedside table into a pile of dirty clothes. What in the world was he doing calling me so early on a holiday?

"This better be good," I said as I answered the phone.

"Get dressed. You have five minutes." He hung up.

What? Did somebody die? Did tickets to something go on sale? I considered going back to sleep, but I was awake now anyway. I pulled on a pair of comfortable jeans, a red and white plaid shirt, and a hoodie and went downstairs.

Dad nodded at me as he slowly chewed a bite of his standard breakfast: plain oatmeal with butter and salt. I think he liked it because it was so bland, though he was always saying that nothing's bland, not when you can really smell it. I nodded back at him, grabbed three store-bought (and therefore safe) blueberry muffins and stuck them in my backpack along with a few bottles of water. If I was doomed to wait in line for tickets to some show, I was going to be prepared.

"I'm going out with Oscar and Melly," I said to him. He nodded again and kept reading the paper. "Be back, oh, tomorrow or the next day. Maybe Friday."

"Have fun," Dad said with a little smile, and turned the page.

Yep, Invisible Girl, that's me. Who said I had only one Talent?

I went outside and sat down on the front porch to wait for Oscar and Melly. I didn't have to wait long. Melly's Volvo (her dad picked it out—highest safety rating for its class, whatever that means) came roaring around the corner in a manner I'm sure her dad never intended. Why Melly ever let Oscar drive is a mystery to me, but maybe she was hoping he'd get in a fender bender so she could get a new car. She really wanted a Prius, like all the conspicuously eco-conscious Hollywood people were driving now.

"Get in!" Oscar yelled out the window as he slammed on the brakes.

I hopped in the back. "Where're we off to? I brought muffins."

"We're going downtown to the York," said Oscar as he sped off. "We're going to save Easton West, if she's still alive to be saved."

"Are you insane?" I looked from him to Melly. "Melly, you're not seriously going to let Oscar drive your car downtown. That's just suicide."

"Don't be silly," said Oscar. "I'm not that crazy. We're going to take the train."

I was still arguing with him when he pulled into the Metra station. He parked the car, got out, and opened the door to the back seat. For once, his timing was perfect. The train was pulling into the station. He must have actually looked at a schedule.

". . . And it's a stupid idea," I finished. Oscar sighed and shook his head, then picked me up and slung me over his shoulder. I tried poking him in the ribs as he carried me to the train, but his jacket was so covered in the patches that he'd collected while traveling that he didn't even feel it. I wasn't even close to being able to fight my way to the ground. Unlike me, he'd lucked out in the half-Asian birth lottery and was tall like his standard-issue white-bread dad. It was completely unfair. His Japanese mom was even shorter than I was.

"Melly," I said, "do something!" I glared at her from my upside-down vantage point.

"I am," she said, and grabbed my book bag and her purse. Traitor. She's usually much saner than Oscar, but if she had one weakness, it was for anything related to Hollywood.

Oscar dumped me into a seat in the back of a mostly

empty train car. "Here's the deal," he said, pulling out his train pass and sticking it in the ticket holder on the back of the seat. "Easton posted last night that the police came and checked on her and that she's peachy keen and everybody should get a grip."

"Okay, good." I couldn't see why that necessitated a trip into the city.

"No, *not* good. If you read Easton like I do—"

"Religiously," interrupted Melly. I snickered, but Oscar ignored us.

"—then you'd know that this latest post had to have been written by an impostor. It doesn't sound anything like her at all! The impostor may have fooled the police, but she hasn't fooled me!"

"Oscar, maybe she was just stressed or something . . . or pissed. Wouldn't you be pissed if the police came knocking on your door?" I knocked lightly on Oscar's head, but he just shook me off.

"But that's not all," he said. "She wrote that she was going to go eat a hot dog. Chicago style." He looked at me triumphantly.

"Um, so? Lots of people do that when they come to visit Chicago. It's one of the things the city is known for—hot dogs, Italian beefs, and those gross tamales."

"Yeah, but she's been an ovo-lacto vegetarian since July. There's no way she'd eat a *hot dog*. She's morally opposed."

"What, she'll dye her dog and cat bright pink but she won't eat a hot dog?" We were pulling into Morton Grove station. I wondered if I should make a run for it.

"She dyed them pink in support of breast cancer awareness," said Oscar. "For serious."

"Tickets?" asked a train conductor.

"All the way to Union Station," said Melly. She and I handed over some money while Oscar waved impatiently at his pass. The conductor pulled out two tickets for us and handed them over, humming a little tune as he went on to the next passenger.

The interruption gave me a moment to think. I didn't really believe the breast cancer thing. I've read Easton's blog a few times and she seemed like your standard airhead gossipmonger to me. But Oscar never failed to amaze me. He really and truly buys into the whole celebrity thing. It's like his religion.

"Well, maybe she couldn't hack being a vegetarian," I said. "It's been, what, two months since she switched? She probably started craving meat and you missed the big announcement. What does it matter anyway? We can't do anything about it." The train pulled out again. I rested my forehead against the window and watched the station disappear. I really should have gotten off.

"I do remember reading about the vegetarian thing," said Melly. "The whole thing seems pretty suspicious, Nat. I read the post and she even talked up Victoria like they're best friends. When does she ever do that? About a girl, anyway."

"Maybe she's realized what a snot she is and decided she

needs more women friends."

Oscar snorted but then turned serious. "You have to do something," he said. "It's your duty."

"It's *my* duty? What are you talking about?" I turned away from the window to look at him.

Oscar tapped the seat in front of him for emphasis. "You've seen *Spider-Man*," he said. "'With great power comes great responsibility.' It's your *duty* to do something about Easton. You're the only one on the planet who could've seen that video and known something was wrong. That's kismet."

He had to be freaking kidding me. "Oh, come on, Oscar. This is real life, not a movie. And I am so not a superhero. It was just a stupid video. I'm sure Easton's fine. Maybe she even staged the whole attack as some weird kind of publicity stunt."

I had to admit that evidence to the contrary had piled up a bit, but still. What am I supposed to do about it? And why should I care about some stupid celebrity blogger? If I passed her on the street, she probably wouldn't even notice me unless she had something snarky to say about my hair.

Oscar stared at me, his brown eyes wide and unblinking. Melly cleared her throat and said, "Nat," like she was disappointed in me. She hated it when we fought. Not that it was really a fight. It was just Oscar being typical crazy Oscar. I was surprised, honestly, that he was still going on about the whole Easton thing. Normally, he'd have moved on to whatever the news of the day was.

I turned away and sat there staring out the window as

the suburbs turned into city, Oscar letting out a not so quiet *humph* every five minutes or so. He was going to be insufferable, I could tell. Maybe if I humored him for a while, he'd lose interest and Melly could stop acting like me being the sane one was a bad thing.

"Okay, okay," I finally said as we were pulling into Union Station. "What's the plan?"

"Um . . . ," said Oscar. Great. That meant there was no plan. Normal Oscar operating procedure.

"Fine," I said. "Let's get to the York and see what we can find out." At least it wasn't far from Union Station, probably about halfway between the station and Grant Park. The chances of us actually running into Easton seemed pretty slim to me. She was probably living it up on the town right now, if she wasn't sleeping in after partying last night. I figured we'd go, hang out in the lobby for a while, and go home. Then Oscar'd have to get off my back about it because at least we'd have tried.

I'd never been in the lobby of the York before, but it looked pretty much exactly how I imagined it would: fancy. Like, living-room-of-the-rich-and-famous kind of fancy. The only way the three of us would have stood out more is if we had walked in on our hands. My ratty hoodie made me look like a homeless person comparatively, and Oscar looked more like a street performer than a guest. At least Melly looked as beautiful as always. Maybe people would think she belonged. We sat down on one of the posh leather sofas and tried to look inconspicuous.

Oscar picked up a magazine from a side table and held it up in front of his face. Upside down. "See anything?" he stage whispered as his eyes panned back and forth across the room.

"No," I answered back in a normal tone of voice, though I did see the concierge, an older guy with dark gray hair and the tiniest mustache I'd ever seen, staring at us suspiciously. Yes! We were going to get kicked out of here in no time at all. I restrained myself from cheering.

"I'll watch the elevators," said Melly. She picked up a fashion magazine too, right-side up, and pretended to read.

Oscar flipped magazine pages abnormally fast as his head swiveled back and forth from the front door to the entrance to the hotel's bar, The Sax. He looked like he could take flight at any minute. I watched the concierge, who watched Oscar. A few minutes later, Oscar's craziness got to be too much for the poor guy. He walked our way with that look that adults get when they're about to do something unpleasant. We'd been kicked out of places before, but never quite as fast. It had to be a record. Goes to show what a fancy place it was.

I smiled helpfully at the concierge as he strode purposefully in our direction. Oscar hadn't even noticed him yet.

Then Melly let out a little gasp. "It's her!" she said and nearly dropped her magazine. I turned to look at the elevator and she was right. Of all the dumb luck. There was Easton—or whoever it was who looked and sounded exactly like Easton—click clacking out of the elevator in some neon-pink Jimmy Choos.

"Oh, Richie!" Easton sat down on the edge of the concierge desk, crossed her legs, and started jiggling her toe up and down. "Where do you think you're going? I have a problem here!" She snapped her fingers.

The concierge had stopped short as soon as she'd called out his name. The look on his face went from slightly displeased to absolute horror. Then he straightened his shoulders, wiped the terror-stricken look off of his face, put on a smarmy smile, and turned around to face Easton. "On my way, Ms. West," he said brightly and headed over to her.

Easton frowned at him. "There are only five towels in my room. We talked about this."

"My apologies, Ms. West, I'll—"

"And the tulips are *wilted*."

"So sorry, I'll—"

"Not to mention the lack of bubble bath."

"I'll have—"

"And where's my dog walker? She should have been here five minutes ago! Do I have to do everything myself? What am I paying you people for anyway?"

The concierge snapped his fingers at a uniformed hotel guy who was standing by the front desk. "You!" he said. "Bring some towels, fresh flowers, bubble bath, and chocolates up to room 2930 right away." He turned back to Easton. "I'm sure the dog walker will be here momentarily, Ms. West. I'll call to check. Is there anything else I can do for you?"

"No," she said icily. She hopped off the desk and walked to the elevator, clearing her throat and looking pointedly at the concierge. He leaped forward and pushed the elevator button for her. Easton didn't bother to say thank you or anything else to him; she just tapped her toe until the bell dinged. Then she got in and left.

Wow. What a total witch.

"That can't be the real *Easton*," Oscar hissed, his eyebrows drawn down to a point between his eyes. "I know Easton and she's nowhere near that cranky."

I don't know about that. He'd been reading her blog to us for a while and she always sounded kind of snarky to me, but maybe not quite so evil-rude. Her brand of snark usually seemed more clever than mean. Maybe Oscar was right.

What was I *thinking*? Oscar was *not* right.

The concierge was still standing there staring at the elevator door, just breathing and standing, probably trying not to slam his fist into the wall. I hoped he wouldn't remember us right away. I wanted to be thrown out, but not by anyone in that frame of mind.

Oscar dropped the magazine and turned to me. "We have to find out what happened to Easton. We have to save her if she's not dead. We can't let that impostor take over her life."

"Maybe she's possessed," I said. "Or maybe she's got a concrete wedgie."

Melly snorted.

Oscar ignored me. "Okay," he said. "I've got a plan. The only way to find out the truth is to talk to Easton's cat. So we have to get Nat up to her room."

"How are we going to do that?" asked Melly.

"Yeah, I'm not about to go knocking on her door," I said.

"Oh yes, you are," said Oscar. "You're going to be the dog walker."

Four

"THE CAT WHO FRIGHTENS THE MICE AWAY IS
AS GOOD AS THE CAT WHO EATS THEM."
—GERMAN PROVERB

"The dog walker?" I shook my head at Oscar, but he just blinked innocently at me, batting those long eyelashes of his. There had to be a way out of this mess. "In case you hadn't noticed, the concierge was about to kick us out. There's no way he's letting us in the elevator." I nodded at the concierge, who had wandered over to the front desk. He looked like he was retelling the horror story that was Easton to a desk clerk, but he kept glancing over in our direction. He was probably spoiling for a fight after his run-in.

"I'll take care of him," said Melly. "Just let me turn on my Marilyn Monroe. Or maybe more Hannah Montana gone bad. He looks like he might be more into skeevy than sexy. You guys just go do your thing." She stood up, tossed her hair a few times, and strutted toward the concierge. A group of businessmen came in at the same time and approached the front desk to check in. All of the desk clerks became suddenly busy helping them. Was the world conspiring against me?

"Okay," said Oscar. "Let's go."

"Wait," I said. "What if he's not into jailbait?" I mean, Melly is beautiful, but she doesn't look a day over sixteen.

Oscar snorted and grabbed my hand. He pulled me to the elevator and pushed the button.

I looked back. Amazingly, Melly already had Richie practically eating out of her hand. He was smiling and laughing as she leaned in toward him and twirled some of her hair around her finger. Dirty old man.

The bell dinged and the elevator doors opened. Oscar pushed me in before I could say another word, and then he hit the button for the twenty-ninth floor. The doors opened again on the right floor before I could even finish protesting.

"I'll keep watch and hold the elevator. You go and talk to the cat." Oscar pushed me out in the direction of the suite.

I followed the signs and stopped in front of room 2930. No one was around. I could not believe I was about to do this. Taking a step back, I looked at the elevators. Oscar waved and gave me a thumbs-up.

The things I do for my friends. I knocked on the door.

Nothing happened.

Did I have the wrong room number? I knocked again and this time the door flew open. Easton, cell phone glued to her ear, stared at me blankly. Her pink hair was standing on end like she'd just pulled on it. "What?" she demanded. "What do you want?"

"Uh, dog walker?" I said.

She waved me in the room. It was more like a mini apartment than a normal hotel room. At least, not like any hotel room that I'd ever been in. The front part was a living room, complete with leather couches and a fancy marble-topped coffee table. Off to one side was a kitchenette with marble counters. A door to the left was open and I could see an unmade bed with pink clothes heaped on top of it and a trail of pink shoes leading to it. The rumors were true. She really did wear nothing but pink.

The dog was sitting on the couch, looking at me expectantly. She looked like a furry pink cupcake, lime-green leash already attached. A plastic pink cat carrier was sitting on the floor by the couch. Easton walked by it and the cat let out a bloodcurdling screech that made both of us jump. Easton kicked at the carrier. The cat hissed.

Just wait until I get out of here. You are going down, human!

I had no idea how I was going to talk to the cat with Easton in the room. Even if she went into the bedroom, she would still be able to hear me. It's not like I could communicate with them telepathically or anything. I walked slowly over to the dog and made a show of petting it and calling it silly dog names while I looked at the cat out of the corner of my eye. The cat hadn't bothered to even look at me yet; he was keeping a baleful glare focused on Easton. Considering how bugged-out his eyes were, I wondered how she could ignore him at all. He had to be one of those fancy breed cats that always win at cat shows.

"I don't care what time you do it, just do it," she spat into the phone. "I want it done yesterday. And stay out of the upstairs!" She paced near the carrier again and the cat let out another howl and tried in vain to swipe at her ankle. "Freaking cat!" screamed Easton. "Watch it, you mangy bag of fur! I'm going to toss you out that window!"

"Um," I said.

Easton whirled on me and pulled the phone slightly away from her ear. "What?" she said. "You got a problem?" She took a step toward me like she was ready to throw me out the window too.

"No. Just—would you like me to walk the cat too? I can take them both if you want." That's when the cat finally noticed me. He crammed his face up against the door of his carrier and stopped hissing.

Easton looked at me a minute. "Sure, yeah, whatever. Get him out of my face." She began pacing again, giving one more kick to the side of the carrier. A rhinestone glued to the side went flying off. Someone had gone a little nuts bedazzling it.

I picked up the carrier and the dog's leash and walked to the door. Was I actually going to get away with it?

She hung up on whoever she was talking to. "Wait," she said. "Dog walker."

Crap. I should have walked faster. I turned to look at her. She had one hand on her hip and her toe was tapping.

"I've got to leave for filming—I mean, the set. We famous people don't get a day off." She attempted a smile, but it came across more like a grimace. "You can drop the cat and dog off with the concierge. I'll make sure he knows what to do with them."

Yeah, I bet she would. I managed a nod and went out the door. I ran all the way to the elevator, the dog yipping excitedly. Oscar punched the button as soon as I was in.

"You did it! You did it!" he said and jumped up and down. The dog yapped louder.

Shut up, Fergie, the cat said. The dog immediately stopped barking and sat down on top of Oscar's foot. The cat peered up at me through the bars. *So, you want to tell me what's going on? Who are you? Are you with her?*

Oscar looked from me to the cat. "Is it talking to you? What did it say?"

"He," I said really quickly. Never call a cat an "it" if you want to keep your skin intact. "Nothing yet. Give me a second." I bent down to look in the carrier. "I'm Natalie," I said. "We're not with Easton." I caught a whiff of some strong perfume and something else.

That's not Easton, said the cat firmly. *I'm asking if you're with her.*

"Um, no," I said. "We're not with her. In fact, that's why we came to find you. That's why we're here."

The elevator dinged and the door opened on the lobby. Oscar stuck his head out and looked to the left and right and back again.

"Melly still has the perv talking to her up at the desk.

And hey, perfect! There's a group of tourists coming in. Get ready to go in one . . . two . . . three!" He sprinted out of the elevator and headed straight out the front door, nearly taking out one of the tourists on the way.

I poked my head out and followed more slowly. Why in the world did everything of Easton's have to be so pink? I mean, how much more noticeable could I be, with a pink dog and a pink cat in a pink cat carrier studded with rhinestones? Maybe I shouldn't have worn the lime-green hoodie today. We looked like sherbet on parade. I matched Fergie's leash.

"Don't make a sound," I whispered to the cat, who passed it on to the dog. I kept my head held high and walked as fast as I could without going too fast. A bellman by the door gave me a curious look, but I held up the leash and shrugged, and he didn't say anything. I made it through the door, looked back to make sure no one was looking, and then ran down the block. The cat carrier banged into my knee with every step, with the cat letting out a small growl each time.

"This way!" yelled Oscar, pinwheeling his arms in the air. Someone should seriously explain spy stuff to him. Attracting attention like that was the last thing we needed. I sighed and followed him around the corner. "We did it!" he yelled again and pumped his fist. A guy in a suit stared at him and moved to the edge of the sidewalk to get around us. Wouldn't be the first time.

The cat hissed softly. *Your friend sounds like something ran over his tail,* he said.

I grabbed Oscar's arm and pulled it down. "Oscar, shut up! Half the city's heard you by now."

"Oops, sorry," he said. "I just can't believe it worked!"

"Why don't you go get Melly?" I looked around for some place less conspicuous than the street corner. "I'll be over there at that sidewalk café."

Oscar took off and I lugged the carrier over to the café. I picked an outside table in the far corner underneath the awning and behind a large potted palm tree. I stuck the cat carrier in a chair and put my backpack over the top of it to try to hide the pinkness of it all.

Let me out of here, said the cat. *I've been in here for two days.*

"I can't," I said. "Look, here comes a waitress now. I'm probably not even supposed to have pets here."

I am not your pet, hissed the cat. I shushed him and pushed my backpack more toward the front of the carrier so it hung over the door a little.

The waitress came up to the table and sniffed at me suspiciously. She looked pointedly at the cat carrier and then down at Fergie, who wagged her little pink tail.

"Um, there's a performance artist doing something in Millennium Park today. Have you seen her stuff? I'm giving the—um—props a break." I held my breath.

She sighed but handed a menu to me. "Just keep them contained, okay? And if anyone complains, you've got to go."

"Thanks," I said. "Sure." I glanced down at the menu. I had only about ten dollars on me and I was going to need money for the train ride back. Melly probably had some cash, but Oscar was perennially broke. At least he had a Metra pass. The waitress turned to walk away. "Um, hey," I said. "Could I get three lemonades?"

She sighed, turned around, and took the menu back.

"Art doesn't really pay much," I said lamely. She nodded and left.

So who are you again? the cat asked.

"I'm Natalie," I said. "Nat. My friend—"

The loud one?

"Yeah. Oscar. He showed me this video of you attacking Easton—"

The cat hissed.

"Sorry, the person who's impersonating Easton. And I heard what you were saying. Oscar's a big fan of hers and dragged me down here to see what was going on." I looked around to make sure no one was watching me talk to a cat. "So, what is going on?"

We got here a few days ago. Easton left us in the hotel to go meet up with one of the actors from that film she's here to cover. When she came back, she wasn't Easton anymore.

"How can you tell?"

The cat hissed again. Talk about pitching a hissy fit.

"She looks just like Easton to me," I said. Even if human cloning were legal, who'd want to clone some celebrity blogger anyway?

Cats are obviously better suited at detection than humans. I

46

can tell. That . . . person . . . is not my human. She doesn't smell the same. She may look the same, but she's not. She didn't even know what our names were. She had to look them up on the computer.

Oh. Yeah, that would be a pretty good clue. "What is your name? The dog's Fergie, right?"

I'm Rufus Brutus the Third. Easton calls me Tiddlywinks. Fergie's the dog's real name and human name. She doesn't have much imagination. She's just a dog.

Fergie sat up at her name and wagged her poofy pink tail. Yeah, she didn't look like the sharpest tool in the shed, that's for sure. But maybe it was the pink fur.

"Tiddlywinks?"

Rufus pushed his face up against the carrier door again and glared at me malevolently, his yellow-green eyes practically glowing. *I said* Easton *calls me that. You may call me Rufus Brutus the Third.*

"Right," I said. "Okay, Rufus Brutus the Third." Delusions of grandeur, anyone? "Any ideas on who this Easton impostor is? And whether or not the real Easton is okay? And why someone is impersonating Easton to begin with?"

Before Rufus could say anything else, Oscar and Melly came running across the street and joined us at the table.

"That was pure awesome!" said Oscar. He high-fived Melly. "We are rockin' the casbah!" I rolled my eyes, but didn't say anything because the waitress was coming back with our drinks. She set the lemonades and the bill on the table and left without bothering to ask if we wanted to order anything else. She must have served broke teenagers before.

"So what have you found out so far?" asked Melly, taking a sip of her lemonade.

I introduced Rufus Brutus the Third/Tiddlywinks and Fergie and summed it up. Not like I'd learned a lot so far anyway. Rufus was more of a hisser than a sharer.

Oscar leaned over so his head was directly in front of Rufus. "Who would do this to Easton?" he asked, loudly and deliberately like he was talking to a five-year-old who didn't speak English. It was a good thing Rufus was contained. I saw his eyes narrow.

"You can talk normally," I said before Rufus came unglued. "He's not deaf or dumb. He's just a cat."

Your friend is an idiot, Rufus said. *But tell him I don't know who did this. All I know is that she keeps disappearing and leaving us in the hotel room. She calls someone named Alan a lot and complains. But it's very strange. She sticks her hand in a bag of hair before she makes the call and she uses a different voice. Before you ask, no, I don't recognize the hair or the voice.*

I relayed all of that weirdness to Oscar and Melly. "Do you think your Easton is still okay?" I asked Rufus.

Rufus was silent for a minute. Then he extended his claws again and didn't bother to draw them back. *I think so,* he said. *Because the impostor keeps threatening to kill her whenever I get a scratch in.*

FIVE

MONDAY, SEPTEMBER 7, 11:46 A.M.

"OF COURSE CATS ARE SMARTER THAN DOGS.
DO I LOOK LIKE I FETCH?"
—RUFUS BRUTUS THE THIRD

Fergie began barking and jumping around like she'd suddenly been possessed. She looked like some kind of demented fluffy pink tennis ball.

"What's she saying?" Melly asked me.

"I don't know," I said. "I don't speak Dog. Just Cat." Every now and then I could get a word out of what a dog said, but usually it sounded like barking to me. Dogs and cats could talk to each other, apparently, though mostly they didn't like to. Meep said most dogs were slow and it wasn't worth bothering to talk to them. I was pretty sure dogs probably said the same thing about cats. Of course, Meep could be pretty stupid sometimes.

She says the dog walker is across the street, said Rufus. *Be quiet, Fergie, she might hear you.*

Fergie quieted down, not a moment too soon. Some girl with four dogs in tow was on the other side of the street,

49

headed toward the York. They were pulling her along, and at the rate the collie was going, they were going to be at the hotel soon. Very soon.

"Oh crap," I said. "We've got to get you guys back before the dog walker figures out you're gone."

I am NOT going back.

"What do you mean?" I asked.

I think I was pretty clear. I am not setting foot in that room again. I've been in this prison for days. I've even soiled myself. I am NOT going back.

I leaned over to look at him more carefully. I didn't smell cat pee, but I did smell perfume. A lot of it. It was really floraly, and not in a good way. And what? Was that hairspray? Close up, I could see that his fur was sticking out in every direction.

"What happened to you?" I asked, rubbing at my nose.

He was quiet for just a second. *She got me back into this cage by emptying a can of hairspray on me. And she sprayed me with perfume a few times.*

A few times? Smelled more like an entire bottle. I guess whoever the impostor was, she was pro animal testing. "Well, we still need to get you back," I said. "We can't take you with us."

"What's going on?" asked Melly.

"Rufus says he won't go back." I looked across the street. The dog walker was picking up some poop, but she was still dangerously close to the corner. I stood up and grabbed the carrier and Fergie's leash. "We've got to go!"

50

I will scream like you have never heard a cat scream, said Rufus. *Everyone within the block will hear. You don't want that, do you?*

I stopped. His eyes were boring holes into my soul. I didn't doubt he would do exactly what he said. For a not very large cat with a weird round head and funky, tiny folded ears, he was pretty intimidating.

"But—"

Besides, you may be useful. You can help me find Easton.

I sighed and looked from Melly to Oscar to Rufus. "What do you guys think?" I asked.

"No idea," said Oscar. "I've only heard half the conversation. But I'm all for whatever the cat says. Whoever that is up there is evil. Eeeev-viiiillll."

"What about Fergie?" I asked. Did I have to think of everything? "How are we supposed to smuggle a pink dog and a pink cat all the way back to the suburbs? What're we supposed to do with them when we get home? And what about the dog walker?" She'd finished picking up the poop and was untangling the leashes of a really overweight bulldog and a poodle. But she was getting closer to the corner.

Fergie will be fine with the impostor, won't you, Fergie? She can be our eyes and ears on the inside.

Fergie let out one quick yip and panted. Rufus had her trained well. He was obviously the brains in the operation, which left Fergie as the not very muscular muscle.

"I don't think—"

Melly cleared her throat and jerked her head in the

direction of the dog walker. She and Oscar looked at me like they were waiting for instructions.

Frick on a stick. I closed my eyes for a moment. "Okay, okay. Let's do this."

I dumped the water bottles and muffins out of my backpack and opened the door to the cat carrier. Rufus immediately poked his head out but paused when I held up my hand. At least he was listening to me—a little. That was more than I got out of Meep. Or my human friends, for that matter.

"I'm not lugging that smelly cat carrier. It's too noticeable." I mean, really. Hot pink with rhinestones? And the Eau du Cat plus whatever nasty perfume she'd sprayed him down with wasn't helping. "And we're riding on Metra. I don't think they even allow animals. So you have to go in here." I held open the top of my backpack. Rufus sniffed loudly once, but climbed in.

Oy. Out of the carrier, he smelled even worse. I was going to have to fumigate my backpack after this. Some perfumes should be outlawed as chemical warfare.

"Oscar, Melly, you guys get going to Union Station. I'll meet you on the 12:35 train, okay? Last car. Can you get me a ticket?"

Oscar saluted. "What're you going to do?" he asked.

"I'm not sure yet," I said. I just knew it would probably be easier to do whatever it was without Oscar's help. He and Melly took off after one last sip of lemonade. I threw down the money for the bill and an extra dollar tip for the waitress. It probably wouldn't make up for ditching the cat carrier there, but it was the best I could do. I looked across the street, where the dog walker was stopped at the corner waiting for the light.

I slung the backpack over my shoulder and caught up with the dog walker. "Hey," I called out when I was close enough. She turned and saw Fergie and came to meet me.

"What's up?" she asked. "Did She-Who-Shouldn't-Be-Named finally decide to replace me?" She bent down to pet Fergie, who went into a total paroxysm of glee. I will never understand dogs.

"Um, no," I said. "She was running late and Fergie had to . . . you know, go, so I said I'd walk the dog and meet you. You can give Fergie to the concierge when you're done." I held out the leash and the dog walker took it.

"Huh. I'm surprised she didn't just let poor little Fergs go in the room again." She pulled the poodle back from his in-depth sniff of my backpack and rear end. I shuffled a few steps backward before the poodle could get any closer to Rufus.

"Yeah, me too," I said and let out the breath I'd been holding. It looked like she'd bought the story. "Well, have fun!" I turned to go. That was easy.

Nice job, said Rufus. He poked his head out of the top of the pack. *You're a pretty good liar.*

"Um, thanks," I said. Coming from a cat, that was actually a compliment.

"Hey, wait!" yelled the dog walker. "Is that Tiddlywinks? Hey, where are you going? Stop!"

I didn't bother to turn around. I just ran.

SIX

"ANYBODY CAN EXERCISE . . . BUT THIS KIND OF LETHARGY
TAKES REAL DISCIPLINE."
—GARFIELD THE CAT (JIM DAVIS)

I found Oscar and Melly on the last train car. I flopped down next to Oscar, completely out of breath, and dropped the backpack on the facing seat opposite, right next to Melly. Let her deal with the smell for a while.

"What happened?" asked Melly. "Are you okay?"

"She saw Rufus as I was leaving. I had to make a run for it." Stupid cat.

Rufus poked his head out. *It doesn't matter. They would have discovered my absence soon enough.*

"Yeah, well, I could have done without the exercise."

Well, I could have done without feeling like a milkshake. You really ought to work on your pacing and stride.

Nice. Exercise advice from a cat who probably sleeps more than he walks. The train took off and I let out a sigh of relief. The dog walker had really followed me for only about a block, and had given up when the bulldog had gotten tangled up with Fergie. Or maybe Fergie had done that on purpose. I don't know. Rufus had been yelling something at her. But I couldn't shake the feeling that everyone was staring at me, looking for the catnapper. I put my feet up on the seat opposite me and sank down as far as I could.

"So, what now?" asked Oscar. "Whose butt do we kick next?"

"First things first," I said. "Where are we going to stash Rufus?"

Oscar looked at me like I was nuts. "He goes home with you, of course. You're the only one who can talk to him."

"My mom is allergic to cats."

"But you've got a cat," said Melly, while Oscar said, "D'oh!"

"I know *that*," I said. "Meep's a designer cat. She's hypoallergenic. Mom's really allergic to cats, but they figured the only way to support my Talent was to get a cat, so they found Meep for me. Paid the big bucks for her too." Probably a good thing. Otherwise, I'd have no one to talk to at home.

"Oh," said Oscar. "Well, *I* can't take him. Fluff would chew him into little bitty pieces. He hates cats." That was true. Oscar's dog was a huge Doberman and had a serious chip on his shoulder about cats. I'd tried to have Meep talk to him once to find out why, and Fluff had nearly gone through Oscar's screen door trying to eat poor Meep. That had cost me some serious tuna.

"I can't take him," said Melly. "My dad would freak. He's

got some big meetings set up at his home office this week with some investor people. I'm not even supposed to be home if I can help it. I've even got blanket permission to sleep over at Oscar's house or your place."

Monkey snot. Monkey snot on a stick. "Okay, okay. I'll take him tonight, but we've got to figure out something better."

"So," said Melly. "I think we should be logical about this." She pulled out a notebook and a pen from her bag. "What do we know so far?"

That I should never listen to my friends. Or cats. And, apparently, I was never going to make it as a cross-country runner.

"Not much," said Oscar. For once, I agreed with him completely.

"Well," said Melly, scribbling, "that's not entirely true. We know that someone is impersonating Easton West."

"For reasons unknown," I said.

"And that the real Easton is alive," she continued.

"Presumably," I said. Rufus hissed at me.

"And the impostor has a bag of hair that isn't Easton's." Melly wrinkled her nose as she wrote that part down.

"Which is pretty high on the grossness scale," said Oscar. "I mean, even if it was Ty's hair? Still gross."

"And the impostor talks to someone on the phone named Alan." Melly stopped writing.

"And has a seriously bad attitude," I added.

And I am going to scratch her eyeballs out, said Rufus.

I didn't bother to relay that information on. This cat was a serious handful. I opened the top of my bag so I could give him the evil eye. "You are not to leave my room when we get to my house. At all. You got it?"

I'll be requiring some decent food and a litter box, he said. *If you have that in your room, then we are agreed.*

It was going to be a long night.

Oscar and Melly dropped me off at home and left to do some Internet research at Oscar's house to see if they could figure out who Alan might be and what else they could dig up. Oscar was the king of the Internet, after all. I went in the back-door, hoping to avoid everyone. No luck. Emmy was in the kitchen.

"What're you up to?" she asked.

"Nothing. What are *you* up to?" I walked around her and grabbed a couple of bowls, some cat food, and a glass of water. Meep wasn't big on sharing her food. Or her house, probably. I grabbed a can of tuna too. A bribe was in order.

"I'm getting a snack. Why'd you come in the back door?"

Geez. Suspicious much? "No reason. Why're you so annoying?"

"Why're you so grouchy?"

I grunted at her and left the kitchen, juggling all the stuff. The best policy to take with Emmy was to ignore everything, deny everything, and stay out of her sight. She was nosy squared. Mom should have never given her those *Harriet the Spy* books when she was younger. Of course, she'd been, like, three when she read them. Overachiever.

Meep woke up from her midafternoon windowsill nap when I shut my bedroom door and locked it. She stretched and yawned, then came to attention as she caught a whiff of Rufus—or, rather, the perfume-plus-hairspray explosion. It was giving me a headache.

What's up? asked Meep. *Who's in the bag?*

I set the backpack on the floor and opened the top flap. Rufus shot out on full alert. When he saw Meep, he sat down all prim and proper and started cleaning his shoulder—or tried to. There was so much hairspray on him that his shoulder fur was kind of flared out in solid wings. Cat politics. I guess I could have warned him that Meep's not big on protocol.

"Meep," I said, "meet Rufus Brutus the Third. Rufus, meet Meep."

Meep stretched again and then ambled over to sniff Rufus's butt. She was a lot like a dog that way, though I'd never tell her that. I like my bed not peed in.

Where'd you find this one? asked Meep. *He smells.* She cocked an eye at the tuna I was carrying. *I hope that's for me?*

Rufus flattened his ears and sat up straighter. *I'll have you know I was being held against my will. I am perfectly capable of bathing myself in normal circumstances.* He bared his teeth slightly.

Time for some distraction before they got in a literal or

figurative pissing fight. I divvied up the tuna and set both bowls down. "Snack time," I said. "Play nice, Meep. It's not Rufus's fault he stinks—or that he's pink."

Pink? Meep looked up from her tuna. *What are you talking about?*

Oh yeah. I always forget that cats can't see shades of red. I guess it's a good thing Easton hadn't dyed Rufus lime green. *That* he would have noticed and he probably wouldn't have been pleased.

"Nothing," I said, and flopped down on my bed. As soon as I did, my cell phone went off. Lady Gaga again. I stuck it under my pillow. Oscar could wait.

Rufus finished his tuna first, which I wasn't surprised at. The Easton impostor probably hadn't been feeding him. He went back to trying to clean himself, keeping one eye on Meep. Meep gulped the last bite, looked pointedly at me and wrinkled her nose.

I sighed. "Rufus, we've got to get you a real bath. I think you could sit there all day doing that and you'd still reek." Besides, who knew if that stuff was okay for cat consumption? If they didn't even want to test it on animals, they probably wouldn't recommend they ingest it either.

He looked offended, but he didn't argue. His tongue probably felt shellacked.

"Meep, can you check and see if anyone's between my room and the bathroom? I know Emmy's home, but I'm not sure about Mom and Dad."

Fine, said Meep. *But I want more tuna later.*

I held open the door just enough for her to get through and closed it again after her. Meep came back a minute later and scratched at the door.

All clear, she said. *I don't see anyone.*

I opened the door and motioned for Rufus to follow me. We were almost at the bathroom when Emmy's face materialized in front of me with an evil grin. She stepped away from the wall and shook off the stripes of the wallpaper.

"Emmy!" I yelped. "Meep, you said you didn't see anyone!"

I didn't, said Meep. *You didn't say anything about smell. Besides, her stink is all over the house. How was I supposed to know?*

"I knew you were up to something!" Emmy said. "Where'd that cat come from? Why's it pink? What's going on?"

I heard a door shut somewhere in the house. "Gah!" I said. "Everybody, in the bathroom! Now!" I pushed Emmy ahead of me and Rufus and Meep ran between our legs. I shut the door and locked it.

"Mom's gonna kill you," said Emmy. "You know she's allergic."

"I know that!" I put my hand over my eyes and counted silently to ten. "Look, Emmy, it's a secret, okay?"

"Why?"

I removed my hand and looked at her. Maybe I could try the truth? She did have a soft spot for animals in distress. Whenever we ran into cats wandering around outside she'd make me ask them if they were lost. "Oscar and Melly and

I are trying to find this cat's person. She's been kidnapped. The owner, that is, not Rufus."

Emmy looked at me doubtfully and put her hands on her hips.

"Fine," I said. "I'll owe you one, okay? Anything you want. Just help me hide the cat from Mom."

Emmy smiled her evil smile again. I was doomed, but at least Rufus was going to get a bath.

E A S T O N   W E S T ' S   B L O G

Monday, September 7, 9:35 P.M.: I was planning on posting today about the incredible time I'm having on set watching Victoria do her thing. But instead, I have some terrible news.

For the second time in two days, I've had to deal with the Chicago police. This time, apparently some crazy fan has stolen my beloved Tiddlywinks. Be on the lookout for a short girl with dark hair and a pink cat.

I am, of course, completely inconsolable. Victoria has so kindly offered to put me up at her house in the suburbs so I can be alone in my grief. ♥

seven

"a man Has To Work so HarD so THaT someTHing of His personaLiTy
sTays aLive. a TomcaT Has iT so easy, He Has onLy
To spray anD His presence is THere for years on rainy Days."
—anonymous inTerneT QuoTe, ofTen incorrecTLy aTTriBuTeD To aLBerT
einsTein, WHo Was proBaBLy Too smarT To mess arounD WiTH caTs

Oscar and Melly were waiting for me on the right side of
the concrete front steps in our standard meeting spot outside
school. It was a little chilly out, so everyone else was hurry-
ing inside, making Oscar and his pitch-black hair and green-
streaked bangs even easier to spot than normal. He's nearly
six feet tall, which really isn't fair. We're both half Asian, and
I barely crack five feet. Even worse, Emmy inherited Mom's
height. She's already taller than me.

"Nat!" Oscar yelled as soon as he saw me. "Why didn't
you call me back last night? Get over here right now, girl!
You have to see this!" He waved his open laptop around in
the air and nearly took off some guy's head. The stream of
people around him eddied even farther out. By the time I
fought my way through to join my friends, it was like we
were a little island of freakishness.

"So what did you guys figure out?" I asked.

Melly shrugged and gestured to Oscar, who swung his laptop around and stuck it right in my face. Easton's blog was on the screen. I pushed the laptop back a few inches away from my nose. "Can you break it down for me, Oscar? The bell's gonna ring anytime now."

"Basically, she says you kidnapped her cat and that she's going to be recovering from the trauma at Victoria's house." He closed his laptop and stuck it in his messenger bag.

"Great."

"She notified the police too, and they're on the lookout for a short girl with a pink cat." Oscar sounded way too happy about the news.

"Lovely."

"Something wrong?" asked Melly.

I yawned. "I owe Emmy big time, my backpack still kinda smells even after I washed it, and I got no sleep with all the arguing Meep and Rufus were doing last night." I had the bad feeling I was going to come home to a room completely shredded. I'd threatened Meep and Rufus both, but some territorial urges can't be denied. "Not to mention there's probably a wanted poster with my name on it somewhere. What could be wrong?" The only luck I'd had so far was that Mom had been out until late working on something, so no huge allergy attacks. Yet.

"We did find out a couple of possibles named Alan. I made a list." Oscar handed me a sheet of paper folded into a tiny triangle. "I thought we could run them by Rufus after school and see if anything jogs his memory."

"Okay," I said. "Sounds good." Not really, but if it helped get my life back to normal, I was for it.

Oscar gave me his thousand-watt smile. "I knew you were on board," he said. "Come on, Cat Girl, what are we standing out here for? It's cold!"

He looped his arm through mine and reached back to pull Melly along for the ride too. I looked around, but at least no one seemed to have caught his Cat Girl comment.

Not that anyone generally paid any attention to us anyway.

♥

For once, I was glad that the first half of my school day didn't include Oscar or Melly so I could put the whole Easton fiasco out of mind. I had trig first period, which is plain evil as far as scheduling goes. No one should be expected to do math first thing in the morning. There were only two good things about the situation: it was my best subject (even if it was way too early and I was the only sophomore in the class) and Ian Abbott sat right next to me.

Not that I'd ever admit it, but I was glad Melly wasn't as good at math as I was. She and Oscar were both in geometry, along with the rest of the tenth graders. Most boys had a way of completely forgetting I was in a room when Melly was around. Even the juniors and seniors. Ian seemed different, but you never knew about testosterone. It addled the brain.

He wasn't her type anyway. She had a thing for tortured

artists who also happened to work out a lot. Ian was tall and lanky, but there wasn't anything tortured about him. He always seemed to have a sly grin on his face, like he'd just thought of this hilarious joke that he was about to tell you and it would be so funny you would pee your pants. And he knew you would, which was why he was smiling to begin with.

The only remotely tortured thing about him was his dark wavy brown hair. It always looked like he'd woken up, combed it through once with his fingers, and then said the heck with it. Some days it was all I could do not to reach over and fix his hair while we were in class.

I slid into my seat a few minutes before the bell rang and smiled at Ian. He grinned back and wrinkled his nose at me. His nose was a little too big for his face, just like his grin, but instead of making him look clownish, it gave him a devilish air. Or maybe that was his eyebrows. They had a natural arch to them.

"Hey, Natalie," he said. "What did you get for the last problem? I swear I did it five times and got five different answers."

Mr. Beck was not afraid of ruining a student's holiday weekend. In fact, I think that's what he aimed for. I shuffled through my backpack and came up with last Friday's home-work, which thankfully hadn't absorbed the lingering odor of cat and perfume. I handed it over to Ian and he compared it to his.

"Great. Not one of my answers matches up with yours."

"I could be wrong," I said. Doubtful, but possible. Let's be honest: I rock trig.

"No, I'm sure you're right. After all, super-geniusness runs in the family, doesn't it?" He wiggled one of those perfect eyebrows at me.

I took my paper back. "That's just my little sister." And my mom, but who's counting?

"She's a senior, right? How old is she?"

I nodded once, held my breath, and went back to digging in my backpack. "Twelve." I dug out some pencils, but when I came up for air, he was still looking at me expectantly.

"I saw her do her chameleon thing in the hall once. It was totally cool. Your whole family has Talent, right?"

I nodded again and braced myself for The Question. I guessed I should be glad it had taken this long to come up between us, since I'd been in geometry with him all last year, though it had only been since trig that I'd worked up the courage to actually sit next to him. Usually, the Talent thing is the first thing people ask me when they find out what my last name is. Viv hadn't been shy about her Talents. Her levitation skill had figured prominently in the senior prank last year. People were still talking about it.

He didn't disappoint. "So, what's your Talent?"

"Sorry," I said, looking down into my backpack again instead of at him. "Classified." That's a complete lie, but one that always worked with the non-Talented. People always believed anything that sounded like a conspiracy theory. Besides, it made my Talent sound much cooler than it was.

"Oh, yeah," he said. "Sorry."

"No problem!" I said as cheerfully as I could manage. "Emmy's really not supposed to show hers off in public, but she's twelve, so whaddaya do, right?"

"Yeah, my little brother is ten. I know exactly what you mean. He still picks his nose in public." He looked a little uncomfortable after I'd blown him off, but that was still better than what I'm sure his reaction would have been if I'd actually told him I could talk to cats. Not that I ever told anyone.

At least, not since kindergarten. I'd learned *that* lesson quickly. Luckily, the kid I'd told had moved away soon after and I hadn't had to live with the taunts for long. A month of being meowed at was enough for me. I didn't tell Oscar or Melly until we'd been good friends for half a year—and I'd made them pinky swear first.

I decided to change the subject. The last thing I wanted was for Ian to feel awkward around me. I felt inept enough for both of us. "So, are you ready for the test this week?"

He leaned back in his chair and groaned. "No! Not even close. And knowing the Beck-Man, he'll load us up with more homework tonight. The man is evil."

That was probably true. Mr. Beck was notorious for his homework. The bigger the test, the more he'd pile on us right before it. He called it practice. Right now, I'd call it an opportunity.

"I could help if you want. I mean, I'm not doing anything after school today." At least, nothing that I wanted to be doing. I hoped he didn't notice me swallow the sudden flood of saliva that had hit my mouth.

"Really? That would be great! You always kick my butt on the tests. You really don't mind?"

"It's Tuesday. I don't have anything more exciting going on, and I've gotta do the homework anyway." And I'd do an entire book full of problems to hang out with Ian outside of school.

"My house or yours?"

"Yours, if that's okay. My house is a little crazy." Like an insane asylum crazy, plus one stuck-up pink cat. The last thing I wanted to do was bring Ian into that mess. That would've been about as bad as telling him I talk to cats. Maybe worse.

He scribbled his address and phone number on my notebook, which was convenient since I wasn't about to sound like a stalker and admit that I already knew where he lived.

EIGHT

TUESDAY, SEPTEMBER 8, 11:20 A.M.

"WAY DOWN DEEP, WE'RE ALL MOTIVATED BY THE SAME URGES.
CATS HAVE THE COURAGE TO LIVE BY THEM."
—JIM DAVIS

The day was definitely looking up. Melly could now officially get off my back about making a move on Ian. (She just didn't get it. It was easy for her. She never had to make the first move. Guys came to her.) I'd even snuck a quick nap in my third period art class during a video about pointillism.

"Guess what?" I said as soon as I joined Melly and Oscar at our usual lunch table.

"You've come up with a plan to help Easton?" mumbled Oscar around a bite of his tuna fish sandwich. Half of it was already gone. He was always the first of us to arrive at lunch, being both incredibly food motivated and having a class two doors down from the cafeteria. How he managed to stay stick thin, I'll never know.

"No, much better." Easton was the last thing on my mind. "I've got a homework date with Ian Abbott!"

"Woot!" said Melly, and gave me a high five. Oscar stood

70

up and did his crazy dance, waving his arms in the air. A teacher gave him a warning look from across the cafeteria and he sat back down, thankfully. At least he wasn't wearing his kilt today.

"Melly, you'll give me a ride after school, right?" I didn't have a car. Though even if I had one, I wouldn't be able drive it. My mom was requiring me to complete seventy-five hours of supervised driving time on my learner's permit on top of the time I'd already spent in driving school this past summer. Since neither she nor dad ever actually wanted to set foot in a car with me, I'd probably be eighteen before I got my full license.

"Wait," said Oscar. "You mean today? You can't go today."

I took a deep breath and counted to three silently while Oscar wagged his finger in my face. "*What* are you talking about?"

"You promised you'd talk to Rufus!"

I pushed his hand away and opened my yogurt. "Look, I want to find Easton and get rid of that cat as much as you do, but it can wait for two hours."

"The clock is ticking," said Oscar. "There's no telling what that impostor is doing to Easton West. Right. Now."

I looked at Melly for help. There was no way I was canceling my homework date with Ian to talk with an annoying cat about his equally annoying owner.

Melly cleared her throat. "I've got news too," she said. "I signed us all up as extras in the movie!" She passed out

71

sheets of paper to me and Oscar. "These are the releases. You have to have a parent sign it and be sure to bring it back tomorrow. There's a cafeteria scene, so technically we're rehearsing right now!"

"Awesome sauce!" said Oscar, the prospect of his big acting debut enough to divert him for a moment at least.

When he was done fist pumping, she continued. "I'm a little bummed, though. They're only going to be shooting a few scenes here at the school with background extras—that's what we'd be. The rest of the shoots are going to be on location around the city."

"Don't worry," said Oscar. "You come to school tomorrow looking hotter than hot, and I know you'll have the director drooling all over you. They'll probably hire you on the spot, if Ty doesn't propose first." He ate the rest of his tuna sandwich in one bite. I threw a napkin at him. He took the hint and wiped his chin.

Melly winked at me. "You never know," she said. "Maybe you're Ty's type after all."

That launched Oscar into a discussion of Ty's soulful brown eyes and whether or not he looked better blond like in his last movie or his usual dark brown. I smiled at Melly. She had my back.

But I'd be on my own with Ian tonight.

NINE

TUESDAY, SEPTEMBER 8, 3:43 P.M.

"THOU ART THE GREAT CAT, THE AVENGER OF THE GODS, AND THE JUDGE OF
WORDS, AND THE PRESIDENT OF THE SOVEREIGN CHIEFS, AND THE GOVERNOR OF
THE HOLY CIRCLE; THOU ART INDEED . . . THE GREAT CAT."
— A HYMN TO THE EGYPTIAN GOD RA

Melly dropped me off at Ian's house with a promise to pick me up at 5:30. I took a couple of deep breaths, swallowed the last of the breath mint Melly had pushed on me, and knocked on the door.

A little kid answered and just stood there staring at me. He must be the nose picker Ian had told me about earlier.

"Um, hi? I'm Nat. I'm here to study with Ian?"

"Ian!" The kid yelled at the top of his lungs, nearly blowing my eardrums. "There's a girl for you at the door!"

"I'll be right there!" Ian yelled back.

The kid didn't budge an inch, just stayed right in the middle of the doorway staring at me. Nice. I stared back at him. I knew how to play the game. I've got a little sister.

Then an orange and white tabby cat strolled up to the door, looked up at me, and blinked in surprise. I don't know how or why it works, but cats all immediately know that they can talk to me as soon as they see me. I've asked Meep about it before, but Meep's got the attention span of a gnat and I've never gotten anything more out of her than "we just know," which is her answer to lots of things.

Hello, the cat mewed at me. *I didn't know Ian knew anyone interesting. This one is Jasper. If you take one step toward him, he'll scatter. He's like a rat that way.*

I was getting tired of standing on the stoop, so I did what the cat suggested and took a quick step toward Jasper. His eyes opened wide and he disappeared somewhere into the house.

"Thanks," I said, and went inside and closed the door. "I'm Nat." I'd learned long ago that cats are really particular about introductions. They find it unutterably rude if you don't introduce yourself.

I'm Purr Daddy. You can call me PD. The humans here call me Pebbles. He let a delicate shudder ruffle the fur across his back as he said it, though I personally thought "Purr Daddy" sounded stupider than Pebbles. But I'm not a cat.

"Nice to meet you," I said.

What are you doing here?

"I'm here to study trig with Ian." Another lesson I learned a long time ago: cats are nosy and will give you no peace until you tell them what's up. It's best to get it over with up front unless you have a reason to lie, but then you'd better have a really good poker face, since they could usually tell when you were lying. Not quite as reliable as Viv's built-in lie detector, but most cats could spot a lie a mile away.

Oh, he said, and studied me intently for a moment. *He always feeds me on time, not like the little rat. I like Ian. He's okay.* He wound between my legs and rubbed his head on my shin, then looked up at me from between my purple Converse All Stars.

He sings in the shower, you know. Mostly reggae. Won't do it in front of people, though.

"Um, okay," I said. I was saved from saying anything else by Ian clumping down the stairs. PD sat on my foot.

"What're you doing at the door? Where'd Jasper go? Didn't he invite you in?" He noticed PD sitting on my foot. "Oh, I hope you're not allergic to cats or anything."

"I'm okay with cats," I said, and lightly shook my foot. PD stretched and stood up. "Your brother took off somewhere."

"Sorry," he said. "I was just, uh, upstairs."

Bathroom, said PD. *Combing his hair, by the looks of it.* He looked up at me and purred. I could swear he winked.

Ian's hair was remarkably tamed. It still stuck up in back, but the front looked like he'd actually won the battle for once. It made me want to mess it up.

"Well," he said. "I set everything up in the dining room. Mom said we need to be done by six because of dinner. Is that okay?"

"Sure, my friends Melly and Oscar are picking me up before then." I shouldered my bag and followed him into the dining room. It was nice and comfortable with cushiony seats and flowers on the table, completely unlike mine at home, which was often covered in research paper stuff in between (and sometimes during) meals. Ian's stuff was spread out at one end of the table along with a pitcher of lemonade and some crackers, cheese, and chocolate chip cookies.

"Wow," I said, sitting down in the chair next to his. "Nice! I don't have it this good at home. I need to study at your house more often!" Oops. I hoped he didn't think that was too forward, but seriously. Cookies?

He ducked his head and blushed a little. "My mom always says that you think better on a full stomach than an empty one." Oh, too cute. But I decided then and there that he should never ever meet my mom, not until some far off day after we'd fallen in love and were about to get married. Maybe not even then.

We got to work on the trig. The test was likely to be of epic proportions based on the amount of homework Mr. Beck had given us. Ian actually was doing pretty well on the problems, though he had a tendency to mix up the reciprocal of a function with its inverse.

Ian's mom came by after about an hour to refill the lemonade and the plate of cookies. It was easy to see where Ian got his looks from. He had her eyelashes and the same dimple in his chin, though her hair was a lot neater and blonde-ish. She patted him on the head and then went back to the kitchen, probably to make some more cookies. I should be so lucky.

"Your mom is really nice," I said.

"She's okay. Mom works part time as an office manager and my dad works at Wrigley Field. Just back office stuff, nothing interesting. It must be a lot cooler to be in your family, with everyone having a superpower."

"Talent," I said automatically, then winced. Mom had ingrained that in my head. She always said that superpowers were for comic books. "It's not really all that cool, trust me. I'd rather my mom could bake cookies as good as your mom." The last time my mom had made cookies, I could have donated them to the field hockey team to use as pucks.

Ian didn't look convinced, but he went back to work. I was really flubbing up this not-date homework date royally. I sounded so stuck up, correcting him like that. I doodled in my notebook while I tried to think of some way to get things back on track.

Then Ian's mom yelled at him from the kitchen. "Ian, I need you to give Pebbles his pill now."

"Aw, Mom, can't I do that later? We're right in the middle of trig!" He shot a dirty look at Pebbles, a.k.a. Purr Daddy, who had wandered in a while ago and was sunning himself on a windowsill. Ian whispered to me, "I hate giving him his stupid pills. He always freaks out. It's like trying to wrestle a chainsaw."

PD licked a paw and winked at me. Such a cat.

"No, I need you to do it now. We're supposed to give him the pill at the same time every day."

"Can't Jasper do it? We're busy!"

"You want to trade, you trade. But that means you're back on litter box duty. Besides, it will take you all of two seconds."

"All right already!" Ian got up. "Crap. I'll be right back. Can you keep an eye on him for me so he doesn't get away? Last time I had to dig him out from behind the couch. I don't know how he always seems to know what's coming."

"Sure," I said. Maybe this was my chance to impress Ian. After all, if there was any Talent that I could be said to have, it was with cats. I waited until I thought Ian was out of hearing range.

"PD, how about you let me give you the pill and you take it nicely?"

He blinked at me. *Why?* he purred. *I like to play with Ian. It's the only exercise I get these days. And besides, the pills taste awful.*

They taste awful? I could point out that he'd spent the better part of the last twenty minutes licking his hind end, but I figured that wouldn't get me anywhere. Cats aren't much for logic.

"Because it's good for you."

Like I believe that. That's what they said before they took the boys.

The boys? "What're you talking about?"

You know, the boys. The furry dice. My balls. He rolled over flat onto his back and flicked his tail at the nether region he'd been so assiduously cleaning.

Oh. The boys. Who knew? Male cats were more like teenage boys than I'd ever thought.

"Well, this isn't like that. These pills actually do help you. And, you know, I just—"

PD stopped licking himself to really stare at me. *Hmm-mmm, you're in heat for him, aren't you? How cute!*

I blushed. Called out by the cat. My life was hitting a new low. "I'm not in *heat*," I whispered at him. "I just *like* him, that's all." PD rolled around on the floor, chuckling, which sounded a bit like he was going to cough up something nasty. "Look, what do you want? How about some tuna?" That always works with Meep. I think she'd sell her soul for tuna.

PD stopped rolling and perked up his ears. Ha ha, I got him! But then he surprised me.

Not tuna . . . but I'll think of something. It's a deal.

Now that worried me. PD was obviously smarter than Meep. But how bad could it be? Either way, before I could change my mind, Ian was back with a pill bottle, a box of bandages, and a stoic look on his face.

"Can you cover the door for me, Nat? He's bound to make a run for it."

Now was my chance. "Hey, Ian, why don't you let me try? I'm pretty good with cats."

"Oh no, I couldn't let you do that. He'll rip you to shreds.

I know he looks cute and everything, but he's like a little demon in a fur coat."

I took the bottle from him and got a pill out. It was now or never. "I bet I can get him to take it on the first try. And if I can't, you can take over and I'll do the next ten problems. How's that?"

Ian looked doubtful, which, I had to say, was a really adorable look for him. "He's never taken it on a first try."

"Well, I bet I can get him to. You in?"

"Sure, but be careful." He grinned at me. "Number 18 looks like a real headache of a problem."

I smiled and turned to PD. He'd better not back out on me now. "Come here, Pebbles," I cooed and wiggled my fingers at him. He stretched and yawned, but then jumped up on the table and ambled over to me, to Ian's amazement. I scratched him a few times behind the ears and tapped him on the nose lightly. Might as well put on a good show.

"I've got a treat for you," I said and held up the pill. PD meowed, playing along, but gave me the evil eye from the side Ian couldn't see. I held the pill out to him and he knocked it back like it was a piece of sushi. I gave him a few more pats on the head as Ian stared at me, openmouthed.

"I can't believe it! How did you do that? He's like demon spawn normally, I swear!"

PD purred and jumped down to twine his way back and forth around my ankles. Geez, what a ham. I am so not ever introducing him to my cat. He might give Meep some bad ideas she would be too stupid to think up on her own.

"I told you, I'm good with cats."

"Well, I guess the next ten problems are mine, huh? You won that one fair and square." Ian sat back down next to me and picked up his pencil.

"Actually," I said, as PD jumped in my lap, "I was thinking maybe something else."

"Oh?"

"How about a movie? Maybe this Friday night? I've been wanting to see that new alien invasion movie." I held my breath. Would it work? I'd thrown in the most guy-sounding movie that was out.

"Sure," said Ian with a smile. "You earned it, between the homework help and getting Pebbles to take his pill."

PD poked his head up and headbutted my arm. *You're pretty crafty for a human. I like that.* Then he settled back down and started kneading a hole in my jeans.

Yeah. And he was pretty crafty for a cat. That was two favors I owed now and I wasn't sure whose was going to be worse to pay back: Emmy or PD.

TEN

"ANYONE WHO CONSIDERS PROTOCOL UNIMPORTANT
HAS NEVER DEALT WITH A CAT."
—ROBERT A. HEINLEIN

I walked in the door at home and the first thing I heard was
"Aaaaachooo!"

"Bless you," I yelled out, not thinking anything about it.
I was halfway down the hallway to my room when Emmy
grabbed my arm and pulled me into her room. Rufus was
lounging on her bed, licking himself. He didn't even bother
to nod at me.

"Where have you been?" she demanded.

"Not that it's any of your business, but I was doing trig
homework at somebody's house." I shrugged off her hand.
"What's your problem?"

"AaaaaaaaaaCHOO!" Sounded like Mom, probably in
her office.

"That's the problem," said Emmy. "But it's yours, not
mine." She pointed at Rufus. "Your little buddy there is giving Mom a serious allergy attack."

"Oh, crap," I said, finally remembering. I poked my head out into the hallway. Mom was standing in the doorway of her office, holding a handful of wadded up tissues. Her nose was stoplight red and her eyes looked bloodshot even from down the hall.

"AAAaaaaaaa . . . AAAAAAAaaaa . . . AAAAA-CHOO!" The force of her sneeze made her lose balance and she sagged against the doorframe of her office.

"Um, bless you," I said. She blurrily focused on me. Kind of.

"Oh, Nat," she said. "I didn't hear you come in. Can you get dinner tonight? I just need to rest my eyes for a minute. I don't know what I'm coming down with, but I don't want you girls to get it. I don't want you to miss any school. I felt fine when I came home, but it hit me after that. I think I'm going to have to stay home from work tomorrow."

Oh, man. That was huge. Mom never missed work. Ever. She missed birthday parties and award ceremonies, but she never ever missed work. I'd forgotten just how bad her allergies were. No wonder they'd shelled out the big bucks for Meep. Designer cats weren't cheap.

"Sure, Mom," I said to her back as she turned around and shuffled into her office. I stepped back into Emmy's room and closed the door.

Emmy poked me in the arm. "He's gotta go," she said. "Mom'll figure out she doesn't have the flu soon enough."

"What's he doing out of my room anyway? Rufus, I told you to stay in there and not leave."

Rufus stopped his licking just long enough to glare at me. *I was bored*, he said.

"Emmy—" I said.

"What? He kept meowing at your door. It was annoying." She shrugged.

I sighed and picked up Rufus and tucked him in my backpack, then poked my head back in the hallway. I heard another sneeze and a small, sad little moan come from behind Mom's closed door. I hurried across the hall to my room.

"If you don't fix this by tomorrow, I'm telling," Emmy called after me. I slammed my door. Frick on a stick. I had to get Rufus out of the house. Sooner or later Mom would figure it out—or wind up in the hospital.

Where in the world was I going to hide a pink cat?

♥

I managed to keep Rufus contained in my room all night, though Meep was no help. They both complained constantly about having to be in the same room together. By the time morning came around, I felt like I got about two hours of sleep. Rufus flat out refused to stay outside while I was at school or actually go outside at all. Apparently, the suburbs just didn't cut it for him.

These paws have not touched grass in years, he said. *And they aren't going to start now.*

Melly pulled up outside and honked her horn. Poodle farts. I grabbed Rufus, stuffed him in my backpack again, and ran for the door. I passed Mom in the hallway and she let out a giant sneeze as I went by.

"Hab a good day at schoolb," she said. "Pay attention to your teaschers."

Well, at least she'd have a better day now that I was getting Rufus out of the house. My day? Somehow, I didn't think it was going to be very good.

I tossed my backpack onto the backseat of Melly's car as I climbed in. It slipped across the leather and banged against the door on the opposite side.

Hey, said Rufus. *Watch it! I'm delicate!*

"Is that the cat?" asked Oscar from the front. "You're taking him to school?"

"I had to. It was either that or Mom was going to sneeze a hole through a wall." I opened the bag so Rufus could stick his head out. "I couldn't think of anything else to do with him."

"Cool," said Oscar. "This'll be fun."

Sometimes I don't know what planet Oscar is on. "So, did you figure anything else out last night?" The last I'd heard, Oscar and Melly were doing more research on guys named Alan that were connected with Easton in any way.

"Not much," said Melly. "She dated a guy named Alan Partridge once, but that was, like, five years ago. He was her tennis instructor when she was a teenager."

"Pretty hot," said Oscar. "I'd return his volleys!"

Like he really would. Oscar was mostly all talk. His last boyfriend had burned him bad. I whacked him in the back of the head. "Get your hormones under control, would you? Have we got anything else to go on?"

"Did you get anything else out of Rufus?" asked Melly.

I glared at the cat. He bared his teeth and gave me his version of a cat smile. "No. Just attitude. He said she talks on the phone a lot, disappears for hours at a time, and smells like makeup." Which describes just about any socialite, as far as I know—and at least half the girls at my school, if not all of them.

Your backpack still smells, said Rufus.

"Just don't pee in it and make it worse," I said. I'd washed it again last night, but there was still a slight lingering odor about it if you put your nose right on it.

"What?" said Melly. She turned around in her seat and the car swerved. "Rufus isn't peeing in my car, is he?"

"Eyes! Road!" I said. "No, he's not peeing in your car. Just drive!"

"Okay, okay," said Melly. "Did you guys get your permission forms signed?"

"You better believe it," said Oscar.

I was drawing a blank. "What form?"

Melly groaned. "To be an extra? Nat, how could you forget?"

"Oh," I said. "Well, I was a little busy trying to keep my wheezing, sneezing mom from discovering that it was my fault she couldn't breathe. Not to mention making dinner and keeping Emmy from telling on me." I dug down into my backpack past Rufus and finally came up with the form. He had put a claw or two through it, but other than that it was okay.

Getting a little fresh, aren't you? asked Rufus. *You could have asked first.*

I ignored him and spread the form out on my lap. I'd learned how to do Mom's signature back in middle school when she was always forgetting to sign permission slips for things. I scribbled a messy "Allison Ng" across the bottom and held it up so Melly could see it in the rearview mirror.

"Okay? All better?"

"Yes," she smiled at me in the mirror. "I couldn't do it without you!"

"Five more miles and I can see Ty," said Oscar. "Drive faster, would you, Melly?"

I sighed. "What about the whole Easton-Rufus thing? How about some focus, you guys?" I really wanted this cat out of my house—and my life. Meep may be stupid, but she's not half as annoying as Rufus. He's classic cat, whereas she's practically part dog.

Oscar made a face at me. "I am a child of the times," he said. "I can totally multitask. Besides, Easton is supposed to be here covering the movie, so maybe she'll be on set while they're filming." He stuck his tongue out at me. "And seriously, girl, it's Ty McKenzie. He's hotter than . . ." He paused. "I don't even know how hot he is, he's so hot."

You people are strange, said Rufus.

Yeah, and that coming from a pink cat with a weird round head and an attitude the size of Texas. This day could not end fast enough for me. But at least I'd get to see Ian first thing. God bless trigonometry.

Now there's something I never thought I'd say.

♥

I stuck my Rufus-filled backpack between my feet as I sat down in trig. I'd warned him—repeatedly—that he was not to even let a whisker show, but I didn't trust him. I figured I'd be able to feel him move if I kept the bag there. I set all my books and notebooks down under the desk, except for my trig stuff. With Rufus in my pack, I was carrying almost everything else. Pity my locker was on the other side of the campus.

Ian came in right after me. "Hey, Nat," he said. "Sleep good?" He sat down and smiled at me, a corner of his mouth higher than the other and one eyebrow raised. Wow, that was entirely too shmexy for this early in the morning. My day was looking much better already.

I smiled back. "Okay," I said. "You?"

"Visions of functions dancing in my head," he said and laughed. "Thanks to you."

"Oh, so you were dreaming about me then, huh?" Ha, look at me. Taking a flirting page out of the book of Melly. I put my hand on my face and leaned on my elbow to hide the blush I could feel threatening to come out.

He winked at me. "Yeah, you must have done a 'number' on me yesterday."

Oh, we were just made of cheese. I was trying to think of some funny but flirty comeback when Rufus poked a claw all the way through my book bag and into my leg. I jumped and knocked my notebook onto the floor. Why had I let that stupid cat talk me into removing the claw protectors on his paws? Maybe that Easton lookalike had the right idea. If I didn't know I'd lose a finger or even a hand in the attempt, I'd try to trim those claws. But if Rufus was anything like Meep, clipping his toenails was completely out of the question. She hated it worse than bath time. I'd yet to meet a cat that didn't, though there were rumors they existed.

"You okay?" Ian asked. He picked up my notebook and handed it to me.

"Um, yeah," I said. "Peachy. My leg just fell asleep, I guess." I kicked like I was trying to wake my leg up, but it didn't dislodge Rufus' claw. He let out a little yelp and dug in harder. I coughed to cover up the noise. I reached down and shifted my bag to unhook him, all the while smiling at Ian like a clown on drugs. He just looked at me with that one eyebrow climbing higher and higher.

"Frog in my throat," I said. I wished once again that my cat talking was telepathic. If it were, I'd be giving Rufus a piece of my mind—a big piece. I shoved the bag back under the chair, not caring if I ruffled the fur of his precious highness.

"Oo-kay," said Ian. "Do you need some water?"

"No, I'm fine," I said. Stupid cat. Mr. Beck saved me by coming in the room waving a handful of papers.

"Okay, people," Mr. Beck said. "Are you ready? What do you say we take a test today?"

I loved how he made it a question, as if we had any choice at all in the matter. He handed the stack of tests to a guy named Shackerman and told him to pass it out. Ian looked at me a little nervously and I gave him a thumbs-up. Hopefully the tutoring yesterday helped him and he'd want to do it again. Melly always said the way to a guy's heart was through his stomach (she could make a mean cupcake), but I hoped you could get there through homework too.

The test was pretty easy. I hoped Ian was doing as well on it as I was. I peeked his way a few times and saw him chewing on his pencil, but he wasn't obviously sweating bullets or anything. If my tutoring had helped, that had to be a good thing, right?

I was almost done with the test when I felt Rufus moving around. I poked him with my toe. He stopped for a second and then started shifting around again. I looked around, but no one seemed to have noticed. Mr. Beck was staring at the clock and humming. I dropped my pencil on the floor and leaned down to get it.

"Stop it," I whispered. "Someone is going to see you."

I have to use the facilities, Rufus whispered back.

"What?"

I have to pee!

I faked another coughing fit to cover up Rufus' outburst. Ian looked over at me and raised his eyebrow again. Mr. Beck did too, but it wasn't nearly so cute on him.

"Problem, Miss Ng?" he asked.

"Just a little cough," I said. Now half the class was looking at me. I felt my face turn red. I hoped Ian couldn't tell ... much. "Um, could I go to the bathroom?" I coughed again, doing my best to sound like I was hacking up a fur ball. "I think maybe I just need some water."

Mr. Beck sighed. "All right, Miss Ng, but no loitering in the hallways. You've only got another ten minutes to finish your test."

I nodded and coughed again. I leaned over to get my backpack and stood up to leave. I was two steps away from the door when Mr. Beck cleared his throat.

"You can leave the backpack," he said. "We are in the middle of a test here, Miss Ng."

I wished he'd quit with the "Miss Ng" thing. It was really annoying, especially since he could barely pronounce it. He drew it out too long. How hard was it to just say "ing"?

"I, um, need it," I said.

Now everyone in the class was looking at me. My face felt like it was on fire.

"You 'need' it?" asked Mr. Beck. He raised his eyebrow again. Someone should really tell him that's not attractive on an old guy. At least, not one with a double chin and really bushy eyebrows.

"Yeah . . . ," I said and stopped. I couldn't think of a good reason to give that didn't involve a cat about to pee on my homework.

Shackerman giggled. "Lady troubles," he said loud enough for everyone to hear. Oh, God. My face went from fire to molten lava.

Mr. Beck's face did too. "Just go, Miss Ng. But hurry back."

I rushed out the door. Hurry back? I might never return. This stupid cat was ruining my life.

eLeVeN

"CATS, FLIES, AND WOMEN ARE EVER AT THEIR TOILETS."
—FRENCH PROVERB

I hurried down the hall to the bathroom and pushed through the door. No one was in there, for once. At least one of my prayers had been answered. I went in the stall farthest from the door and opened the bag so Rufus could get out.

"Don't even talk to me," I said. "Just go."

Go where, exactly? Rufus looked around the stall. It was standard school issue: chipped green paint, dingy gray tile, and a toilet with water stains around the base.

"Oh, for . . . here." I picked him up and held him over the toilet. He immediately tried to climb up my arms toward my head. "Ow! What are you doing?"

What are you doing? There's water in there!

"Duh! It's the toilet! Hold still. I won't let you fall in. It's the only place I've got for you to go!" I grabbed him firmly around the middle and tried to force him back down to the seat. He went whirling dervish on me and wound up

93

clinging to my shoulder with all four paws—and his claws.

"Agh! Let go! I told you, I'm not going to let you fall in! You have to have seen a toilet before. I mean, *come on*! You're not a kitten!"

Rufus finally released my shoulder and I dropped him onto the ground. He landed on a stray piece of (hopefully unused) toilet paper that was lying on the floor. I tried to get a look at my shoulder. It felt like a bad acupuncturist had gone crazy on me.

This place, he said, *is absolutely disgusting.*

Like a litter box isn't pure nasty? "It's a public high-school bathroom. What did you expect? It's all we've got." He gave me a wicked look. "Look, there's a seat, okay? I'm just going to hold you up on it so you can go. I promise I will not drop you. You will not get wet. So do you have to go or not? I've got to get back to class."

If I must. But if one drop of water lands on this fur, I will carve you into little pieces.

Yeah, like he hadn't already. I could see at least one pinprick of blood coming through my T-shirt already and there were bound to be more. I picked him up again and held him over the toilet. Just as he was getting his feet firmly planted on the seat, I heard the door open.

Frick. "Just do your thing and don't say anything," I whispered. It was a good thing I'd closed the stall door out of habit.

"Oh, wow, I haven't been in a bathroom this gross since

high school," said a voice that sounded strangely familiar.

"Well, Victoria's camped out in the teacher's lounge bathroom, so this is it. Alan seriously needs to have a talk with her. She's a total—"

"Shhhh, Claire! Someone might hear you."

"Oh, I don't care, Candace. Everyone knows she's turned into a huge diva. It's ridiculous. I don't care if she is the love interest. This is Ty's movie, not hers." A toilet flushed.

Claire? Candace? It must be Claire Ryan and Candace Grace! They were B-level teen starlets. I vaguely remembered Oscar mentioning they were in the film too. But Alan? Who was he? I tried to take a peek through the crack between the door and the wall, but I couldn't move far enough to see without dropping Rufus. He hissed. Quietly, thankfully.

"Sorry," I whispered.

"I worked with her on her first movie, you know," said Candace. "I thought she was pretty nice."

"Yeah, well, fame does some funny things to people. She could act back then too." A stall door banged open.

"Seriously. Hey, have you seen Easton? I told her I'd do an exclusive, but I haven't seen her on the set since the day she got here."

Rufus finally started to pee. He obviously really had to go. He must have drunk a gallon of water this morning, from the sound of it.

"No, I haven't seen her," said Claire. "Did you hear about her cat being kidnapped? It even made *The Daily*

Show. Supposedly, Easton's staying at Victoria's place to recuperate."

"Total weirdness. I swear I saw them about to throw down the first day Easton showed up on set, and then I haven't seen her since. I thought she was here to write about how bad Victoria sucks now."

Someone turned the water on for a few seconds and then turned it back off. There was a moment of silence, and a small horrified gasp. Claire said, "Do you smell *that*?"

Two words: cat pee. Actually, five words. Prodigious amounts of cat pee.

"Shhhh," said Candace. "Let's just go, okay? Don't be rude."

I heard the door swing shut behind them. A few moments later, Rufus finally stopped peeing. *You can put me down now,* he said.

I put him directly back in my backpack. I wasn't going to take any chances and besides, I had only, like, three minutes to get back to class and finish my test. Good thing I had only one more problem to do.

Honestly, if I didn't have to turn my test in and pick up my books, I'd skip going back entirely. At least Candace and Claire hadn't actually seen me. Even though I didn't know them, I still didn't want them to think my pee smelled like cat pee. That was just wrong.

TWELVE

"THE CAT PRETENDS TO SLEEP, THE BETTER TO SEE."
—FRANCOIS-AUGUSTE RENE DE CHATEAUBRIAND

I met Melly and Oscar outside the cafeteria after dumping all of my books and notebooks in my locker. Rufus wasn't as fat as Meep, but he was heavy enough. And when you added his weight to all the books I normally had to cart around, the result was nothing short of a big backache. Dropping off my books didn't seem to make a difference, though. I was starting to think he must have smuggled some cans of tuna in there or something.

"I've got news," I said. "I heard Claire Ryan and Candace Grace talking in the bathroom. They said they haven't seen Easton on set since the day she got here."

"You saw Claire Ryan and Candace Grace?" Oscar jumped up, his eyes as round as bowling balls and his hands flapping. "What were they wearing? How did they look?"

"I don't know," I said. "I only heard them pee. I didn't actually see them. Rufus had a bathroom emergency."

"Oh," said Oscar, momentarily deflated. "Well, how did they sound?"

"Gross!" said Melly before I had a chance to say it.

"I meant their voices, you goons! Get your minds out of the toilet!"

Oscar and Melly followed me into the cafeteria. "You're missing the point, Oscar," I said. "They said they haven't seen Easton on the set at all since the first day. So there's no way we're going to run into the lookalike here."

We got in the sandwich line and I ordered two tuna sandwiches.

"Hungry?" asked Oscar.

"One's for Rufus," I said. "Duh."

"Oh yeah! I forgot all about that. How's that going?"

"Don't ask." I should have made Oscar carry the stupid cat around all day. At least Rufus had kept his head down for second period, but in my art class, he'd started sneezing like crazy. He'd said it was the smell of paint, but whatever it was, I'd had to fake sneeze all through class to cover it up. By the end of the day, the entire school was going to think I was some allergy-prone weirdo with "lady troubles."

We sat down and I opened the backpack enough to stick the tuna sandwich in. Rufus didn't even complain for once, he just tore into it. I was seriously going to have to throw away my backpack after this craziness was over. He wasn't exactly a delicate eater.

"Are you guys as excited as I am?" asked Melly. "Only

a few hours to go until we get to be extras in a real movie!"

"You know it," sang out Oscar. "I am R-E-A-D-Y ready!"

"So, how's it work?" I asked. I'd given Melly my permission form in the car after faking my mom's signature, but I hadn't actually read it, so I really had no clue.

"We're just going to be background extras. That means that we may or may not even be in the movie. Like, they're going to have a bunch of kids around for 'color,' but there's no guarantee we'll actually be in the shot." Melly sighed.

"And they'll feed us!" said Oscar the bottomless pit. "Craft services, here I come!"

"No, I meant, like where are we supposed to go and stuff like that?" Not like I was ever going to be doing this again. I didn't care about the really technical details.

"Oh! We're supposed to meet at the auditorium for a costume check right when school lets out and then come back here to the cafeteria. They're shooting a lunchroom scene. That's why they need all the extras."

"Costume check?"

"Yeah, they make sure no one is wearing any kind of logo on their T-shirts and stuff like that. Maybe give out some clothes if someone shows up in something really inappropriate."

"Like that freshman girl who's always being sent home for the tiny skirts," said Oscar. "You think she'd learn. I mean, seriously, no one wants to see your thong."

"How long is this going to take?" I was hoping to have some new place to dump Rufus at tonight. There was no way

I could bring him home again, and so far, I had absolutely no idea what I was going to do with him. He'd suggested a kitty hotel, but I'd looked them up and they were super expensive, especially the one he said he wanted to go to after I read him the descriptions. Like he needed catnip brought to him on a pillow.

"We should be done by six o'clock. Maybe seven. The cafeteria scene is pretty short." She lowered her voice and pulled some papers from her bag. "I snitched some of the pages for today's shoot from the guy I turned the forms in to. Ty is Freddy and Victoria is Molly."

"Rock on!" said Oscar. He grabbed the pages from Melly and started to pore over them. "You wait and see, Melly. You're going to wind up starring in this movie. I just know it."

I'd bet ten bucks that Oscar already knew the pages by heart. It always surprised me how his brain worked. Stuff that would take me hours to commit to memory he could get in seconds. But ask him to do a math problem? It wasn't pretty.

Sometimes it amazed me that the three of us had become such good friends. Oscar and Melly had the whole starstruck thing in common, but I was honestly not all that interested in any of it. Who wore what when and why and all of that just didn't excite me. Of course, when we'd first started hanging out, Oscar's celebrity addiction really hadn't started yet and Melly had been a scrawny tomboy with semipermanent scabs on her knees from daredevil stunts on the playground. A lot had changed over the years. Yet here we were, still together even if we did drive each other a little nuts. In a good way.

"Make sure you read the pages, Nat," said Melly as we were getting up to go. "**We should all be prepared. It could** give us an edge."

"Yeah, sure," I said. She gave me an I-don't-believe-you look, so I took the pages from Oscar and started reading on my way out of the cafeteria. It was okay. Kinda normal teen movie stuff. I knew what they were talking about only because Melly had made us watch the Ferris Bueller movie twice this past weekend in preparation.

I wondered if Ian was into old movies. Melly had a collection of, like, every teen movie ever made, and her dad had built a theater room down in their basement so she could study up on them. That could work as a second date, couldn't it? Assuming we actually made it through the first one okay. Also assuming it was safe to bring Ian around Melly and Oscar in their natural habitat. People thought Oscar was crazy at school, but it was nothing like as weird as he could get out of school. It might take some warm-up time for Ian to appreciate the jaw-dropping awesomeness that the full-on Oscar experience brought to your life.

I was folding the pages up to stick them in the front pouch of my backpack when Emmy appeared out of nowhere and grabbed my arm. I nearly dropped the backpack and Rufus let out a grumpy growl.

"Watch it!" I said. "What're you doing?"

"Was that the cat?" asked Emmy, her eyes wide.

"Shhh! Yeah, I couldn't leave him at home, not with mom there."

"Well, she's not there now. She's *here*. I just saw her heading to the principal's office."

"What? Why?" Surely Mr. Beck hadn't called about the whole trig thing? He'd seemed okay when I got back to class. He just wouldn't look at me, unlike stupid Shackerman, who'd given me a huge wink. The jerk. I hated that guy.

"She said she was feeling better. I guess because Rufus was gone, so that makes sense now. And since she wasn't at work, she thought she'd come in to complain about the movie thing. You know, because of my test being moved and all that? Oh my God, Nat, what am I going to do? If she really gets the movie shoot canceled and people find out it was my fault, I'm dead!"

Holy hairy llamas. She wasn't the only one. I'd be guilty by association.

"You've got to do something!" Emmy had a death grip on my arm, but that was second to my own realization that there was actually something one of my sisters couldn't handle. Imagine that. A chink in her armor.

Inspiration, though sketchy, finally came to me. "You go find Principal Johnson and delay him. I saw him in the cafeteria a few minutes ago." He'd made me nervous too, what with Rufus in my bag. He had a knack for figuring out when you were up to something. "I'll deal with Mom."

"Okay," said Emmy. "I'll try." She paled even more and turned to go.

"And Emmy?"

She looked at me.

"If this works out, we're even. Got it?"

She nodded and scampered off like a scared rabbit. Heh. Depending on how painful the next ten minutes were, maybe I should have said that *she* would owe *me*.

THIRTEEN

"EXERCISE IS FOR DOGS."
—RUFUS BRUTUS THE THIRD

I ran down the hall toward the principal's office. Mom would've had to come in through the main door, since it was the only one accessible during the day for visitors. I had a chance of getting to her before she got to the office if I cut through the library.

I almost ran over a freshman carrying a stack of books, but I saw Mom ahead of me walking in that stiff I'm-going-to-kick-butt way she did whenever she was about to go medieval on someone. I slowed down.

If you do that again, I'm going to use your back as a pin cushion. I told you before, I don't enjoy the sensation of becoming a milkshake, said Rufus.

"Shhh!" I whispered over my shoulder. "I'm sorry, but if you say another word, I'm totally going to dunk you in the toilet." He let out a low hiss, but didn't say anything else. "And I'm sorry for this too, but you're just going to have to suck it up." I let the bag slip down my left arm and I stuck my right hand in the top and rubbed it all over Rufus, making sure I came in contact with his skin. That's where the dander was. Then I shut the top up tight again before he could bite me.

"Mom!" I said as I caught up to her. "What're you doing here? Are you feeling better?"

"Oh hi, Natalie. Yes, I suppose it must have been one of those twenty-four hour things. I'm feeling fine now." She stopped walking as I stepped in front of her. "Shouldn't you be in class?"

"I just got out of lunch. I've got a few minutes. It's, um, good to see you!" Would she buy that? I patted her on the shoulder for good measure, hoping some of Rufus's hair would stick to her cardigan.

"Well, thank you. It's good to see you too." She looked at me quizzically, like she was trying to determine if I was up to something—which I was. Good thing Viv wasn't here to rat me out.

"I just don't get to see you during the day usually, you know. So it's good to see you." I smiled big and hoped she hadn't noticed the sweat popping out on my forehead. I really sucked at lying.

"Right," said Mom, ever the literal one. "I'm usually at work while you're at school."

This wasn't going exactly well. How was I supposed to get Rufus's dander on her? If I kept up this inane conversation,

I could bet the next step would be for her to frog-march me to the school nurse and have me checked for mind-altering substances.

"So, um, what are you doing in school?" That would be the obvious next question, right?

"I'm here to talk to your principal about the movie being filmed here. It's just unacceptable!"

Uh-oh, maybe I shouldn't have gone there. She looked fired up.

"I don't know what he was thinking when he okayed it, but he certainly didn't ask the PTA!" Did a principal need to get permission from the PTA to hold an event at his school? I didn't know, but Mom sure thought he did.

Was it possible to reason with her? That wasn't the route I normally chose, but it was apparent that just proximity to Rufus's dander wasn't doing the trick.

"It's really not a big deal," I said. "They've kept the disruptions to a minimum, you know. And most of the filming stuff is taking place after hours and on weekends."

"Anything that interrupts the school day is a big deal, Natalie." She raised her eyebrows at me like she couldn't believe I would suggest otherwise.

"But it's a good extracurricular activity, don't you think? It's, um, allowing us to experience firsthand what the movie business is like. And some of the students are really excited about being able to act as extras. That's an opportunity they wouldn't normally get, especially not in a safe environment

106

like school, don't you think?" I'd thrown in every buzzword I could think of.

Mom looked at me closely, her blue eyes blinking rapidly like she was trying to process what I'd said. It obviously wasn't computing for her. "Are Melly and Oscar caught up in this movie-making thing?"

Busted. But maybe I could keep her talking long enough for Rufus to have an effect on her. "Yes, but you know how much it would mean to Melly to be discovered. This could be her chance."

"Natalie," said Mom gently, "I've told you before what I think of Melly's dream. That's all it is—a dream. You both would be better off concentrating on your schoolwork and real life."

I shuffled my feet. The halls were starting to thin out. In about one minute I was going to be late for my biology class. Emmy had B lunch, so hopefully she was still on Principal Johnson's case, but I wasn't sure if I could trust her to keep him occupied. She was such a suck-up. She never did anything she wasn't supposed to.

"Dreams aren't necessarily a bad thing," I said. Though in my mom's world, I guessed they were. If you couldn't put some kind of quantitative value on it, it wasn't real.

"Of course not, but school is not the time or place for—" Mom stopped and sighed. I think even she was realizing what a stick she sounded like. "Natalie, I'm sure you'll understand when you're older."

Like I hadn't heard that before. Apparently, once I hit twenty-one, I was going to have some kind of epiphany and the world would suddenly make sense. Or maybe it wouldn't be until I was thirty. Mom had never been too clear on that point.

"But you really ought to be getting to class. I'll see you at home and we can talk about it some more then, okay?" She stepped around me and sneezed.

"Wait!" Oh man, just when Rufus was finally starting to get to her!

"What now, Natalie?"

I had to do something. I reached up and put a hand on either side of her face, trying to position my right hand as close to her nose as I could without actually covering it up. It wasn't too hard to do that, since I could barely reach her face anyway, she was so tall. I pulled her face down to mine and kissed her on the cheek.

"I just want you to know that I, um, really appreciate what you're doing for me and Emmy. I know you're only doing it for our own good, even if I don't agree with you." I let her go and stepped back. Now there's something I never thought I'd say. Would she buy it or would she drag me off to the nearest research lab to conduct tests on the alien that had obviously taken over her daughter's body?

Mom touched her cheek and came away with a cat hair, but I don't think she noticed. "Why, Natalie. That's so sweet of you!" Were her eyes actually tearing up? Wow. I think I just seriously bought myself some brownie points. She wiped at her eye and blinked. Was it my imagination or did her eye start swelling immediately?

"You okay, Mom?" The guilt started welling up just a little, looking at that eye. It was *definitely* swollen. Maybe even a little red.

"Fine," she said, and sneezed again, then sniffled.

"Maybe you're still sick? You really ought to go back home." I stepped back. "I don't want to get sick."

"Maybe you're right." Mom sneezed again. That Rufus. Boy, he's got some powerful dander. I felt a little bad about infecting Mom again, but not too much. I knew she was going to feel better as soon as she got away from Rufus. Well, and washed her face.

"Maybe you should go take a nice hot bath and have some soup." I grabbed her arm and started leading her down the hall back to the front door. At first she pulled back, but then she sneezed three more times and let me lead her along. "And tonight is Dad's night for dinner. You should take it easy."

"Well, I—" She sneezed again and stopped resisting completely. "Hmph. If this doesn't clear up by tomorrow, I'm going to have to call the doctor. Okay, Natalie. If you start feeling sick too, call your father, okay? We don't want to infect anyone else."

"No problem," I said. "I mean, I feel fine, but I'll call Dad if I need to." I gave her back one final pat and watched as she went off down the hall. Then I made a run for biology.

FOURTEEN

"HONEST AS THE CAT WHEN THE MEAT'S OUT OF REACH."
—OLD ENGLISH PROVERB

The wardrobe lady deemed my jeans acceptable, but made me change shirts because of the little blood specks that had seeped through. I told her they were ketchup so she wouldn't be totally grossed out, though I had no idea how I would have gotten ketchup on my shoulder. She gave me a sleeve-less black and white striped shirt with a really weird collar and lace fringe and told me to keep the collar up. I'm not sure what look she was going for. I looked like I had neck wings.

Then she sent me to the makeup lady for some extra eye-liner. She seriously layered it on, so I looked like Cleopatra after a crying jag. Very cringeworthy. I hoped I was one of the extras who didn't make it into the movie. The good news was that even if, by some miracle, the Easton impostor actually did show up, the chances of her recognizing me were pretty slim.

Melly and Oscar were accepted as is, which completely

astonished me—about Oscar, anyway. Melly looked kind of on the preppy-pretty side today, but Oscar was his typical slightly grunge, slightly punk self. I guess with his hair being what it was, he was going to be typecast anyway. Maybe that was why they'd stuck me in a strange shirt, to go with my kinda funky dip dyed purple hair.

When we got to the cafeteria, there were already a bunch of kids in line. It looked like half the school had shown up. I even saw Ian over in a corner with a bunch of other juniors. I was debating about heading over that way, even after the whole trig debacle from the morning (not to mention the hideous shirt and eyeliner), when a guy with a clipboard came up to us.

"Okay," he said. "What do we have here? Did you already turn in your slips?"

Melly gave him our names and he checked us off a list. Then he looked us up and down, spending an extra long time on Melly. "You," he said, pointing to her. "Let's put you on table three. That's over there." He pointed to a table right next to the one that was obviously the actors' table, based on all the lights focused on it. Melly squealed and took off without even waiting for us.

Oscar and I started to follow. "Wait a minute," said the guy. "You two, you're on table five. That one." He pointed to another table a few tables down from Melly's, kind of close to the cash register. There were already a few kids sitting there, including two junior girls who were either really emo or had also had a run-in with the makeup lady, and a senior guy with a nose ring, an eyebrow ring, and probably a few other metallic embellishments in places I didn't even want to think about. Clearly, we had been relegated to the freak table while Melly was all set to enjoy herself in the land of the "cool" kids.

Oscar and I looked at each other and then trudged over to the table and sat down. "Hey," said the guy with all the piercings. We nodded at him. I'd seen him around before, but I didn't know anything about him other than that he was a senior. The two depressed-looking girls just ignored us. I sat my book bag with Rufus in it on the seat between me and Oscar. Luckily, Rufus was still in a tuna coma from lunch. I hoped it was going to last through the shoot.

"Isn't this movie about a guy who *isn't* cool?" I asked Oscar. "Isn't that why he wants to re-live Ferris Bueller's day?"

"Yeah," said Oscar. "But there's regular uncool and movie uncool. We're real-life cool. You can't bottle that."

Apparently, we were uncool to these people in any situation. Melly had been deemed worthy, and Ian too. He was seated at her table. She finally noticed that we weren't sitting with her at the unpierced kids table. We waved to her. She made a face like she was going to get up and move, but then Ty McKenzie came in and she sat her butt back down. Betrayed by my best friend for a teen star! But I can't lie. Ian was at that table. I'd probably have stayed too.

Ty took his place at the table by Melly's. Oscar started

hyperventilating, as did pretty much every girl in the cafeteria. I noticed that Melly was mostly keeping it together, trying to act cool. But I could tell she was freaking out because she kept almost picking at her nails and then stopping. She'd broken herself from the habit by sheer willpower when she was in middle school, but it still popped up every now and then when she got stressed out.

"Okay, kids!" said the same guy who'd relegated us to the freak table. "Listen up! My name is Jason and I'm the AD."

"Ah," said Oscar. "The assistant director." He nodded like he knew what he was talking about, and the pierced guy looked at him with new respect.

"We've got a tight schedule today, so I need you to listen up. Everyone needs to take his or her assigned positions. If I didn't give you one when you came in, come see me. Now, in all of the shots we're going to be taking today, we need you to be as quiet as possible unless I say otherwise. But we want you to act natural, like you're eating or talking with your friends. Do not look directly at the cameras. I know most of you have never acted before, so I've got Candace Grace and Claire Ryan here to show you how it's done."

The two girls I'd heard in the bathroom stepped forward. If I remembered right, they were actually both twenty-two, but they looked like sixteen-year-olds, if sixteen-year-olds commonly had boob jobs. They smiled at all of us and waved to a couple of guys who were wolf whistling in the back of the cafeteria. Then the girls started chatting with each other without making a sound.

"So cool," said Oscar. "I can totally do that."

I snorted. It would be a miracle if Oscar made it through five minutes without making a sound. But maybe the excitement of being on a movie set would hold him in check. I kind of doubted it.

The girls finished, gave another wave, and we all politely applauded. It didn't actually look that hard.

"Okay," said Jason. "That's how it's done. We'll also be doing a short panning shot as Ty and Victoria walk to their table. They're going to be doing lines while this is going on, so I want to stress again how important it is for you to be as quiet as possible. That also goes for applause at the end of a scene. Even if the director has said, 'Cut,' I expect all of you to sit quietly. There are no exceptions." He looked around the room with a stern glare. I elbowed Oscar and he studiously ignored me. The safe bet would be that we were going to get kicked out by the end of filming.

"Okay then. Alan will be out in a second and then we're all getting started. Now would be a good time for a bathroom break if you need one."

"He said Alan!" I said to Oscar. "Did you hear that? Who's Alan?"

"A. F. Leonard, the director," said the pierced guy. "Alan Francis. He's why I'm here. He directed *Rough Diamonds*. Incredible movie. I'm not much of a Ty McKenzie fan."

"D'oh!" said Oscar, and whacked himself in the fore-head. "I should have realized that! Thanks, man!"

"No problem. It's Garrett, by the way."

I noticed how Garrett was only looking at Oscar and not at all at me or the two emo chicks, who were huddled as far away from us as they could get. Hmmm. I wondered if Oscar had noticed. It didn't seem like it. He just dived right into movie talk instead of flirting. Maybe that was his way of flirt-ing? I didn't often get to see him do his thing.

"*Rough Diamonds* was awesome. But you have to give Ty credit for *Cyber Runner*. He totally pulled that one off."

"Um, not to interrupt, Oscar, but can we get back to our little Rufus problem?" I smiled at Garrett so he wouldn't think I was totally ignoring him. He didn't even look at me.

"Who's Rufus?" he asked Oscar.

"Oh, Rufus? He's—"

I kicked Oscar under the table. "Nobody," I said. I smiled at Garrett again. "Hey, isn't that the director over there?" He turned to look where I was pointing. Some longhaired guy had just walked in, but I had no idea if it was really the direc-tor or not. I pulled Oscar's head down next to mine. "We're back at zero," I whispered. "We already knew Easton knew the director guy. That's probably how she wound up on the set, right? So it tells us nothing."

"I don't know about that," said Oscar. "Didn't Rufus say something about her always changing her voice when she talked to him on the phone? And demanding stuff? Easton's

115

super famous and rich as all sin, but what's she going to demand from him? He's the director!"

"Hey," said Garrett, "that is Alan! And there's Victoria Welling too."

Even the emo twins turned to look. Victoria was in the lead and she looked like she was reading Alan the riot act about something. I couldn't hear her from here, but neither of them looked happy. Actually, Alan looked unhappy. Victoria just looked constipated.

Then she turned and looked right at me and froze. Her face broke into something I could only describe as a snarl. Geez. The shirt wasn't *that* bad.

FIFTEEN

"THE PROBLEM WITH CATS IS THAT THEY GET THE SAME EXACT LOOK
WHETHER THEY SEE A MOTH OR AN AX-MURDERER."
—PAULA POUNDSTONE

Jason, the AD (as he liked to remind us constantly), walked us through a test shot as practice. Ty, Victoria, Claire, and Candace were all on their marks or whatever. Ty and Victoria had lunch trays in front of them with sandwiches and fruit. I couldn't tell from here if it was fake or not, but it looked way better than the sandwich I'd eaten at lunch. Claire and Candace were apparently supposed to have brought their meals. Claire only had a yogurt but Candace had the full sushi setup with chopsticks and everything. If she had been a real teenager at our school, she'd have been laughed out of the lunchroom. Not to mention, where would she have kept *raw fish* refrigerated all morning? In her locker? Whoever was in charge of props had obviously never gone to a public high school.

Melly's table was right next to theirs and the camera was pointed right at her. Well, at the actors, with Melly right behind them. I could tell by the way she was practically vibrating in her seat that she was totally flipping out, but she was holding it together pretty well. Ian's back was to the camera, which meant he was more or less facing me. He looked really cute in the blue shirt the costume lady must have given him. He hadn't been wearing it this morning. It looked like they'd made him brush his hair too.

Alan, the director guy, was sitting behind a big monitor on one of those classic director's chairs. I didn't know they actually used those in real life. His name wasn't written on the back, though.

I had to admit this was kind of cool. It felt like we were in the middle of one of those behind the scenes things on a DVD. I would never ever, however, admit this to Oscar.

"Okay, kids, when it's time for you do your thing, I'll yell out 'Background!' and I expect you to shut up immediately. Remember, don't look at any of the cameras." Jason pointed to the biggest camera, which was trained directly on Ty. "Just act natural."

Yeah, natural. I doubted if he really wanted that. He wanted movie natural, not regular high-school natural.

Jason walked back over near the director. "Then Alan will say 'Rolling!' or 'Roll film.' Sometimes he'll jump right to 'Action,' but either way, it means things are underway."

He walked over to the actors and nodded to Ty. "Let's go ahead and walk through a few lines and then I'll turn every-one over to Alan."

Ty nodded. Then, without even stopping to mentally prepare himself or whatever it is that actors do, he turned to Victoria and started his lines.

"I'm going to do it," he said.

Victoria looked blankly at him and picked up her sandwich. "Do what?"

Claire and Candace slowly walked by the table and crossed behind Ty. From the angle of the camera, I guessed they were kind of in the background of the shot.

Ty leaned over and looked intently into Victoria's eyes. "Do something about my life, that's what!" He glanced over his shoulder at Claire. She was dressed as a typical queen bee movie hottie: short plaid skirt, tight-fitting white Oxford shirt halfway unbuttoned, and some low red heels. Basically, hot girl a la Britney Spears in the early days. I doubted Principal Johnson would actually allow that outfit on a real student.

"Trina is never going to notice me. No one is ever going to notice me unless I do something—something big."

Victoria glanced from Claire (who, apparently, was playing the character named Trina) to Ty and made an exaggeratedly sad face. If I had to guess the plot, I'd say she was the always-a-bridesmaid best friend, but the eventual love interest of Ty's character. They'd stuck some clunky glasses on her and pulled her hair back into an unflattering messy ponytail, the hallmarks of the "ugly" girl who always gets a makeover by the end.

"Like what?"

"Remember that old movie we watched last weekend? The one about Ferris Bueller?"

"Yeah?"

"*That's* what I'm going to do."

"Cut!" yelled Jason, making everyone except the actors jump. They were probably used to it. "Okay, kids, you did good with the keeping quiet, but I need you to not watch the actors and hang on their every word. Remember, this is supposed to be an average school day for you. Ty isn't Ty McKenzie, he's Freddy Barnes, okay?"

"That was awesome," whispered Oscar. "Just like in the script."

Garrett immediately perked up. "You have a copy of the script?"

I pulled the slightly crumpled pages out of my backpack and held them out. Oscar grabbed them from me and passed them to Garrett like I wasn't capable of doing it myself. Or maybe he wanted to be the one to give them to Garrett.

"Just this scene. My friend Melly got them," said Oscar. "She's over at the good table." He nodded in Melly's direction.

"Cool," said Garrett, reading the pages under the table.

"All right, Jason, it's my turn," said Alan. "Let's take it from the top, shall we?"

What happened next was the most boring hour or so of my life, ever. Alan had the actors do the scene a bunch of times using different inflection in their voices, sometimes changing a line or two or just changing how Claire walked by. He gave them some pep talks, even sat at the table once and showed Ty how he wanted him to look. Between takes, Victoria was constantly hounding the director for some perceived slight in shooting her, or alternately, she complained when he corrected her acting and asked her to act more natural. I saw Candace and Claire roll their eyes more than once.

The actors eventually got through more dialog than the first run-through, though it took longer because of Victoria's interruptions. But after listening to it five or six times, I was already sure I didn't need to see the movie to know what was going to happen. Ty (a.k.a. Freddy) was the so-called loser at school with a crush on a hot girl. Victoria (Molly) was his best friend with a crush on him. He decides to go all Ferris Bueller, goes on crazy adventures with Victoria, and attracts the admiration of Claire (Trina). But in the end he realizes that Victoria's the girl for him. Classic ugly duckling teen story. In real life, Freddy's antics would make him a laughingstock, his "ugly" best friend would ditch him as soon as she got the makeover, and the crazy stunts he pulled would get him expelled. And the hot girl? She was probably dating the captain of the football team.

That wasn't entirely true. The captain of our cheerleading squad was actually dating the captain of the basketball team.

I was bored out of my skull, but Melly still seemed perky as ever and Oscar was even behaving himself. Between takes, he and Garrett chatted about Alan's other movies, and which movies Ty had sucked in. Rufus snored a little, but luckily it happened between takes and no one noticed. I was just thankful he was still asleep.

They finally set up for the next take, which was apparently the scene before the one we'd just watched them film a bazillion times. In this one, Victoria and Ty were walking to their lunch table. They were actually going to pass right by ours. Oscar nearly hyperventilated when he heard that, but quickly controlled himself. That was probably Garrett's influence. If it was just me at the table, he probably would have done his happy dance.

They did a practice run first, with the camera tracking them along the way. While they were setting up the camera, I noticed Victoria staring at me again. Even Garrett noticed.

"Did you, like, send her bad fan mail or something?" he asked. "With naked pictures?"

"*No*," I said. "I barely even watch her movies, except the ones Oscar makes me go to." She was kind of creeping me out. Of course, she'd been arguing off and on with Alan the whole time, so maybe she just didn't like anyone. Well, other than Ty. She could barely get through her lines half the time, she was making such goggle eyes at him. Way more than the part called for.

"Okay," barked the Director. "I'm not liking the dynamic here. Victoria, let's have you on the other side of Ty. And pause here to do your lines instead of walking through them." He put down some masking tape in an X pattern only a foot away from our table, right behind my back. Oscar started primping his hair. Great. Now I really was going to be in the movie. Like, visible. Stupid neck wings.

"Let's walk through one more time. On your marks, please, everyone."

Jason gave all of us the evil eye again and we all settled down quickly. He'd already kicked Shackerman off the set for not shutting up fast enough. Served him right.

Ty and Victoria walked from their starting mark to the new spot Alan had put on the floor. They ran their lines and then continued on to their table. Then Victoria came unglued all over Alan.

"I should be standing on the other side. It's closer to the camera. He's blocking me." Ty stood back, looking supremely bored, as she got in Alan's face for yet another diva attack. Easton had been totally right about her.

That's when my good luck with Rufus apparently ran out. He woke up. I could tell because my backpack wiggled and thumped as he struggled to poke his head through. Luckily, everyone's eyes were on Victoria and Ty.

I hunched over the bag. "Stop it! What are you doing? Do you have to pee again?" I poked Oscar in the side. He looked confused for a minute and then leaned over too to help me cover things up.

No, hissed Rufus. *I smell the impostor! Let me out!*

What? "Who do you smell?" I looked around. I didn't see the Easton lookalike anywhere. There was a crowd of people near the door, but it looked like the same crowd that had been milling around the whole shoot. Maybe the lookalike was over there?

Rufus successfully poked part of his head out of the top of the bag and turned his practically rabid-looking eyes on me. *I know what I smell! Just a moment ago I smelled her! Where is she?*

I looked at Oscar and whispered. "He says he smells the lookalike."

"Hey, what's in the bag?" asked Garrett. He half stood up on the other side of the table to see if he could get a look. I leaned over farther.

"Nothing," I said, at the same time that Oscar said, "Oh, that's Rufus." I punched him in the arm and nearly fell on the floor.

"Rufus?" asked Garrett.

He looked really confused, but I couldn't blame him. He probably thought we had the world's smallest little person in my backpack or that we were totally insane. Maybe both.

"Background!" yelled Jason. Garrett sat back down.

I put my hand over Rufus's head and pushed him back into the bag. "Stay," I whispered as threateningly as I could.

"Rolling!"

Victoria must have lost the argument with Alan. She was on the side closest to our table. She and Ty walked, stopped, and started their lines.

Then Rufus exploded out of my bag. *Banzai!* he howled.

Die, impostor, die! He landed on top of Victoria's head and did his best impersonation of a blender.

She screamed. Not that I could blame her, seeing as how I'd removed the claw protectors. She windmilled her arms and tried to bat him off her head. For just a moment, the whole room was dead silent except for Victoria and Rufus. Then absolute epic pandemonium broke out.

Ty reached out to attempt to help Victoria, but then Jason jumped on him and pulled him back. "No, you're the lead!" he screamed. Meanwhile, some of the equipment guys came running over, but then they just kind of stood there shouting out not so helpful advice like "Throw it off!" and "On your left!" No one wanted to grab the whirling pink dervish that Rufus had turned into. All of the extras were yelling, except for a few kids who had broken into hysterical laughter. The director was just screaming incoherently. Some people were running for the door.

Oscar was looking at me, totally aghast. "Do something," he yelled. He grabbed me by the shoulders and started shaking me. So much for staying cool in front of Garrett.

I pushed him back and stood up. What was I supposed to do? Everyone knew not to grab a fighting cat. You'd just get clobbered.

"Rufus," I yelled ineffectually. "Stop it! What are you doing? Get off of Victoria!" I picked up my backpack and tossed it halfheartedly in the direction of Rufus. There was no way I was getting him back in it, not right now. Probably ever.

This is the impostor, Rufus snarled back at me in between yowls. *I don't know whom she's trying to fool, but this is her and I'm taking her down!*

"How are we supposed to find out what's happened to Easton if you take her down?" I yelled back at him. He just kept up the attack. There was no reasoning with him normally, and with him in bloodlust mode, I had no chance.

As soon as I said the name Easton, Victoria turned to me. She somehow managed to focus on me through the wall of fur and claws. She took a step in my direction, still screaming.

I picked up a drink from the cafeteria table and threw it at Rufus, mostly missing him but drenching the front of Victoria's now blood-speckled shirt. "Oscar, everybody," I yelled. "Throw liquids! As much as you can!" I grabbed one of those little chocolate milk cartons that had been sitting in front of Garrett and opened it all the way. Everyone around us grabbed their drinks too. "On the count of three," I screamed. "One, two, THREE!"

A multicolored wave of every kind of drink imaginable hit Victoria and Rufus. Milk, soda, water, you name it. One of the equipment guys grabbed a full cooler of tea from the refreshment table and came charging in. He dumped it directly over Victoria's head. Rufus shrieked like he was on fire and went down in the puddle of liquid ooze that was spreading out from the epicenter of the blast area.

I jumped on top of Rufus before he could go on the attack again. Someone cheered as I wrestled with him, both of us skidding across the slippery cafeteria floor. My back hit something solid. I rolled over and saw the cooler that the guy had dropped. It had fallen on its side and the top was open. I shoved Rufus inside, then slammed the lid shut.

I got up on my knees and looked up. Everyone who hadn't fled the cafeteria when the melee broke out was staring at me. Victoria was down on her knees with her hands on her head about three feet from me. Her face, hands, and arms were covered in bloody scratches. Her eyes focused on me, and then she pulled a Rufus.

"You! I knew it was you!" she shrieked, and dived at me with her fingers held out like claws.

She hit me like a battering ram. I fell over backward and my head knocked into the floor. Liquid goo splashed up around us like a geyser. I tried to hold her off, but she was determined. I had about given up on getting out of this with my vision intact when someone pulled her off me.

I wiped a combination of milk and orange juice out of my eyes and looked up. Jason and Ian each had one of Victoria's arms. Jason looked mad, but it was Ian's face that made my heart skip. He was looking at me like he didn't know who I was. Alan came running up.

"What the hell is going on here?" he yelled. He looked from me to Victoria and back again. Rufus picked that moment to let out a howl and throw himself at the lid of the cooler. One of the gaffers sat down on it. "And what," continued Alan, "was that pink monstrosity that attacked my actors?"

I decided not to point out that Rufus had attacked only Victoria. But before I could even say anything, Victoria spoke up. "This is the girl who stole Easton's cat." She pulled her arm away from Ian and pointed at the cooler. "And *that's* Tiddlywinks in there."

Rufus let out another howl, but luckily, I was the only one who understood what he actually said because it wasn't repeatable. I didn't even know cats knew words like that or that they'd use them. Cats tended to be more poetic and cryptic about cussing you out. And I was pretty sure Victoria's mom wasn't physically capable of what he was saying.

"Is this true?" asked Alan.

I opened my mouth and then shut it. Ian was still standing right there looking at me with those eyes. Everyone was looking at me, but his gaze was the one that hurt the most.

"Nat, tell him what's really going on!" Oscar stepped forward and pulled me to my feet. I skidded a little in the puddle of goo.

Victoria narrowed her eyes at him and pulled her other arm free. She took a step forward and Oscar and I took a step back. "*I'll* tell you what's going on," she said. "We've got a stalker here, that's what. Alan, you need to call the police."

"They've already been called," he said. "But I still want to know what's going on. Young lady, do you realize how much money you've wasted by delaying our shoot today? Not to mention the mess? And just look at Victoria! She's a bloody mess!"

"I'm sorry," I said. "I didn't know the cat was going to do that."

"Ha!" said Victoria. "She admits she brought the cat!"

Not like I could deny it. Everyone saw Rufus catapult out of my backpack like a furry angel of death.

Oscar leaned over to whisper urgently in my ear, "Nat, *tell* them. Just tell them about your Talent. Have Rufus tell you something only he would know. They'll have to believe you!"

I thought about it and opened my mouth. I looked at Melly. She stood up and held her hand out to me, though I wasn't sure what she was trying to say. I looked at Ian. He looked confused and upset. Well, so was I.

"I'm not a stalker," I finally said. I couldn't bring myself to say anything about my Talent, not in front of all these people. There had to be another way. It was time for some damage control. Just living down what had happened so far was going to be bad enough. Maybe too much. Adding "Cat Girl" on top of that? Social suicide.

Not to mention dating suicide.

Speaking of death, I noticed the guy was still sitting on the cooler. "Hey," I called out. "Get the cat some air, okay?" If he suffocated in there, I'd have no chance of anyone believing my story. As if anyone would believe it anyway. Why in the world would Victoria Welling impersonate Easton West?

For a minute, I didn't think the guy was going to do anything, but then he got up and cracked the lid. Rufus let out a yowl and the guy dropped the lid shut again. Jason gave him a stern look and the poor guy found a book to wedge in between the lid and the side, then sat down again to keep Rufus from escaping. A steady stream of cat cursing issued forth from the cooler.

I was trying to think of anything else at all to say or do when the police arrived, along with Principal Johnson. Alan gave a brief summary of things to the policemen, with Victoria interjecting comments. Melly and Oscar both tried to get me to talk again, but I stared them down. The police finally mercifully said it was time to go somewhere less public. The female officer tentatively grabbed my multicolored, liquid-soaked arm and frog-marched me to the door.

I kept my head down as I walked past Ian and everyone else. Who was I kidding? There was no way I was ever going to live this down.

SIXTEEN

"ONE OF THE MOST STRIKING DIFFERENCES BETWEEN A CAT
AND A LIE IS THAT A CAT HAS ONLY NINE LIVES."
—MARK TWAIN

"Okay, Natalie, give me one good reason why I should bail
you out of this mess and not tell Mom and Dad." Viv widened her eyes at me, making her look even more like a living,
breathing manga character than normal. "And you know I
can tell if you're lying."

She didn't have to remind me. Her built-in lie detector Talent was her most annoying feature. And even when
I didn't need to lie, I would normally never ask my perfect
sister for help. But when the cops had gotten the answering
machine at home (and I'd lied and said my parents didn't
have cell phones), the police hadn't known who else to call.
Honestly, I wasn't really sure if having Viv here was better
or worse for me.

Actually, that wasn't true. I had a chance of survival with
Viv. If Mom found out I'd been suspended from school, she
would kill me. Sure, she'd be mad about the whole police

thing, but messing with my education? I was so dead if Mom found out.

At least, for once, the true story was on my side. Mostly.

So I told Viv the whole story. Everything. She sat there the whole time looking at me like I was insane. When I was finally done, she shook her head and stared at me.

"That's crazy," she said.

"But true."

"Yeah, I know. I got that." Her chair creaked as she slumped down and focused her eyes on the table. We were in a room at the police station. It looked just like in the TV shows: two wooden chairs, a plain table, and an institutional paint job. A fluorescent light above us flickered on and off. I felt oppressed just sitting there. At least I didn't have hand-cuffs on.

There was even one of those one-way window things. I wondered if anyone was on the other side shaking their head in disbelief. The police had said we'd have our privacy, but I wasn't sure if I believed them or not. They'd also told me they'd let me clean up, but all they'd done was give me a couple of paper towels.

Viv seemed to come to some sort of decision. She glanced at the window, then sat up straight and leaned forward, look-ing me right in the eye. "Are you positive that the cat said that actress Victoria was the impostor?"

"Positive," I said. Hello. He went completely Animal Planet on Victoria's head. Cats are many things, including crazy, but they don't do go completely kung fu unless they mean it. And Rufus definitely meant it when he went after Victoria.

Viv nodded. "Okay, but why? Why would a fairly successful teenage actress want to impersonate a celebrity blogger?"

I'd been thinking about that ever since Rufus had come flying out of my book bag. "Oscar said Easton was probably in town to write about Victoria and how she was in the middle of a starlet meltdown, which he said could sink her down to D-list status. I bet she kidnapped Easton and impersonated her to get her to stop. Remember when that Rory actress had her meltdown and Easton wrote about it and posted those pictures of her?" Rory had literally been committed for a while, and when she'd gotten out, she'd sued Easton. She hadn't won, but the fight had gone on for a year. Oscar had kept us up to date on everything that had happened. Rory's last movie role had been as a talking squirrel in an animated feature that went straight to DVD.

"I guess that sort of makes sense," said Viv. "Stupid, but I guess if she's trying to save her career and she had the means to do it, it's possible."

I'd never heard that Victoria had a Talent, but maybe she kept it hidden like I did. Of course, hers was kind of cool. If I had a Talent like that, I probably wouldn't be quiet about it.

Well, unless I was all evil and everything. That could explain a lot. I'd seen the look on Victoria's face when she went for my eyes. If that wasn't evil, I didn't know what was.

"So, here's what we're going to do." Viv tapped her fingers on the tabletop. "First, I'm going to talk to the police and get you out of this mess. Then I'm going to check the registry database to confirm Victoria's Talent. I'll talk to my superiors at the BERM and we'll come up with a plan."

"What do you want me to do?"

"Stay out of trouble. Let the professionals handle it."

Well, wasn't that all big sister of her. "What about Mom and Dad? And school? I got suspended, you know."

"Yeah, I know." Viv looked deep into my eyes again. What was she trying to see? Was this part of her truth divining stuff? Blech. And she wondered why no guys ever asked her out after they found out what her Talents were.

She finally blinked. "Let's leave Mom out of it for now. I want to see what I can find out first. I think we'll have to leave your school situation as is for now. Since they're still filming there, we don't want to tip Victoria off that anything's up. If you go back to school with no consequences, she'll know something is going on." She stared at me again. "You're positive Oscar didn't say anything about your Talent where she could hear?"

"Yes. I'd have killed him. He knows that."

"Perfect. So as far as we know, she really does just think you're some kind of crazy stalker."

Yeah, great. Her and my entire school.

Viv dropped me off at home after grabbing me some dinner at McDonald's. The police had been suitably impressed by her BERM credentials, though one of them made me demonstrate my Talent by calling her husband and having him put their cat on the phone. She wanted to know what the cat's favorite toy was. According to Whiskers, it was the cop's toothbrush, but he told me to tell her it was a polka-dotted mouse stuffed with catnip. *Otherwise*, he'd said, *she'll probably lock me out of the bathroom.* She totally bought the mouse.

Mom and Dad were both in the living room typing away on their laptops with the TV going. This was their normal Wednesday night routine. There was some History channel thing about ancient scientists or something that they liked to "watch" together. It was also the reason why they hadn't answered the phone. After all, it *was* their date night.

I waved at them as I went by and they both nodded, but didn't look away from the show. I'd been counting on that. I'd cleaned up as much as I could at the police station, going through an entire roll of paper towels. I'd finally mostly dried off, but if you looked close, I was pretty sticky.

Dad sniffed. "What's that smell?"

Figures. The supersniffer strikes again, which was weird since I could see he actually had his olfactory inhibitor on for once. He must have forgotten to take it off when he'd gotten home. "I spilled something on myself," I said, and kept walking along the edge of the room. Hopefully, I was in the shadows enough they couldn't see exactly how goopy I was.

If you really looked, it was obvious it would have taken, like, thirty cups of stuff, not just one. Or, you know, a cafeteria full.

He wrinkled his nose. "New flavor? Doesn't smell very good." I did reek. It was a good thing he had the inhibitor on or else he probably wouldn't have bought my story at all. I could only imagine what I'd smell like to him then. But it also meant that I smelled so bad he could tell *something* was up even with the inhibitor on. I needed a shower, bad.

"Yeah," I said. "I wouldn't recommend it."

Mom cleared her throat. "Do you have any homework? You're home rather late."

"No homework tonight," I said. Or for the next two weeks while I was suspended, but I definitely didn't mention that. Hopefully, Viv could clear everything up soon and I could try and put all of this mess behind me. As if I could ever live down a multibeverage wrestling match.

"You sound better, Mom."

"Yes, thanks. I think you were right about the bath. I felt much better after a long soak."

"Big Mac and a large fry?" asked Dad.

"Yeah," I said, waving the McDonald's bag and inching closer to the hallway.

He sniffed again. "And an apple pie?"

"Yep," I said. "You're good!" He liked to play the guessing game. He said it helped keep his nose sharp. Maybe he was wearing the inhibitor to test it again. He did that from time to time.

"A little challenging tonight, with whatever it was you spilled. I really would avoid it in the future, if I were you. Or whatever situation you were in that caused you to spill it in the first place. You should be careful out there." He peered at me and wrinkled his nose.

"Trust me," I said, "I will." That was about the longest parental advice speech I'd ever gotten from Dad. Usually all mandates came from Mom.

I ducked out of the room and let out the breath I'd been holding. Then I snuck into Mom's office to check the answering machine. She forgot to listen to them half the time anyway, but better safe than sorry. Strangely, there were no messages. The police must not have left one after all.

I shut the office door quietly behind me.

Holy spoiled milk, Batman, screeched Meep, who was coming down the hall. *I thought I smelled something rank, but . . . phew! What happened to you?*

"Shhh!" I said. "Be quiet! I'll tell you everything later."

Meep backed away from me, wrinkling her nose. *After a bath,* she said. *I'll smell you later.* She ran off in the opposite direction.

At least I could eat in peace for once without her begging for food. The one crimp in my plan was Emmy, but apparently she hadn't said anything to either of them. Then again, maybe she hadn't heard about it. She hadn't signed on to be an extra (the only extracurricular things she did were the chess club and some future business leaders thing, both activities that Mom approved of as "appropriate" for school) and the whole fiasco hadn't gone down until after school hours, so maybe the story hadn't made the rounds yet.

That hope was dashed as soon as I got to my room. Emmy flew through the door, shut it, and put her hands on her hips.

"Why aren't you in jail?" she demanded.

"Thanks," I said. "Didn't know you cared."

"Well? It's all over the school's online forum."

That made me pause. "We have an online forum?" I didn't even know we had a website.

"Quit changing the subject! Everyone is talking about it. They said you were arrested! Does this have anything to do with that pink cat? Tell me the truth!"

I sat down at my desk and took out my sandwich and fries. I needed a shower, but I was hungry. First things first. "Viv sprung me. And yes, of course it has to do with the pink cat. I told you somebody was in big trouble, didn't I?"

Emmy sat down with a thump on my bed. "Oh man, oh man. I *knew* I shouldn't have helped you with that cat. Mom is going to kill us. We're in *so* much trouble."

"*We're* in trouble? Hello? Who was the one who got hauled off by the police?" I took a bite of my burger. I guess this explained why Emmy hadn't told Mom and Dad. It wasn't my skin she was worried about, just her own. "Don't worry about it, though. Viv is on the case now with her BERM buddies and she said she wasn't going to tell Mom and Dad until she sorted something out with BERM." I ate a couple of french fries while Emmy digested the news. "Oh, but when you go to school tomorrow, don't tell anyone. Viv said to pretend I was guilty." That won't be hard for her. She's been doing that all her life.

"Oh," said Emmy. "Where's the cat? And what happened to you? What's all over you?" She scooted a little farther down the bed from me, like I could contaminate her with goo from my desk chair.

I ignored the question about the sticky glop, though I did smell. It was the milk, I think, or maybe the combination of milk and orange juice. A shower was definitely next on my agenda, right after I finished eating. "I don't know where the cat is," I said. "Did they say anything about him on the forum?"

"No. Mostly it was just all stuff about you and how you got into a throw down with Victoria Welling. And something about JELL-O wrestling."

You'd think someone would have mentioned that a crazed pink cat had attacked her first. Or that I'd saved her from possible dismemberment by orchestrating a liquid deluge.

"There was no JELL-O," I said. "Trust me. And where's my thank you for saving your butt this afternoon?"

"Oh, yeah," said Emmy. "Thanks. Now stop changing the subject."

Nice. See if I do her any more favors. In retrospect, maybe I should have let Mom do her thing at school. If she'd managed to get the shoot canceled, I wouldn't be suspended and I wouldn't have gotten arrested. I'd still be stuck with Rufus, but I wouldn't be coated in goo, going through the third degree with my little sister.

Emmy made me tell her the whole sordid story, but I finally got rid of her so I could get clean. It took me three shampoos and a lot of unsolicited advice from Meep (who always has to go in the bathroom with me, no matter how many times I tell her it's kind of creepy—apparently, it's a "cat thing"), but I finally got all of the residual stickiness out. But there was a good chance I was never going to drink milk or orange juice again.

EASTON WEST'S BLOG

Wednesday, September 9, 7:05 P.M.: The good news is that my beloved Tiddlywinks has been returned to me, and my stalker, a teenage girl who I'm not allowed to name, has been caught red-handed. The bad news is that the wonderfully brave Victoria was injured when she attempted to rescue Tiddlywinks. And yes, this all took place on set!

Victoria's prognosis is good, and like the true professional she is, she'll be back at work tomorrow.

However, I'm very worried about poor Tiddlywinks. I think the ordeal may have been too much for him. I've brought him to a vet and they are keeping an eye on him. I'll be making the big decision about him later today. My only goal is to make sure that he doesn't suffer.

I hope you will understand, dear readers, if I go into seclusion for a while. I am just absolutely devastated by everything that has happened since I came to Chicago. If it weren't for Victoria, I don't know what I would do. ♥

SEVENTEEN

"THOSE WHO WILL PLAY WITH CATS MUST EXPECT TO BE SCRATCHED."
—CERVANTES

After my shower, I called Melly first, since she was the least likely one to scream my ear off.

"Nat! Are you okay? Where are you? I'm at Oscar's. He's practically ready to bake a file in a cake. Wait, let me—"

"NATALIE!" shrieked Oscar. "Are you okay? Don't let anyone make you their bitch! We'll get you out of there!"

I held the phone away from my ear a little. "Guys, calm down. I'm fine. I'm at home."

There was the sound of struggle and a pause that I could only imagine was Oscar and Melly fighting over the phone. Oscar, of course, won. He fights dirty. Melly is too nice. She never sees it coming.

"You're home? Are you on the lam? Did you bust out?"

"Don't be silly. I called Viv. She got me out. And even better, she's going to take care of everything and she's not going to tell Mom and Dad. We can relax now. The professionals are going to take care of it."

"What do you mean?"

"The BERM, goofus! We're off the hook! Our lives can get back to normal now. That psycho cat is out of my house, the authorities are on the job, and as soon as they've cleared things up, I can go back to school." I felt like spinning around in celebration, but I was too tired, so I settled for a nice big flop backward onto my fringed chartreuse bedspread.

There was silence on the other end of the phone for at least half a minute, which was a record with Oscar. "I think Victoria's going to put Rufus down."

"What? What are you talking about?" I sat up.

Melly took the phone back from Oscar. "After the police took you away, Victoria made this huge production out of finding a proper carrier for Rufus and everything. Kept going on and on about how she had to get the poor cat back to her dear friend Easton."

"Such a faker!" Oscar yelled in the background. Poor Melly. Her ears were probably shot.

"And then she did a blog post as Easton tonight, and it doesn't sound good for Rufus. She's got him at a vet, where it sounds like she's going to do something drastic."

Oscar took control again. "She's getting rid of evidence, that's what she's doing! And I bet Easton herself is next. Go read the blog, you'll see what I mean."

I went to my desk and opened up my laptop. Oscar had bookmarked Easton's blog for me before, so I went right to it and read the post. Victoria was tricky and obviously up to no good. How far would she go to shore up her sucky acting career?

"Okay," I agreed, "it doesn't sound good. But the BERM is on it now."

"Rufus will be dead by the time they get around to doing something," said Oscar. "Trust me. My uncle works for the government."

"I don't—"

"And probably Easton's a goner too. What do you bet Victoria's writing up a suicide blog post right now and scheduling it to run after she has the vet give Rufus his lethal injection?"

I closed my laptop. "Look, Oscar, I'll call Viv, okay? That's all I can do. She told me to stay out of it."

"*Humph.*" I couldn't believe he actually humphed me.

I sighed. "Oscar, there's nothing I can do."

"Well, *we'll* do what we can. *We'll* be on set again tomorrow and *we'll* watch her like hawks. Won't we, Melly?"

I didn't hear whatever Melly responded since Oscar hung up on me.

Meep headbutted me. *You're not going to let them kill that cat, are you?* She'd been listening in on my entire conversation, as usual.

"I didn't think you even liked Rufus," I said.

He was okay. He's just a cat, said Meep. Ha. Truer words

144

were never spoken. *He was annoying, but that doesn't mean he deserves to die.*

True enough. If you killed cats for being annoying, there wouldn't be any cats left on the planet. But would Victoria really kill Rufus? Or Easton, for that matter?

eighteen

"THE CAT, HAVING SAT UPON A HOT STOVE LID, WILL NOT SIT
UPON A HOT STOVE LID AGAIN,
BUT HE WON'T SIT UPON A COLD STOVE LID, EITHER."
—MARK TWAIN

I lay awake half the night thinking about what Oscar and
Meep had said. Rufus was definitely the most annoying cat
I'd ever met, but he really didn't deserve to be put down because of it. I hated that phrase, actually. "Put down," like
there was anything nice and gentle about it. Maybe if you
couldn't talk to cats and truly thought they were just emo-
tionless, mindless furry critters, you could justify it. Maybe.
But I knew better. I mean, not that there weren't an awful
lot of stupid cats, but they weren't stuffed animals. They had
feelings and they felt pain.

Morning finally rolled around. I shoved Meep off my
head (she likes to sleep up there like some kind of furry,
purring hat). I got dressed like I was going to school and
went to the kitchen to grab some breakfast. Mom was sitting
at the counter with Emmy, both of them eating cereal. The
kitchen TV was on the local morning show, and thankfully

not the Food Network. But I guess even Mom couldn't mess up cereal.

"It seems that even the northern suburbs have starstruck teenagers," said a chirpy anchorwoman.

"I think you mean stalkers, don't you?" laughed a guy with teeth that were far too big and way too white.

"Geez, Mom," I said. "How about we watch some real news?"

Emmy sat up straight and shot me a look. She reached for the remote, but Mom stopped her. "Hold on, I'm watching that. Besides, it sounds like a cautionary tale. You should both listen." Yeah. Mom was big on "learning experiences," which generally meant listening to stories where some teenagers ruined their lives by not paying attention to their parents. I just looked at Emmy and shrugged. The police had assured us that my name would not be released.

"Yes," said the anchorwoman. "It seems that Easton West, a celebrity blogger, is in town to cover the filming of *Freddy's Day Off*, which is being filmed at our local Shermer High and in locations throughout the city."

"See," said Mom. "I told you girls that no good would come of letting a movie be filmed at your school. I really need to call your principal. I should have just toughed it out yesterday."

Oh, crap. I made a mental note to call Viv and make sure she'd called Principal Johnson. She said she would straighten things out and just swear him to secrecy. Wait, did that involve

147

telling him about my Talent? If so, he needed to be sworn to top-level classified secrecy. I was hoping he'd let me at least have Melly pick up my homework so I wouldn't get too behind. If I kept up on schoolwork, maybe Mom wouldn't be as pissed when she found out what happened.

"Are you sure you're feeling okay today, Mom?" I asked. Maybe I should have brushed Rufus and kept some of his fur around for emergencies. I put some cereal in my bowl and got out the milk, trying to act nonchalant.

"So, this teenage girl was so enamored with Easton that she allegedly kidnapped Easton's cat!" continued the woman with a snarky grin. The segment went to a picture of Easton (apparently an old picture with the real Easton, since Rufus wasn't trying to dismember her) holding Rufus. "And yes, that *is* a pink cat! Tiddlywinks is quite famous in his own right and has his own fan club." No wonder Rufus had such a big head.

"But not only did this local girl kidnap the cat, she's a student at Shermer High! She brought the cat with her to school and was caught red-handed when the kitty escaped from her book bag during the film shoot."

The anchorman laughed. Smarmy talking head. "I guess no one told her not to let the cat out of the bag!"

Emmy groaned and put her hand over her eyes. I felt like doing the same, but I tried to keep my cool so Mom wouldn't suspect anything.

"That's right, Cory! And what makes this story even

crazier is now the cat is being held at the Happy Paws veterinarian clinic in Northbrook under a 'death watch,' and animal activists from the Chicago area have descended on the place to protest!" They cut to a small mob scene outside a vet. People were chanting and holding up signs that read Free Tiddlywinks! A lot of the protestors were waving stuffed pink cats in the air. In other words, utter chaos.

They cut to another shot of Easton (or rather, Victoria looking like Easton) surrounded by news reporters. She was wearing some huge dark sunglasses, probably to hide the fact that she had no tears. I mean, seriously, after watching her yesterday, I didn't know why she was an actress. She couldn't act, not even like a spoiled celebrity blogger, and it's not like that was a stretch.

"You just would not believe the pressure I'm under. The pain!" Easton-Victoria moaned. "Tiddlywinks is my life!"

I rolled my eyes at Emmy, but she had her head buried in her hands. Mom was staring intently at the screen. Maybe if she watched the cooking shows like that, she'd actually be able to cook.

"After his ordeal at the hands of that . . . that *wicked* girl . . . it was obvious that Tiddlywinks is not the same. He's been irrep—irreper . . . deeply wounded. I've agonized over this decision, but it's for the best." She fake sobbed. Emmy raised her head and shot me yet another pointed look.

"Teenagers today," Mom said. She picked up the remote and shut off the TV. "You girls can take a lesson from that."

"What lesson?" I asked. Don't be a sucky actress? Don't watch crappy morning TV?

"Not to get caught up in the celebrity culture. It makes you do crazy things. You know, Natalie, I should really have a word with your friend Oscar's parents."

"Oh no," I said. "I mean, his parents talk to him about it, Mom. It's under control." Not really, but having her talk to them about it? That was a bad idea on so many levels, especially the fact that Oscar might never forgive me. His parents were finally sort of comfortable with him being gay. There was no need to add the doubtful appellation of potential celebrity stalker to the list. Besides, I'm pretty sure they were aware of his celebrity news addiction. It's not like he tried to hide it.

"Nat," said Emmy, "don't *you* think it's a shame what they're doing to that cat?" She stared at me and pointed her spoon, which was dripping with milk, in my direction. "How they're probably going to *kill* him through no fault of his own?"

This from the girl who once tried to flush poor Meep down the toilet. *"Yes,"* I said. "Of course I do." I pushed my half-eaten bowl of cereal away. Like I could eat when I was thinking about what they might do to Rufus. Stupid Victoria. What an ego! It's not like Easton would have been lying about her acting talent—she didn't have any. And she *is* a total diva. What good did her ruse do anyone?

"Well," said Emmy, hopping down from her stool. "Time

150

for *me* to go to school!" She looked meaningfully at me again.

Sometimes I wondered if all super-geniuses were as annoying as Emmy, or if it was just the fact that she was my little sister.

♥

A few hours later, I was standing across the street from Happy Paws watching the crowd of Tiddlywinks (a.k.a. Rufus) supporters. There were even more now than they'd shown on the TV earlier, maybe a hundred or so. Some of them had chained themselves together and were sitting in a big circle in the parking lot. The building itself was small and brick, with a fenced-in area in the back. There was a happy little dog caricature on the Happy Paws sign. It looked pretty cheerful—you know, for a house of death.

I really didn't know what I was going to do or why I was there. I'd left my house around the same time as Emmy since I had to at least pretend to go to school. Then I'd taken the bus to the mall to kill time, and then felt like an idiot when I'd finally gotten there because it didn't open until ten. I'd tried calling Viv to see if she had any news, but I kept getting her voice mail. I'd even thought about going back home, but somehow, I'd found myself walking to Happy Paws instead. It wasn't that far from the mall.

I walked over to the edge of the crowd and stood next to a woman carrying a stuffed pink lion and a sign that read *Save Tiddlywinks!* She even had a pink stripe in her hair. I wondered if she'd still be protesting if she knew Rufus like I knew him.

"What's up?" I asked her. I tried to look inconspicuous. Maybe I should have borrowed something pink to wear.

She dropped her sign and grabbed me in a huge hug. That was when I noticed she had tears running down her face. "Someone just announced they're gonna do it!" she cried.

"What?" I asked, even though I had the sinking feeling I knew what she meant.

"They're going to give Tiddlywinks a *lethal injection!*" She sobbed louder, and some other people around her began crying and wailing too.

What kind of quack vet worked at Happy Paws? How had Victoria convinced them to do it? There hadn't been anything wrong with Rufus other than general pissed offedness the last time I saw him, unless they'd left him in the cooler for too long. But then they wouldn't even be talking about killing him, he'd already be dead.

I disentangled myself from the woman and walked off a few feet. A policeman was standing in front of the door, probably because of all the crazies out front. I tried Viv again on my cell phone. The BERM should be able to stop this. After all, wouldn't they need Rufus to prove their case?

It rang through to her voice mail again. Crapola.

"If I ever get my hands on the girl who did this to poor Tiddlywinks . . ." The woman who had been sobbing on my shoulder just a minute ago had stopped crying. She punched her right hand into her left, which was still holding the stuffed lion. It squeaked, and she looked at it guiltily. She patted it and put it in her bag, then punched her hand again. I backed away a little farther.

I probably didn't have anything to worry about. The newscasters really hadn't described me in any detail. They'd just said I was a local high-school student, probably because I was a minor. Not to mention I wasn't actually arrested, but that wasn't public knowledge.

And not to mention they really *ought* to be mad at Victoria-pretending-to-be-Easton anyway. What kind of person decides to kill their cat off for no reason? But I guess celebrity saves you from a lot of criticism. If I had any pull with the press, I'd be pointing the finger at the cat killer.

I looked around the crowd. Almost everyone there was older, which made sense since it was school hours. But there was another girl on the other side of the parking lot who looked like she could be in high school. Even better, she was carrying, like, five stuffed pink cats, which would normally make her look really weird. In this crowd, she stood out only a little.

I sidled over to the weeper with the violent streak. "Hey," I said. "Didn't they say the girl who stole Tiddlywinks was blonde?" I motioned in the general direction of the girl across the way, and the woman turned to look. Then I tapped another woman next to her. "And didn't they say she, um, was kind of tall and skinny?" Both total lies, but hey, it was for a good cause. I silently apologized to the girl, who I'd never seen before. But if this worked and I saved Rufus, we were all working toward the same goal, right?

"Yeah," said the first woman, narrowing her eyes. "I think they did."

"I bet that's her!" said the other one. "She looks kind of shifty to me. Check out how she keeps petting her stuffed cats."

"Get her!" yelled the first one and took off. "That's the girl who did this to Tiddlywinks!"

That was all it took. The whole crowd started surging at the poor blonde girl, who looked up in surprise, shrieked, and hugged her stuffed animals to her. She didn't even try to run. I think she was too confused by the sudden turn of events.

It might have been the first time in history it ever sucked to be tall, thin, and blonde.

NINETEEN

"CURIOSITY KILLED THE CAT, BUT SATISFACTION BROUGHT IT BACK."
—ANONYMOUS INTERNET MISQUOTE OF A FAMOUS PLAYWRIGHT

The policeman stepped into the fray, but I could still see a couple of employees inside gathered around the door and the picture window in front. They were all staring at the carnage and shaking their heads. Well, at least they were distracted. I felt a little guilty about the blonde girl, but only a little. All the protestors looked kind of crazy to me. It's not like they were protesting outside of a puppy mill or something. This was all about celebrity.

I jogged around the side of the building to see if I could find another way in. I peeked through the side of the wooden gate and didn't see anyone, so I tried the gate. Locked, of course. But I guess it'd be idiotic not to have it locked with the mob out front. I took a deep breath, looked over my shoulder to make sure no one was watching, and climbed the fence. It was fairly high but kind of decorative, so it had plenty of places to grab onto, which was good for me since

I hadn't climbed anything since I was younger than Emmy.

I'd taken only about three steps toward the building when a really huge Doberman came charging straight for me out of a pet door cut into the back door. He was even bigger than Oscar's dog, Fluff, and that was saying something. This dog was like the Mack truck of Dobermans.

WOOF! Woof! Woof! Dude. I could practically feel the ground buckling under his charge.

I held up my hands and immediately stopped walking. "Hey," I said. "I'm just here to rescue someone that's about to be put to sleep, okay?" I held my breath. Would he understand me? Some animals did pretty well with just regular human speech, but there were some that would just look at you like you were speaking Swahili. And only some dogs seemed to understand Cat. I didn't have much experience with large dogs other than Oscar's, and Fluff definitely wasn't much of a conversationalist.

He skidded to a stop about a foot away and lowered his head. *Grroowwwf?* he said.

Hmm. Maybe he did understand me? I spoke slowly. "There's a cat in there and they're going to put him down. I'm here to save him. There's nothing wrong with him. Can you let me by? Please?"

He gave me a long look and then gave me a doggy smile, his tongue lolling out. *GRrrruuuufffuuuu*, he said.

Oh, wow. "Yeah, that's right. Rufus. Can you show me where he is?" The dog turned around and loped to the back

156

door and went in through the doggy door. I tried the doorknob, but it was locked. I tried the window, but it was locked too.

The dog stuck his head through the doggy door and looked at me. *Wrrooof?* He backed up and his head disappeared.

It was worth a shot. I got down on my hands and knees and stuck my head through the doggy door. Good thing he was a Doberman, and a huge one at that. If they'd had a doggy door for a Chihuahua, I'd have been completely out of luck. I pushed myself through and got a face full of doggy saliva before I could stand up. Gross. That was one thing that I preferred about cats—they mostly kept their tongues to themselves.

"Um, thanks," I said, and patted his head. We were in a room with a bunch of vet supplies and stainless steel tables, and cages along one wall. Some of the cages had pets, including cats, but none of them were pink. "Now, can you show me where Rufus is?"

They took him to the death chamber, piped up a scrawny orange and white cat in a cage close to the door. *Two doors down on the left. They don't come back from there, you know. At least, not alive.*

"Oh, thanks." I went to the door and opened it a crack to take a look. I was at the end of a hallway. The front waiting room was directly down the white tile hall. I let the door swing softly shut. If any of the employees turned around, they'd see me as soon as I opened the door.

I'm probably next, the scrawny cat continued. *Ain't what I used to be. At least, that's what my human keeps saying.* He let out a strangled sounding cough.

You're just in here for a teeth cleaning, said a white cat in the next cage. *Stop being such a baby.*

You never know, the first cat said darkly. *You never know. Look what they're doin' to that hoity-toity cat the girl's looking for. He's a lot younger than I am.*

"That's why I'm here," I said. "I'm trying to save him. There's nothing wrong with him."

The white cat snorted. *Oh, I wouldn't say that.*

"What do you mean?" I asked. Maybe Victoria had done something to him after all. Maybe he was brain-dead after being locked in the cooler. Oh, no. Had I killed Rufus? Was it really my fault after all?

Even drugged up, that one's got an attitude.

"Oh," I said. "Uh, yeah. That would be Rufus." I cracked the door and peeked out again. I counted three employees at the front window and another behind a check-in counter. They all had on colorful hospital-style scrubs with pictures of happy-looking little kittens and puppies frolicking around. Killers. How did they sleep at night?

They were all still staring out the front window, but the room the cat had said Rufus was in was only one door down from them. There was no way I could get in there without being seen, even with the diversion going on out front. I needed them out of the room.

Sneaking him out, eh? asked the white cat.

"Well," I said, "I was going to try to. I'm not technically his person, so I can't just go up front and get him."

I figured that, said the white cat. *I saw her when they brought him in. I understand where he gets his attitude from, though he didn't seem to like her much.*

"She's not actually his human either. That's part of the problem. She wants him gone."

The dog interrupted. *Woof! Woof?*

What's that again? asked the orange and white cat. *My dog ain't what it used to be either.*

He says we could help, said a black cat in the corner cage. *I've got a dog at home, though I'm better at ferret.*

"How?" I asked.

My person has two ferrets too, the black cat continued. *Smelly little things, but they're pretty nice. Really preoccupied with chewing, but friendly.*

"No, I mean, what does the dog mean about helping?"

They ignored me and conferred with each other. I peeked out the door again. I could hear some shouting from outside, and one of the employees was shaking her head. I felt a little bad for the blonde, but hey, sometimes you hit the birth lottery and sometimes you don't. Besides, if she really was a fan of Tiddlywinks, she'd probably be glad to have had a hand in helping save him.

Okay, said the white cat. *You there, girl. Let us all out except for Daisy over there on the end. We'll take care of it. Just open the door and give us a few minutes, then go get Attitude Boy and get out of here.*

It was worth a shot. I didn't have any other ideas. I started opening cages. "Why not Daisy?" I asked as I opened the white cat's cage.

The white cat jumped nimbly down to the floor. *Pregnant as a bowling ball*, she said. *We take care of our own. No use endangering the kittens.*

"Oh," I said. I guessed that's why they were helping me free Rufus anyway. Who knew? Meep always seemed pretty aloof when it came to other cats, and I'd taken my cat cues from her. But then, Meep was kind of weird even by cat standards. I figured it was all the weird genetic inbreeding or whatever they did to make her hypoallergenic. Other cats tended to make fun of her. They said she smelled funny.

I finished letting everyone out of their cages and opened the door enough for them all to go through one by one. All told, there were three dogs and five cats. I kept the door cracked open and watched as the white cat and the Doberman led the way.

They all quietly crept to the end of the hallway. None of the employees noticed them. Then as if on cue (apparently, reports of an animal sixth sense are true), they rushed the front door with the Doberman leading the way, barking his head off. He crashed right into the door and it popped open with a bang and a tinkle from the bell they had looped on the door handle. It looked like he'd done it before. The cats and other dogs followed him out, howling and yowling all the way. For just a second, no one moved. Then everyone up front said their curse word of choice and went barreling out the door after the escapees.

I gave it a second to make sure no one else was around and went in Rufus's room. He was in a cage lying on a faded blue towel. He lifted his head as I entered the room and looked at me. Or rather, he tried to look at me. Literally, one eye was going in one direction and the other eye was going in another. With his smooshed-in ears and big round eyes, he looked a lot like an owl—a drunk owl.

"What happened to you?" I asked as I opened the door of the cage.

That evil imposter gave me a double dose of my travel medicine, said Rufus. *But she told the vet it was from being abused while I was kidnapped. Personally, I think she paid off the vet.*

I hesitated before reaching in the cage. "Are you sure you're okay to be moved?"

He focused his left eye on me. *I'll be a lot worse if you don't move me. Where have you been? I've been waiting!*

"Good point." I picked him up.

Crap. I should have brought my book bag. But the last time I'd seen it, it was floating in a pile of assorted liquids in the cafeteria. I hadn't been planning on a rescue attempt when I left the house and I hadn't brought anything useful with me, just my purse, and there was no way Rufus was going to fit in that. And there was no way I could just carry him out. I mean, not only was he pink, but he was probably the most recognizable cat on the planet, especially to the mob of freaks outside the door.

Frick on a stick. I looked around, but there wasn't much in the room, mostly just medical-looking stuff. But there was a stack of folded blankets and towels on a table. I grabbed one and tried to conceal Rufus in it. Not unsurprisingly, he freaked.

What do you think you're doing? Trying to send me parcel post? I can't breathe!

"No, but I've got to hide you in something. Dude, you're pink!" I stopped struggling with him. We probably had only a few minutes left before the employees started coming back.

Rufus took a swipe in the general direction of the blanket and almost managed to snag it out of my hand. I pulled it back and held it out of his reach. It was light blue with little stars on it, kind of like a baby blanket. That gave me an idea. Last year in health class, they'd made us practice swaddling fake babies. I think it was supposed to be a preventative measure or something, along with talks about STDs and carrying around bags of flour and pretending they were kids. (It made no sense to me. I mean, who would ever mistake a bag of flour for a kid?) But I remembered how to swaddle, kind of.

"I'm going to swaddle you like a human baby," I said. "Just hold still. You'll be able to breathe, okay?"

He humphed, but lay there and let me swaddle him. When I was done, he looked like one seriously ugly, furry baby, with only the front of his face sticking out. I hoped that as long as I held him close to my chest, no one would notice. Or maybe they'd just think I was babysitting a really ugly kid. With a lot of pink facial hair. And a lazy eye.

This is ridiculous, said Rufus.

"Tell me about it," I said. I cradled him in my arms like I'd practiced with the baby doll and flour bag, and peeked my head out the door. The front door was still wide open. I walked out the door, went down the steps, edged around the crowd, and kept going. I couldn't tell if the blonde girl was still standing or if the protestors had completely taken her out. The cats and the Doberman were nowhere to be seen either.

A bus was pulling up to the stop at the corner. I didn't know where it was going, but I climbed on anyway, paid, and sat down in the back.

As it was pulling away, I heard some shouting. Then the whole crowd took up the chant. "Tiddlywinks escaped! Tiddlywinks escaped! Hooray!"

TWENTY

"ANYONE WHO CLAIMS THAT A CAT CANNOT GIVE A DIRTY LOOK
EITHER HAS NEVER KEPT A CAT OR IS SINGULARLY UNOBSERVANT."
—MAURICE BURTON

I transferred to another bus that was going back toward home after I got off the first one somewhere in Glenview. It was more crowded than the first bus had been, but I still managed to find a seat in the back next to an older woman in a tweedy-looking pantsuit. She sniffed at me as I sat down.

"You're awfully young to have a baby," she said.

"I'm just babysitting," I said. Like it was any of her business anyway.

She sniffed again like she didn't believe me. "In my day, they had a name for girls like you."

"Um, babysitters?" I said it with as much innocence as I could muster, but I couldn't help letting a little snark slip through.

She looked at me over the top of her glasses and sniffed one more time. "I think you know the word I'm thinking of," she said.

Rufus let out a hissy kind of cat laugh. *She thinks you're a—*

"Shhhh!" I said to Rufus. The lady looked at me suspiciously. I started to hum the "Hush, Hush" song to cover up his cat giggling. You'd think he'd be a little nicer, considering I'd just saved his butt from lethal injection.

"Is there something wrong with your baby?" She reached out a hand and pulled on a corner of the blanket. "He doesn't sound right. Maybe he has a cold. You young mothers don't know what you're doing."

"I told you," I said through gritted teeth, "he's not my kid. And he's fine. Maybe just some allergies or something." Rufus kept sniggering, which actually sounded a lot like phlegmy coughing, now that I thought about it.

The nosy woman leaned over and then pulled on the blanket again. "Let me see," she said. "I'm a grandmother. I know what *I'm* doing—" She stopped as the flap of blanket I'd put over Rufus's face came loose and his crossed, bulging eyes and pink fur peeked out. "Aaaaah!" She shrieked and shrank back in her seat.

Some of the other passengers were looking at us now. "It's okay," I told her as I flipped the blanket back down. "I can explain."

She stood up and looked down at me. "Honey," she said, "I'm sorry, but that is the ugliest baby I have ever seen in my life. It's just not right." She lurched a bit as the bus came to a stop, shook her head at me one more time, and then got off the bus.

A few people were still looking at me with undisguised interest. "He, um, takes after his dad," I said lamely. Rufus just kept laughing.

♥

I finally made it home and went straight to my room, even though no one else was around, not even Meep. I set Rufus on the bed and unswaddled him.

You should have seen your face! He was still laughing.

"Well, you should see yours. Your eyes are still crossed. Besides, you're the ugly baby, not me."

He stopped to consider that. *All of your hairless human babies are ugly, if you ask me. But I want a mirror. What do you mean my eyes are crossed?*

"You can't tell?" I got him a mirror and held it up in front of him. He peered at it, but only his right eye seemed remotely focused on it.

He was silent for a moment. *If my eyes stick like this, that woman is going to pay.* He raised his head and looked at me. At least, with one eye. *Why did you pull me off her? I had her!*

"Rufus, you're insane. We were in a room full of witnesses. You got me arrested!"

He ignored that. *And then you let her take me away! She was going to have me killed!* He swiped a paw at me and I jumped back, but I didn't really need to. His aim was way off. *And she threatened to kill Easton!* He stood up on wobbly legs. *We've got to find my person before it's too late!*

166

"Wait," I said. "Tell me exactly what she said. Tell me everything, from the beginning."

He sat back down after he nearly fell off the bed. *Fine*, he said. *After we left your school, she brought me to a house. Easton was there somewhere; I could smell her. The evil woman—*

"Victoria."

Victoria, then. She had all of our things. She went digging into our stuff, just flinging it everywhere, and found my travel pills. The whole time she was doing this, she was yelling so my person could hear her. She said this was all more trouble than it was worth and that we were both expendable. She said she was going to take care of it all this Saturday when she had a break from shooting. Then she shoved the pills in my mouth and made me swallow them.

I sat down on the bed next to Rufus and stroked his back. His hackles were up. "I'm sorry, Rufus," I said.

I would have taken her out if I hadn't been restrained.

"Of course you would have." I petted him a few more times and then got my phone. "Just hang on, okay? My sister works for the BERM. It's . . . um . . ." How to explain a governmental agency to a cat? "Well, it's kind of like the police . . ." Well, it was, *kind of*. Maybe more like the Secret Service, but would a cat even know what that was? "But they just monitor people with Talents. Anyway, I've told her everything. She's taking care of things. I just need to let her know I rescued you." I called Viv and got her stupid voice mail again. I left another message. Where was she? And why wasn't she returning my phone calls?

Now all we could do was wait.

Oscar and Melly arrived as soon as school was out. I'd sent a text to Oscar and he'd texted back, even though texting wasn't allowed in school. He was such a pro he could actually text with his hand in his pocket. Mad skills.

I gave them the whole story as soon as they came in, with Rufus interrupting me every now and then to make himself look better. Like they could even understand him.

"Wow," said Oscar. "This is a new low for Hollywood. Killing a blogger because they're gonna out you as a sucky actress? Sounds like a B-grade movie plot."

"What did Viv say?" asked Melly.

"Nothing. I've left her three messages so far." I gave Rufus another pat on the head. "So, what's the word at school?" I almost didn't want to ask. I'd been trying really hard not to remember the look on Ian's face as I'd been dragged out of the cafeteria.

"Well," said Oscar, "you're totally famous!"

He held up his hand to high-five me, but I didn't take the bait. That was his dream, not mine. "What are they saying?" I looked at Melly. Surely she at least understood the whole cafeteria scene was not good for my reputation. Not that I'd really *had* a reputation before, but whatever I'd had before was completely shot now.

"Mostly, no one can believe it. And they're wondering why you did it."

Yeah, I was kind of wondering the same thing myself. "Anything from Ian?" I couldn't believe the words had come out of my mouth. I was obviously a glutton for punishment.

"I didn't see him today," said Melly, playing with the fringe on my bedspread instead of looking at me. "Sorry."

I wasn't sure if I believed that or not. Maybe she was just being nice. How was I ever going to face Ian again?

"What are we going to do if Viv doesn't call back?" asked Oscar. "They're filming in the city tomorrow at Wrigley Field. And then it's Saturday, and *then* it's lights out for Easton." He drew his finger across his throat.

Rufus coughed pathetically as he tried to growl. *I must do something*, he said.

"Dude," I said. "Just settle down. You're in no condition to do anything." I wondered how long it would take for the drugs to wear off. The vet had given Meep something once, but it certainly hadn't made her eyes cross. I tried Viv again on the phone, just in case. No answer. What good were the professionals if you could never get in touch with them?

"What do you think we should do?" asked Melly.

"I'm sure Viv will call back," I said, though I really wasn't sure at all. Other than her weekly night at home, I didn't really talk to Viv regularly, especially since she had moved out for college. We weren't like those sisters in the Hallmark commercials. Honestly, I had no idea what her schedule looked like.

Though you'd think she'd call me back after bailing me out and promising to fix everything.

"But what if she doesn't?" asked Oscar again. He attempted to pet Rufus, who responded by trying to bite his hand.

I was about to reassure everyone again that Viv would take care of it, when Melly spoke up. "We'll have to do something," she said. "We have to. If you know something bad is going to happen and you can prevent it, then you have to do something. It's our responsibility as human beings." She stood up, put her hands on her hips, and looked right at me.

I snapped my mouth shut. Ouch. There was the responsibility thing again.

Rufus purred and wiggled in Melly's direction. She scratched him behind his ear but kept her eyes on me. Then Rufus opened his still-crossed eyes wide at me and blinked.

"Oh, all right already!" I sighed. "If Viv doesn't call back tonight, we'll figure something out. I guess we need to find out where Victoria is hiding Easton. Maybe see if we can get some incriminating evidence or something."

"Yay!" Oscar cheered like we weren't talking about taking on a homicidal maniac on purpose. "Skip day!" He pulled out some sheets of paper and handed them to me. "Here's all the notes I took when I was listening to the filmmakers talk about their shoot tomorrow. And some pages from the script that I, um, borrowed."

Wow, Oscar took notes on something. That truly was amazing. Of course, it wasn't school related, but still. I read through as much as I could decipher while Melly intently studied the script pages. His handwriting needed work. I peeked over Melly's shoulder at the script. They didn't really say much either. Maybe I didn't know how to read them. There were only a few pages and it seemed like there had to be more. Who knew what they were going to be filming tomorrow?

"I'm guessing that most of the shooting will be around the press box? Or the ticket booth? And I guess the stands," I said. I didn't remember Ferris ever going in the press rooms, but I supposed the script called for at least doing a few original things in this new movie. "We should definitely be able to catch them filming outside the ticket windows since you don't need to be inside the stadium for that."

"Maybe we can sign up as extras," said Oscar.

"That won't work," said Melly. "The call went out over a week ago. They've already signed everybody up that they need."

Oscar looked at her. "Oh?"

She had the decency to blush. "Yeah. I tried to sign up, but Dad wouldn't let me skip school for it since we have that test in English."

"You've still got the test," I said. "Maybe you guys shouldn't skip tomorrow after all." Not that I wanted to tackle any of this on my own.

"Pfffft," said Oscar, waving his hands. "English shminglish. We're taking the day off with you."

"That was before someone's life was on the line," said Melly. "Besides, I'm not going to tell my dad. Oscar and I can make the test up later or something. And you're still suspended."

Thanks for reminding me. "Well, okay," I said. "So, we don't know what they're shooting tomorrow. If they aren't doing the ticket window scene, they're probably doing one of these other bits." I pointed to the script pages that Melly was still clutching in her hand. "And that means we've got to get inside the stadium."

"Didn't you say Ian's dad works for the Cubbies?" Melly said sweetly. Darn her for paying attention.

"I don't think —"

Oscar grabbed me by both shoulders and put his nose right up against mine. "Girl, this is life or death! Don't think! Do!"

Frick on a stick. For once, he actually wasn't exaggerating.

Wrigley Stadium - Day

FADE IN:
Outside of Wrigley Stadium. Freddy and Molly
walk up to a ticket window . . .

> **TICKET VENDOR**
> Can I help you?
>> **FREDDY**
> Yeah, two tickets to today's game,
> please. (Pause.) Hey, can we get the
> Ferris Bueller seats?
>> **TICKET VENDOR**
> The what?
>> **MOLLY**
> Freddy, give it a rest.
>> **FREDDY**

Freddy turns to Molly and then back
to the window. The ticket vendor is
peering through the window, clueless.

> Hey, if I'm going to do it, I want
> to go all the way.

> (To ticket vendor): You know, the
> seats Ferris Bueller sat in for the
> movie?

> **TICKET VENDOR #2**
>
> Sam, he wants Section 104, row
> three, seat 9.
>
> > **TICKET VENDOR**
> >
> > Oh, sorry. I'm new. Let me see what we've
> > got available there.
>
> > **FREDDY**
> >
> > Great, thanks!

Freddy bounces on the balls of his feet
while Molly looks annoyed.

> **TICKET VENDOR**
>
> I'm sorry, I've got row two, but row three
> is all sold out.
>
> > **FREDDY**
> >
> > Oh no! Are you sure?
>
> > **MOLLY**
> >
> > Freddy, just get the tickets. It's close
> > enough.
>
> > **TICKET VENDOR**
> >
> > So do you want them or not?
>
> > **FREDDY**
> >
> > Yeah, I guess so.
>
> > **TICKET VENDOR**
> >
> > They're $50 each.
>
> > **FREDDY**
> >
> > Ouch. Um, Molly?

Molly rolls her eyes and opens up her purse to pull out a credit card. She hands it to the ticket vendor.

                    FREDDY
         Thanks, Molly, I owe you.
                    MOLLY
         Technically, you'll owe my dad.
                    TICKET VENDOR
         Okay, here you go. Enjoy the game.

Cut to Freddy and Molly walking down the steps to their seats. Freddy is holding the tickets in his hand. He pauses at row three.

                    FREDDY
         Nobody's here yet . . .
                    MOLLY
         Just sit where we're supposed to.
         It doesn't matter.
                    FREDDY
         I just want to do this right. All my life
         I've been close enough. I want to be there.
                    MOLLY
         Freddy, how many times do I have to tell
         you? Real life isn't like the movies. We
         couldn't get in to visit the stock market
         like Ferris did, there's no such restau-
         rant as Chez Quiz so we couldn't eat lunch

where Ferris ate, and the parade isn't until
tomorrow. Life's all about compromise.

Molly passes by row three to sit in row
two. After a moment, Freddy follows her. A
teenage girl is seated next to Freddy.

> **FREDDY**
> Maybe you're right. I don't know. Today
> isn't working out like I thought it would.
> **MOLLY**
> Like I said, that's life.

They watch the game in silence. It's approxi-
mately the fourth inning. The Cubs are up at
bat.

> **MOLLY**
> It's like the Cubs, you know? They haven't
> won the series for over a hundred years,
> but they don't give up. They keep on trying.

A player hits a grand slam and the stands
erupt. You can hear the announcer (Pat Hughes)
screaming, "Get out the tape measure, LONG
gone!"

> **FREDDY**
> Whoooooo!

Freddy stands up and cheers. The girl next
to him is standing and cheering too.
They high-five each other, then Freddy
suddenly grabs her in a hug and kisses her.
Molly stands, stunned. He hugs her too.
The girl laughs and high-fives him again.

FREDDY

You know what, Molly? Life doesn't have
to be like that. Life can be anything you
want. I'm going to prove it to you.

Freddy runs up the stairs and disappears
into the stadium. Molly stares after him.

FADE IN:
Freddy outside the press box area
Freddy is knocking on the door leading to the
press box area. People are passing by on the
concourse. The door finally opens.

WRIGLEY EMPLOYEE

What's going on, kid? This is a restricted
area. Quit banging on the door. We've got
people working in here.

FREDDY

Yeah, I know. I need to talk to Pat or Ron.

WRIGLEY EMPLOYEE

And who are you?

FREDDY

I'm Freddy and I'm the guy who's going to
sing during the seventh inning stretch.

TWENTY-ONE

"WHEN MY CATS AREN'T HAPPY, I'M NOT HAPPY.
NOT BECAUSE I CARE ABOUT THEIR MOOD, BUT BECAUSE I KNOW
THEY'RE JUST SITTING THERE THINKING UP WAYS TO GET EVEN."
—PERCY BYSSHE SHELLEY

Melly and Oscar left only after I swore up and down that I'd call Ian after dinner if Viv hadn't called back. And, of course, Viv didn't call. After Mom's dinner interrogation was over, I asked Mom and Dad if they knew what Viv was up to, but they didn't have any idea either.

Dad was curious as to why I wanted to know, so I told him a friend of mine wanted to go to Northwestern and had questions. Then he said I could ask *him* since he'd gone there too, and I had to think up some college-related questions off the top of my head. Thankfully, he never asked which idiot friend of mine wanted to know which dorms had the best rooms or where the best fast food was on campus, since that was all I could think of to ask him.

"Any other questions?" he asked when I stopped babbling about how the quality of pizza could seriously impact a person's study habits. "Or maybe something else

179

you'd like to talk about? Something bothering you?"

"Nope," I said. "I'm good. I'll, uh, ask my friend if they have any other questions tomorrow." I took a final bite of dinner and put my fork down. At least it was Emmy's turn to do the dishes.

But just as I was about to ask to be excused, Dad asked me another question. "How is Meep feeling?"

"Meep?" He *never* asked about Meep.

"I noticed there's a different kind of cat smell in the house and I haven't seen her today. She usually begs at dinner. Maybe she's sick?"

Emmy's eyes bugged out of her head and she started coughing like she was choking on something. She had actually been trying to help keep Mom away from my room, but the strain of lying to Mom was killing her. I had the feeling she was going to crack at any time. I shot her a look and leaned over so I could pound her on the back.

"I'm fine, I'm fine," she finally spit out, her face flushed.

Normally, Mom would have freaked out about Emmy hacking up a lung, but she was distracted with her own health issues. The Rufus Effect had already hit her, even though I'd brushed him, given him two baths in a row (much to his displeasure), and hidden him in my room. She'd been sneezing all through dinner.

Meep hadn't come out for dinner because she was keeping Rufus company. I think she felt sorry for him, since his eyes were still crossed and he couldn't walk in a straight line. It was the nicest I had ever seen her treat anyone. She'd even tried to give him some of her tuna. I'd think it was love if they weren't both fixed.

"Well," I said brightly to Dad, "now that Emmy's stabilized, I'm just going to go check up on Meep. She seemed okay before dinner, but I'll ask. I'll tell her you were thinking of her!"

"Okay," said Dad, grinning a little. "If you need anything else, I'm here."

I nodded and made my way to my bedroom as fast as I could, trying not to look any more suspicious than I already did.

Any word from your sister? asked Rufus as soon as I got in the door.

"No," I said. "I guess I'm going to have to call Ian."

Well, get to it then. If Rufus were able, I think he'd have his paws on his hips. Patience was definitely not his thing. But he was right. I had promised.

I picked up my phone and took a deep breath. I dialed Ian's number without even using my contact list. Even though this was my first time calling, I already had committed his number to memory from when he'd written it on my notebook in class. I could pretend that I was that good with numbers, but let's face it, I memorized anything that had to do with Ian.

"Hello?" It was Ian. I almost dropped the phone.

"Um, hi," I managed to get out. "This is Nat." You know, the girl who got arrested in front of the entire school.

"Nat!" He sounded surprised, but I didn't blame him. I

couldn't believe I was calling him either. "Are you okay? Is everything all right?"

At least he hadn't asked if I was certifiably insane. Yet. "Yeah, I'm okay. I know all that stuff at school yesterday seemed pretty . . . crazy."

"A little," he said.

"A little?"

He laughed. I shouldn't have prompted him. He must really think I was nuts. "Okay, a lot. Do you want to tell me what was going on?"

Did I? Yes and no. "I really can't."

"Oh," he said. Did he sound disappointed? Mad? I wasn't sure.

"I really want to, but I can't. I'm sorry." I took another deep breath and then stopped mid inhale. Adding "heavy breather" to my list of attributes was probably not a good idea. "Really sorry."

"Okay," he said. He definitely didn't sound happy. "I get it."

No, he totally didn't. How could he? But what was I supposed to say? Viv had told me to keep it quiet. But if I was honest with myself, I had no desire to tell him about the whole talking to cats thing anyway. It would be better if he thought I were some celebrity stalker rather than the weird girl who talks to cats. Right? To steel my resolve, I kept picturing Frog Boy in my head, sitting alone at his lunch table like he had the plague or something.

"I need to ask you a huge favor," I said.

"Okay . . ."

Maybe I should have had this conversation in person. I couldn't tell from his tone what he was thinking. No, wait, that would have sucked even more.

"You know how your dad works for the Cubs?" Well, that sounded stupid. Of course he knew. I could just picture him rolling his eyes.

"Um, yeah?"

"I really need to get into Wrigley Field tomorrow. Is there any way you could get, like, some backstage passes or something from him? Like, three?"

Long pause. "Would this have anything to do with the film crew being at Wrigley Field tomorrow?"

"Yes, but it's not what you think. I promise."

"Nat . . ."

"I swear on my trigonometry book that I am not a celebrity stalker." Please, please believe me.

Another long pause.

"I *really* wish I could tell you everything. And I will, I promise! As soon as I can. But this is really, really important. Like, literally someone's life is at stake."

"Someone's life is at stake?" He sounded really doubtful.

"Yes." I could feel my eyes tearing up a little. Poodle farts. I blinked to hold the tears back. Thank frick he couldn't see me. "Please, Ian, trust me."

"You can't tell me anything?"

"Just that someone's in really bad trouble and this is the

only way I know of to try and save them. If there were any other way, trust me, I wouldn't be asking." Seriously. I'd rather pull my toenails off with a pair of pliers.

"Come on, Nat. Give me something. Anything."

What could I say that wouldn't sound stupid and wouldn't make Viv mad? And most important, wouldn't out me as the cat whisperer? "I can't tell you how I know or why, but Victoria isn't . . . nice."

"That's pretty obvious," he said. "Remember, I was there yesterday and I heard her after you left."

"I am definitely *not* stalking her or Easton West," I said. "Really. Victoria's involved in something bad and I'm trying to help fix it." Oh, man. He wasn't going to buy it, was he?

He sighed. "Okay, Nat. I'll talk to my dad and see if he can leave you passes at the Will Call window. I can't promise anything, though."

"Thank you so much, Ian. Really. You have no idea. I owe you — big time." I slumped down on my bed, completely drained.

"Yeah," he said.

I told him thank you a few more times and then finally hung up. There were fingernail marks in my palm from where I had been clenching my hand. That was by far the most painful phone call I'd ever made. He was pretty nice about it all in all, considering. But I realized a few minutes later that neither one of us had brought up our Friday night date.

The chances of me seeing that alien invasion movie with Ian tomorrow night were right down there with my social status.

TWENTY-TWO

Friday, September 11, 11:30 a.m.

"TO SOME CATS, PATIENCE IS A VIRTUE.
TO OTHERS, SOMETHING TO LAUGH AT."
—NATALIE NG

Oscar and Melly skipped out on school right before lunch and picked me up, and we drove to the train station. I'd spent the morning packing and unpacking an old backpack of Viv's with supplies, like I even knew what spies—or whatever it was you called BERM agents (which we weren't)—should carry.

We were so doomed.

I actually hadn't even pretended to leave for school. I just stayed in my room, but Mom was so preoccupied with her sneezing that she hadn't noticed I wasn't gone when she left for work. I'd been really worried that she was going to stay home again, but her workaholic side had prevailed. That was the first time *that* had worked in my favor.

The hardest thing had been leaving Rufus behind. He had really wanted to go and finish what he'd started with Victoria, but after what had happened the last time I'd taken him with me, there would've been no way I was going to chance it. Besides which, whatever pills Victoria had given him had been potent. His eyes had finally straightened out, but he was still walking like he was a drunken sailor. Meep had promised to keep him company, but ultimately, I'd had to duck out while he was using the litter box so I wouldn't have to deal with him screeching at me.

I'd put on a Cubs baseball cap and a Cubs T-shirt of Dad's. The shirt was huge on me, but at least I wouldn't stick out like a sore thumb. Oscar hadn't quite grasped the concept of blending in. He was wearing black jeans with silver studs down the side and a black shirt with a shredded Cubs T-shirt over the top of it.

"You do know we're going to a baseball stadium, right?" I asked him. At least Melly had worn something normal looking. It wasn't a Cubs shirt, but at least it was red. She looked perfect, as usual.

"What do you mean?" He looked down at his outfit and pointed at the Cubs logo on the front, which was slashed completely in half. "This is very sporty."

Yeah, in some parallel universe. We were lucky there weren't going to be any real Cubs fans at the stadium that day who might take offense to the defacement of their logo or something. I pulled my Cubs hat down lower over my forehead and tucked a few stray hairs back up underneath. It was not a good look for me, but if the movie security people were on the lookout for the crazy celebrity stalker girl, hopefully they wouldn't notice crazy Cubs fan girl in clothes that were too big for her.

We finally made it to Wrigley Field after a Metra train ride, a transfer to the El, and a short walk. There were a few people out front taking pictures of the famous red and white sign that read Wrigley Field: Home of Chicago Cubs, which was pretty normal. There were always tourists checking it out.

We checked all of the ticket windows, but there were no film crew people anywhere to be seen. They must have either already filmed the ticket window part or were going to do it another time, so we were going to have to get into the stadium.

We went up to the will call window. Had Ian been able to talk his dad into leaving some passes? The lady at the window waved us forward.

"Um, hi," I said. "I'm Natalie Ng. Do you have some passes for me by any chance? From, um, Mr. Abbott?"

"Hmmmm." she said, flipping through a box. "Let me see . . ." She kept flipping. My heart sank. Either Ian's dad hadn't come through, or Ian hadn't even asked. Not that I could blame him. But what were we going to do? Maybe we could sneak in somehow?

"It's Ng, spelled N-G," said Oscar. Ah, good point. Maybe she was looking under I. Oscar was lucky it was his mom who was Asian. His last name was Green. You couldn't mangle that.

"Ah, here you go!" She pulled out three lanyards with a

plastic card attached to them and handed all of them to me through the little window. "Remember to leave the passes on where they can be seen. And watch out for the film crew today!"

"Thank you," I said. I couldn't believe it. Oscar let out a cheer behind me. I passed around the lanyards and we walked over to the nearest gate.

"See!" Oscar said. "Ian *wuuuvvvvsss* you! I told you so!"

"Let's just get inside, okay?" I honestly didn't think Ian would do it. Not that I had a backup plan in case of disaster, but I was still amazed. PD was right: Ian was awesome.

There was a huge line of extras at the gate, all wearing Cubs clothes and carrying slips of paper. We finally got to a security guy. He waved Melly in when she held up her pass, but stopped me. "I've got one, too," I said. I held up the lanyard.

"I see it," he said. "But I need to check your backpack."

"Oh, okay," I said, and held it out to him. He put it on a table and started digging around inside. He pulled out my dad's video camera.

"You've got a stadium pass and I'm assuming you're not an extra, but you do know you can't use this to record any of the filming, right?"

"Right," I said. "We're, um, here to, um . . ."

"We're filming a short promotional spot for a local charity," Oscar said smoothly. "We won't be near the film crew at all, just in the offices."

"Okay, but if you're caught filming around the movie

crew, they will ask you to leave," said the guy. He set the camera aside, then peered into the bottom of the bag.

"What's this?" he asked.

"What?" I wasn't sure what he meant. I'd packed some dark sunglasses (more potential disguise), my cell phone, my keys, a regular digital camera, a notepad and pen, and an extra (non-Cubs) shirt that actually fit me so I could change later.

He pulled out two black wooden sticks hooked together with a chain. "Nunchucks? Seriously?" He looked at me like I was crazy. Oscar started whistling.

"Uh . . . ," I said.

"Miss, you can't bring weapons into the park. I'm going to have to confiscate them." Oscar stopped whistling.

"Wait," he said, "Can we, like, coat check them or something? They're my dad's."

"Sorry, we don't have a coat check for weapons." The guy stuck the nunchucks in a box under the table. He put everything else back in my bag and handed it to me. "No foolishness from you three, okay?"

"No, sir," I said. "Sorry about that." I whacked Oscar in the back as we went through the gate and joined Melly, who'd been standing there waiting.

"What were you thinking?" I asked him when we were out of earshot of the security guy.

"Victoria totally attacked you last time. I thought she was gonna claw your eyes out. I figured we could use a weapon, you know, just in case."

I really didn't even know what to say to that. His heart was in the right place. Sort of. But *nunchucks*?

"Why does your dad even own nunchucks?" asked Melly, which was exactly the same thing I had been thinking. I mean, his dad was complete white bread. Not that I could imagine my dad with nunchuks. He may work for the BERM, but he wasn't a field agent by any stretch of the imagination.

"I dunno." Oscar shrugged. "He has a secret desire to be a ninja? He's got some throwing stars too, but I didn't bring those."

"Good thing," I said. The security guy probably wouldn't have let us in. The nunchuks had been bad enough. And what would I have done with throwing stars? I wasn't Batman.

We wandered around the lower stands, the doors to the locker room, and the concession areas, but saw no sign of a film crew or any of the stars. There were a lot of people wandering around in Cubs stuff, but I couldn't tell if they were extras who'd answered the casting call or what. It looked like it was time for us to go up to the press area and see if they were filming there.

We found the entrance to the press boxes and showed our passes to a guy who happened to be walking out at the same time. He just glanced at the passes and waved us through without really looking at them. I let out a sigh of relief. Maybe everything would work out after all. Things seemed to be going so well, other than the nunchuks. I imagined how we'd find them filming, conceal ourselves, and get a video of Victoria saying something damaging or giving a clue as to where her rental house was. I already knew it had to be near Northbrook or Glenview somewhere. After all, why would she have brought Rufus to a vet far away from her house? It wouldn't make sense. And then I could get in touch with Viv and give her all the details and that would be it. Case closed.

Of course, I knew I was dreaming.

TWENTY-THREE

FRIDAY, SEPTEMBER 11, 1:45 P.M.

"BEWARE OF PEOPLE WHO DISLIKE CATS."
—IRISH PROVERB

Just like I'd hoped, we found the film crew without much trouble. There was a narrow hallway with a few offices and a small break room/cafeteria-looking area leading up to the actual press boxes. It wasn't really a very big area. That meant there were a lot of people and equipment crowded into a tiny spot, which was mostly good for us. Everything was so harried and packed, and we were just three more bodies in the way.

They were running a scene where, apparently, Ty's character was talking the announcer guys into letting him sing during the seventh-inning stretch. I'd been to only a few Cubs games in my life, but even I knew the seventh-inning stretch was a big deal at Wrigley Field. It was a huge tradition.

They had big name (and no name) celebrities come perform. Basically, some famous person would sing "Take Me Out to the Ball Game" and the crowd would sing along. And, you know, stretch after sitting for so long, I guess. Baseball games always seemed interminable to me, but the hot dogs were good. Dad wasn't very sporty, so I was spared having to watch them on television, at least.

It soon became apparent that watching them film the same scene over and over wasn't getting us anywhere. Victoria wasn't even in this scene. We needed to be somewhere where we could catch her off guard. Off movie camera and less public. With all the movie security people around, we couldn't even take our own camera out without risking getting thrown out. We moved back along the hallway to talk it over.

"I vote for the dressing room," Melly said.

"What about the craft services table?" asked Oscar. It was set up in the break room behind us.

"You're just hungry," I said, and punched him in the shoulder.

"True," he said. "But everyone winds up by the craft services table sooner or later."

They both looked at me like I should be the one making the decision. Like I had a clue. Finally I told Oscar to go over by the craft services table, and Melly and I would try to find Victoria's dressing room. After all, they might have the girls' and guys' areas separated, so Oscar wouldn't be able to get close anyway.

Not to mention he looked pretty conspicuous in his punk Cubs outfit, even around the movie people.

We split up, and our luck still looked good. We watched

as Oscar slipped into the break room and took up station by the food. He busied himself with straightening stacks of sandwiches and lining up bottles of water. No one questioned him at all.

Melly and I mingled with the people nearest the filming. When a lady I recognized as the costume designer walked by us, I poked Melly. She nodded and we followed the woman around the corner and down the hall to a section of offices, making sure to stay way back. Hopefully, she wouldn't recognize us. I'd even tucked the purple-streaked portions of my hair well up into the hat so I'd stand out less. She might not have recognized me without my neck wings anyway. The woman flipped through a rack of clothing in the hall, grabbed a Cubs shirt, and went back to the filming, not even glancing in our direction.

It really seemed like our good fortune was holding. A few of the office doors had paper signs taped on them. One had Victoria's name right on it. We'd actually found the dressing rooms, and even better, no one was hanging around in the hallway. They were all back where the action was.

Melly and I looked at each other. I knocked on the door, ready to run if it actually opened. Nothing happened and we didn't hear any noise from inside, so Melly opened the door and I followed her in. It looked like some poor guy's windowless office had been commandeered for Victoria. The desk (really, a glorified table) had a large three-part lighted mirror set up on it, and it was covered in makeup and curlers and hairbrushes. Another clothing rack had been shoved up against one wall, and a bookcase had been pushed out of the way near it. It wasn't a huge office to begin with, and with so much of Victoria's stuff sprawled on the desk, it looked like people from that TV show about hoarders had come through and made themselves at home.

"What do you think?" I asked.

"Not a whole lot of options," said Melly.

We looked at each other and then the clothing rack. I rearranged the clothes on it so all the longer pieces were on the side closest to the bookcase, and we shoved ourselves behind the rack. As long as no one pulled out a piece of clothing directly in front of us, we'd hopefully be okay. I pulled out Dad's video camera and made a space to stick it through and aimed it at the desk.

Then we waited.

"This is pretty cool," whispered Melly. "Though I really thought the dressing rooms would be nicer than this."

"I imagine you've got to make do with what you can when you're on location," I said, almost sounding like I knew what I was talking about.

Then the door burst open. Melly and I froze. I turned the camera on as quietly as I could and looked through the viewfinder. It was Victoria and the crazy eyeliner makeup lady. The door slammed behind them and Victoria sat down in the chair. Perfect. She was right in my sights. Amazingly, all of her wounds from the day before were completely gone.

She looked good as new. Either her Talent had taken care of them or the film crew used some seriously good makeup for moviemaking. What kind of Talent could she have, though, that both healed and allowed her to impersonate someone? It had to be Class A. At the very least, she was probably multi-Talented like Viv.

She leaned in toward the mirror and made a face as she looked closely at her eyebrows. She whirled on the make-up lady. "You're useless. You missed two hairs right here." She stabbed a finger at her left eyebrow. The poor makeup woman backed up and held up a brush like a shield.

"I can—" she started to say.

"Forget it! Just get out of here! I'll take care of it my-self! It's no wonder Alan didn't want to give me a close-up!" She spun back around and makeup flew off the table as she started digging around in the pile, presumably looking for tweezers. The makeup lady left without another word.

I tilted my head slightly and widened my eyes at Melly. She looked back at me and wrinkled her nose. Seriously, Victoria was a starlet needing a serious come down. Hopefully, we'd be the ones to do it. I zoomed the camera in on her face. After we send a copy to the BERM, I was so going to stick it up on YouTube.

"Stupid people," she mumbled to herself. "I have to do everything myself." She leaned in so close to the mirror that her eyeball was practically touching it. She plucked out the two hairs, letting out a shriek with each one. Drama queen.

Finished, she sank back in her chair and stared at herself in the mirror. "What a freaking mess," she said to herself. "The stupid cat is missing again. I've got to take care of that idiot blogger today. At least it gives me an excuse." She sat up straight and said in a whiny voice, "I just can't go on without my beloved Tiddlywinks!" She slumped back down and was quiet for a minute, not taking her eyes off herself in the mirror. Homicidal freak. How could someone talk so casually about killing someone else? I guessed if you could do it to a cat, a human being was the next step up.

Then she leaned forward and breathed deeply, staring intently at herself. "I can do it. I am successful, rich, healthy, and happy. I am powerful. I am in charge. No one can stop me from getting what I want. People fear me."

I managed to hold back my laughter. For a classic villain, she was a total dork. I zoomed the camera back out as she kept repeating her mantra over and over again. Melly let out a small snort, but Victoria was too wrapped up in herself to notice.

Then my cell phone went off with "I Am Woman." Holy flying pancakes. Of all the times for Viv to finally call me back. Why hadn't I turned my ringer off? I fumbled with the camera and passed it to Melly, then plunged my hand in my backpack. Where was the damn phone?

It didn't matter. By the time the phone stopped ringing as it went to voice mail, Victoria was in front of us ripping clothes off their hangers and throwing them on the floor.

"You again," she practically snarled, peering at my face under the brim of my hat. She reached through the few remaining shirts hanging up and grabbed each of us around a wrist, yanking us both out. I went sprawling on the floor, but Melly managed to stay standing, barely. Victoria let go of me as I went tumbling, but she had Melly's wrist firmly in her grasp. "What do you want?" Victoria demanded.

I scrambled to my feet and backed toward the door with my book bag in my hand. "We're on to you!" I said. "We know you're planning to kill Easton West!"

Victoria stopped. "I don't know what you're talking about. You don't have any proof of anything. In fact"—she snatched my dad's camera from Melly's hand—"I'll take this."

"That's what—" I started to say, but Melly shook her head at me. She was right. Why tell her what we know from Rufus?

"Fine," I said. "You're right. Whatever you say. Why don't you let Melly go and we'll get out of here."

For a moment, it looked like Victoria was going to do just that. Then her eyes narrowed at me and she tightened her grip on Melly's wrist. "Why aren't you in jail? Why did the police let you go?" she asked. "I told them I wanted to press charges." She took a step in my direction, dragging Melly with her.

"Um, I've got a good lawyer?" I must not have sounded too sure, since her eyes narrowed even further. Craptastic.

"I don't believe you," she said.

"Maybe they just thought I was a better actress than you," I said, and leaped forward to try and grab the camera.

I almost got my hand on the strap, but then she shoved forward and hit me in the chest with the camera. I heard something crack and hoped it was the camera instead of one of my ribs. It hurt bad enough that I wasn't sure. She pulled her hand with the camera back up over her head like she was going to bash me in the head next. Melly jumped, trying to grab her arm, and Victoria gave her wrist a vicious pull. From the way she was able to keep hold of Melly, who yelped as I backed up, Victoria was stronger than she appeared.

Then I almost fell into both of them as the door slammed into my back.

"Oh! Sorry!" said Alan, the director. "Didn't know anyone else was in here. We're ready for you, Victoria."

Victoria dropped the hand with the camera behind her back. "Of course, Alan. I was just getting ready when these fans showed up," she said. She looked from me to him to Melly and then smiled. Uh-oh. I ducked my head so he couldn't see my face. "Hey, Alan, don't you think Melly here would be perfect for that little scene you were planning with Ty and a Cubs fan in the stands? I heard that the girl you wanted to do it didn't show."

She turned to me. "You wouldn't mind, would you?" she said, and grinned an absolutely evil grin. "I'd really love to get to know Melly here better, and I could keep an eye on her during shooting so you wouldn't have to worry about *anything* happening to her."

It was the way she said the last part that seriously worried me. I rubbed the sore spot on my chest.

"I don't—" I started to say, but Alan interrupted.

"You're right! She'd be perfect." He stepped forward without even looking at me and took Melly's chin in his hand, moving her face from side to side. "Just the right look. What do you think, Melly? Are you up for it? I'd just need to get a permission form from your parents. How old are you anyway?"

"You've already got one," squeaked out Melly. "I go to Shermer High."

"Melly!" I said. She looked at me, her eyes big and round, and shrugged. Oh my God. I couldn't believe it. She was going along with Victoria's ploy because she had a chance at being in the movie! Was she nuts? Who knew what Victoria was going to do to her when the cameras stopped rolling!

"Sorry," said Alan, barely registering that I was in the room. "I only need one. But maybe next time!" He put an arm around Melly's shoulder, apparently not noticing that Victoria still held her by the wrist. "Let's go talk about it out on the bleachers, okay? The second unit is getting ready to shoot now."

"Sure!" said Melly. She smiled excitedly at me and gave a little finger wave from the side Victoria didn't have a death grip on as the three of them swept out the door.

Holy cheese on a cracker. What was I supposed to do now? Melly was certifiable. She'd just willingly turned herself over to the enemy. Did she want to be an actress bad enough to *die* for it?

TWENTY-FOUR

"Never Trust a Human."
—RUFUS BRUTUS THE THIRD

I found Oscar eating some chips by the craft services table and told him what had happened. At first, he was excited for Melly, until I whacked him on the forehead.

"Ouch!" he said. "Okay, okay, I get it. Victoria's evil, blah, blah, blah. Still, what's she going to do while they've got the cameras rolling? And we'll keep an eye on her too. You'll see, it'll be fine. Melly's gonna be in the movie!" He did his happy dance, whacking his hip into the table and knocking over a small tower of soda cans. I pulled him away from the table before he could do any more damage.

We found Alan, Melly, and Victoria as they went out into the stands. We were stopped at some caution tape by a security guard who gave Victoria a thumbs-up sign as he stepped in front of us.

"Sorry, no can do, kids," he said. "You'll have to watch your friend from here." He crossed his arms over his chest, which was wholly unnecessary seeing as how his chest alone was as big around as the two of us together. Probably bigger.

Oscar looked ready to argue, but I pulled him away. The dude was seriously beefy. Oscar looked like a toothpick next to him. We stood off to the side and watched as Alan walked Melly (and the ever-present Victoria) over to Ty McKenzie.

"Oh. My. God," said Oscar. "He's introducing her to Ty!" He was so excited he didn't even jump up and down, just sort of vibrated in place.

Melly looked like she was holding it together pretty well, though I could tell even from where I was that she was nervous. Like, two seconds away from squealing. Ty held out his hand to shake hers and Victoria was forced to let go of Melly's wrist or look like a real freak.

"Run, Melly, run," I whispered under my breath, but she just shook Ty's hand and giggled. Victoria looked my way, grinned, and waved. She knew she had me. Or rather, she had Melly—hook, line, and sinker.

"Like she'd run," snorted Oscar. "This is the kind of thing she's been dreaming about all her life!"

"Being held hostage by a homicidal maniac?"

"No, Nat." Oscar patted me on the head. "Being on a *real* movie set with *real* actors with a *real* chance to be in a movie. We were talking about it on the phone last night. She was hoping we could wrap the Victoria business up quick so she could really get a close look at the shoot and maybe even drop off some headshots with someone. But this is way beyond that!" Oscar did another happy dance and threw in a twirl for good measure. "Melly is *so* lucky!"

Both of my best friends were crazy.

Oscar and I watched as they sat Melly down right next to Ty, with Victoria on his other side. A bunch of extras were directed to sit around them. Then some of the movie people passed around drinks and hot dogs as well as various Cubs paraphernalia. Basically, one section of the stands was filled in, while the rest of the stadium was pretty much empty.

Then Alan talked to everyone, but especially to Melly. With all of the noise from the extras, I couldn't hear anything he was saying, but I saw Melly first go completely red and then completely pale.

"Can you hear anything?" I asked Oscar.

"No," he said. "But it's either really good or really bad. Did you see Melly's face? Wait. Oh. My. God. Did you say it was for Ty's scene with a Cub's fan?"

"Yeah," I said. "Why?"

Oscar didn't reply. He squeaked out "Just watch!" and leaned as far forward over the caution tape as he could without falling over.

They finally set up for the first take. After Alan gave the word, Ty, Melly, and some of the other extras stood up and cheered like the Cubs had just hit a home run. Since there was actually nothing happening on the field, it looked rather odd. Then Ty turned and high-fived Melly, grabbed her in a giant bear hug, and laid a huge kiss right on her lips. After that, he turned to Victoria and squished her in another big hug.

Oh. Wow. This was part of the scene from the script that Oscar had stolen. Melly was the "attractive teenage girl." I felt a little weak in the knees myself. Ty McKenzie had just kissed my best friend.

Oscar let out a strangled sound next to me. "It *was* . . . he did . . . oh my . . ." He gulped and sat down right there in the middle of the aisle. Finally, he recovered enough to speak. "Nat," he said, looking up at me, "next time I want to stake out the craft services table instead of going with you, just hit me, okay?"

All told, Ty kissed Melly no fewer than ten times as Alan filmed Victoria's reaction to it from different angles. Each time, Oscar practically fainted. I was actually really impressed with Melly because she *hadn't* fainted. It looked like she really had the makings of an actress, if we could just get her away from Victoria in one piece. I'd seen Melly in a bunch of school plays and even community theater stuff, but this was so different from that. She was a natural.

Then they filmed Ty running up the stairs. It was weird how everything was all out of order. The kissing scene had come before the press box stuff, and they'd filmed that first. How did the actors keep everything straight? And it was no wonder Ty was so built. Alan had him run up the stairs at least half a dozen times. It was actually kind of mesmerizing. How did his hair manage to flop so perfectly?

I shook my head and scanned the stands. I grabbed Oscar's arm. "Oscar! Where's Melly? Where's Victoria? Do you see them?" I didn't see either one of them anywhere. What were we doing watching Ty?

Stupid question. I knew exactly why we were watching Ty—the same reason Jason had been reminding all of the extras to look at the field between each take. There was a reason he was the star of the show.

Oscar looked too and shook his head. "Nope. I don't see them. Maybe they went back inside?"

We ran back to where they had been filming earlier. A few extras were hitting the craft services table, but I didn't see Victoria or Melly. Her dressing room was empty too.

I finally grabbed someone wandering around with a clipboard. "Hey, have you seen the girl they used in the stands? The one Ty kissed? Or Victoria?"

The lady checked her clipboard. "Don't know about the girl, but it looks like Victoria's not scheduled for anything else for a while. She probably left. She usually doesn't stick around any longer than she has to."

Oscar and I looked at each other. Holy bat fingers. Victoria was on a kidnapping spree and now she had Melly.

TWENTY-FIVE

FriDaY, SepTeMBer 11TH, 4:44 P.M.

"THere IS NOTHING a CaT DOESN'T KNOW,
especially THe THINGS YOU DON'T WaNT US TO KNOW."
—MeeP

Oscar and I sat staring at each other in my room, Rufus and Meep in standard cat bread loaf poses between us. We'd immediately run outside the stadium, but with no idea what direction Victoria had gone with Melly, there was nothing we could do. Oscar had managed to locate his dad's nunchuks and steal them back from the box without the security guy noticing, but that was the only thing we could remotely call a success for the day. We hadn't gained any real information and we'd lost Melly, not to mention my dad's camera. Well, at least that wasn't a big loss. He didn't use it much. I'd checked the card and the last thing he'd recorded had been Emmy's tenth birthday party. We hadn't really captured anything hugely incriminating to use against Victoria, either, even if we could have found the camera again.

I dialed Viv's number but, of course, she didn't answer. It was ridiculous. No wonder the newspapers were always filled with stories about terrorist threats. You couldn't reach the authorities even when they were your own sister!

That's when I remembered that I probably had a voice mail. It was Viv: "Nat, just a quick message. I've got a couple of classes and then a department meeting downtown and an interrogation they want me to sit in on. My battery's about dead, but I'll get back to you as soon as I can. I checked the registration database and there's no record for Victoria Welling. I thought at first she might be an unregistered, but we both know how unlikely that is since the BERM started infant testing over twenty-five years ago. So, just for kicks I did a search on the database for Talents matching what you'd told me. And bingo! There it was! There are only two people registered who have any kind of Talent similar to what you mentioned. And one of them I happened to notice was from the same town as Victoria. Remember how we watched that behind the scenes thing on one of her movies and she talked about being from Gun Barrel City, Texas? I remembered it because it was such a weird name. Anyway, some girl named Regina Fedorka was registered, and she had a record a mile long with all kinds of petty theft and even an assault and battery charge. What do you bet she changed her name when she left home to become an actress?"

There was some noise like she was interrupted, and then she came back.

"Oh, I forgot, the registry mentioned that the subject she's impersonating has to be alive and she's got to touch them on a regular basis, otherwise she turns back into herself. It's only a Class B Talent. Anyway, that means that Easton is alive and well. I'll talk to you later. And stop freaking out! You left me, like, a billion voice mails. I haven't even had time to listen to them all! Everything's going to be fine. We're on the case."

Whoa. I had Oscar listen to the message too so I wouldn't have to repeat it all. Then Rufus made me play it for him too.

So, Rufus said, *your sister, who was supposed to save the day, is unreachable and probably hasn't even listened to half the messages you left her. Am I getting that right?*

"Yeah," I said. "And Victoria's real name is Regina Fedorka." I could see why she'd changed her name, even without the criminal record. You'd never get a starring role with a name like "Fedorka." My head was reeling, trying to take it all in. "I wonder if Easton had discovered something about her past?"

"I know you don't think so," said Oscar, "but Easton really is a good investigative reporter."

I snorted. How many crack investigative reporters wear six-inch pink heels?

"Seriously," he said. "I bet she figured it out. She came out here to break a story on Victoria's acting. If she stumbled onto a story about a stuck-up actress with a Talent for shape-shifting who also happened to have a lengthy criminal record, it'd be like hitting the jackpot. She'd have been all over that."

Absolutely, said Rufus. *My person is very talented.* He glared at me.

"Okay, okay," I said. "Easton is amazing. But what are we supposed to do now?"

Oscar pulled out his cell phone. "It is time," he said theatrically, "to call the cops." He dialed 911 then handed the phone to me. "You talk," he said. "They make me nervous. Besides, you've already met them."

Yeah, if that's what you want to call being arrested.

"911, what's your emergency?"

"Um, hi," I said. "I'm calling about a kidnapping. Actually, I guess, *two* kidnappings."

"Two kidnappings?" the lady asked. There was a pause. "Okay, please provide me with all of the details."

"Okay." I took a deep breath and tried to organize my thoughts. "First off, that blogger Easton West was kidnapped by Victoria Welling. You know, the actress? Well, it turns out Victoria's real name is actually Regina Fedorka and she's got a criminal record. Easton probably figured that out and that's why she was kidnapped. You know, to shut her up. We were, like, gathering evidence and then she—Regina—also kidnapped my best friend Melly. Are you following this?"

There was a pause. "Let me get this straight," she said. "You're calling to report the kidnapping of a blogger and your best friend . . . by an actress?"

"Yeah, Vic—sorry, *Regina* kidnapped Melly a couple of hours ago from Wrigley Field. We think she's holding everybody at a rental house somewhere in the Northbrook area or maybe around Glenview. Oh, and she can shape-shift."

I heard some typing on the other end of the line. "I see that this number was recently input into our system as having made a false 911 call. You do realize that fake emergency calls are against the law, don't you, young lady?"

"I explained that one! It was a butt dial. But this is for real—"

"I'm going to be lenient this time, but I've flagged this number. If you make any more false reports, you *will* be criminally charged. Do you understand?"

"Wait!" I said. "There are some officers who know what I'm talking about! When they arrested me and my sister came—she works for the BERM—to bail me out—"

Click.

That didn't go entirely well, I take it, said Rufus.

I handed the phone back to Oscar. "I wouldn't use your phone to call 911 again," I told him. "Ever."

"What now?" asked Oscar.

"I have no idea," I said.

"You could tell your parents."

"They won't even be home for a few more hours. They almost always work late on Fridays. They're workaholic freaks. Besides which, they're useless." And I also had less than no desire to tell them. They probably wouldn't believe me, not without Viv to back me up, wherever she was.

"Call the BERM directly?"

"I guess I can give it a shot." It was worth a try.

Oscar looked up the number on the Internet and I dialed the phone. After going through about half a dozen automated voice prompts, I finally got a real person on the phone. I started out by explaining that my sister worked there in the hope that would lend some legitimacy to my story.

"Genevieve Ng?" the woman repeated for about the fourth time.

"Yes, that's my sister. Sometimes she goes by Viv? Anyway, we need to get in touch with her or her supervisor."

"Let me see," she said. "Okay, I'm connecting you now." *Click.* Three rings later and I was in Viv's work voice mail. I left a message and then called the main number back again. Five minutes later, I was finally back on with the same woman who'd transferred me.

"Hi," I said. "I just spoke with you a few minutes ago. You connected me to my sister Viv's voice mail . . ."

"Please hold," she said.

Some elevator music came on. I rolled my eyes at Oscar and he shrugged. Then click.

"She hung up on me!" I tried again, but this time I went right to being on hold. Then another click. I hung up the phone. "Aaaaggggggggghhhhhh!"

Oscar patted me on the shoulder. "Do you want me to try?"

"Fine," I said. "You try." I left my room to get a glass of water and cool off. When I came back, I got there just in time to see Oscar throw the phone on the bed.

You people obviously have no clout.

"Okay, you were right. That was useless. But we have to do something! That crazy Regina woman has Melly, and there's no telling what she'll do! If she can look like anyone at all in the world, she could just kill everyone and disappear and start over!" Finally, Oscar was getting it.

"Well, what are we supposed to do? We can't just go door to door looking for kidnap victims. Even if we found the right house by some miracle, Regina could disguise herself as someone else and we'd never know." I rolled Meep over and scratched her on her tummy. Sometimes that helped me think and it had the added benefit of keeping her happy too. "Do you even know how many houses there are between Northbrook and Glenview?"

Why don't you ask? purred Meep, looking up at me.

"Ask who? I don't think 411 has that kind of information. Besides, who really cares how many houses there are?"

No, stupid. She means, why don't you ask the cats? said Rufus.

"What are you talking about?" I really had no idea, but Rufus and Meep were looking at each other like they'd revealed some incredible pearl of obvious wisdom.

Cats know everything, said Rufus sagely.

Whatever. "Fine." I made an exaggerated bow to my cat. "Meep, where is Regina holding Melly?"

Oscar, Rufus, and Meep all gave me a look like I was insane.

Not me, said Meep. *You know I don't talk to cats.*

213

Rufus rolled over to get some tummy love too. *You need a savvy cat*, he said. *Someone more like me, but who knows other cats around here. Someone who gets around.*

Where was I going to find a cat like that?

TWENTY-SIX

Friday, September 11, 5:23 P.M.

*"There is, incidentally, no way of talking about cats
that enables one to come off as a sane person."*
—Dan Greenburg

"I cannot believe I'm doing this," I said for probably the
fiftieth time as I opened the passenger's side door. I looked
back at Oscar, who had commandeered Melly's car. It's
not like she was using it. He gave me a thumbs-up from
the driver's seat. Rufus and Meep, in the back, peered at
me through the side window from up on their hind legs.

I rang Ian's doorbell. In what felt like hours later, he
answered it.

"Nat," he said. "Um, hi. Did you get the passes this
afternoon okay? Everything work out with your life or
death thing?" He looked a little confused to see me. Or
maybe just confused that I had the guts to show up on his
doorstep.

"Oh, um, yeah, thanks for the passes. We got them fine.
The other thing, though . . . it didn't go as planned. We could
really use your help."

"I don't think my dad's got any more access than what he gave you," said Ian.

"It's not about the ballpark," I said. "It's about PD."

"PD? What's that?"

Oh, yeah. Crap. What was it they called Purr Daddy? "Oh, sorry! Pebbles. I need to, um, see Pebbles."

The confused look changed to completely baffled. "You need to see my cat?" he said slowly and deliberately. He stepped back from the door a little like whatever I had might be catching.

"Yeah," I said miserably. "Can I please see Pebbles?" At least Dad would be happy about me killing all my chances of ever having a date in high school. Maybe I could find one once I went off to college.

"I don't know if that's a good idea. Maybe . . . maybe you should go." He moved to close the door, but I held out my hand to stop him.

"Okay," I said quickly without giving myself time to think about what I was about to do. "Do you really want to know what's going on? I'll tell you." I had no choice, not with Melly's life on the line. And maybe I could just go to college somewhere far away where they had no idea who I was. Like in another state. Or maybe another country.

"Sure," he said, though he didn't invite me in. So I stood on his stoop and told him an abbreviated version of the whole story, starting with the video and ending with us driving over to his house to enlist the help of PD.

He listened to the whole convoluted mess without interrupting, but his eyebrows kept climbing higher and higher until I feared they would disappear into his unruly mop of hair and never be seen again. There was complete silence for a minute.

"So," he said finally, running a hand through his hair. "You talk to cats. And there's a crazy shape-shifting kidnapper actress out there somewhere who's holding Melly and Easton West hostage. Does that about sum it up?"

"Yes," I said. "And Meep and Rufus suggested that we use the cat network to find out where Regina is hiding them." I felt stupid for even saying the words "cat network," but I didn't know what else to call it. I shoved my hands in my pockets and kicked my toe at the edge of their cheerful little flowery doormat.

"Natalie," he said, "you know you sound totally insane, right?" The door creaked a little as he shifted his weight. Was he going to shut it in my face?

And yes, *of course* I knew all of this sounded crazy. There was no part of any of it that sounded remotely like normal life. Like a normal person's life. But that wasn't my life. It never had been. I mean, my little sister was doing calculus when she was three. My first good friend was a cat. My older sister was a human lie detector, and my mom had more patents than most people had cookbooks. My dad could smell what you had for dinner two days ago if you didn't brush your teeth well enough. I was a freak from a family of freaks.

Tell him he's wearing his SpongeBob boxer shorts, the ones with the holes. His mom keeps trying to throw them away.

I looked past Ian to see PD saunter into the front hall. "I can't say that," I said.

"What?" asked Ian. He turned to look at PD. "Are you saying that Pebbles just said something to you?"

Okay, fine. Tell him he had Fruit Loops for breakfast.

"PD says you had Fruit Loops for breakfast."

Ian looked momentarily surprised. "Lots of people eat that for breakfast," he said, but he was keeping one eye on PD and one on me.

But not everyone pours orange juice over them, said PD. *Milk I understand, but orange juice I really don't get. The smell is unbelievable.*

"In orange juice," I told Ian. "Fruit Loops with orange juice." Gross.

He stared at me with eyes as big as baseballs. "What did he tell you a minute ago?"

"I'd rather not say," I said. Underwear is just so personal.

"No," he said. "Tell me."

I was already in dateless territory. Might as well go whole hog. "Um, SpongeBob," I said, covering my eyes for a moment. "SpongeBob underpants."

Ian's face went to immediate lobster red, but so did mine. I should have made something else up. He'd never have known the difference.

"He told me before you like reggae. When I was here

218

to do homework." That's what I should have said. It would have been much safer.

"Wait," he said. "You talked to him last time you were here?"

I looked down at the doormat again. It actually said Have a Nice Day under the sunflowers. *That* wasn't going to happen. "Yeah. A little."

I could practically hear the wheels turning around in Ian's head. "Is *that* why he took his medicine from you so easily? Because you told him to?"

"Um . . ."

He's got you on that one. Just tell him you're in heat for him, said PD. *It can't hurt.*

This was rapidly becoming the most painful conversation I had ever had, even worse than the phone call when I asked him for the passes. "Yeah," I finally said. "I asked PD if he'd take the pill for me so I could trick you into a date with me." I forced myself to look Ian in the eye. "Because I really like you."

He looked at me for a beat, his brown eyes wide. "Why didn't you just ask me?"

I just raised my eyebrows at him. Was he kidding me?

This is charming and all, said PD, *but didn't I hear you say something about someone's life being on the line?* PD walked over to Ian and headbutted his ankle, then looked up at me.

"Right," I said. "Um, Ian, can we talk about that later? Right now, I really need PD's help."

"I'm coming too," said Ian. He grabbed a jacket from

the hooks by the door. He bent down to pick up PD, but PD gave him a look that you didn't need to understand Cat to get. Then PD stuck his tail straight in the air and led the way to Melly's car. I scrambled after him and opened the back door. PD jumped in. Ian, a bemused look on his face, followed after him. I climbed in the front passenger's side without a word. As soon as we were in and our seat belts were on, Oscar gunned it. All three cats went flying.

"Hey, Ian, welcome to the party," said Oscar.

"Um, hi, Oscar. Do you know where you're going?" asked Ian, holding on to the back of my seat with both hands.

"No," I said, and whacked Oscar in the shoulder. "Slow down, Oscar. I need to talk to PD!"

"Oh, okay," said Oscar. He barely let off the gas.

"This is so weird," said Ian. He was staring down at the cats, who had all climbed back on the seat and were looking right back at him.

This is the boy you talk about in your sleep? asked Meep. *Hmmmm.*

PD let out a cat giggle. *She's in heat for him*, he said to Meep. All three of the cats laughed.

"What are they saying?" asked Ian.

"Nothing," I said. "Just . . . you know, cat stuff."

Liar, said Rufus.

I ignored him. "Okay," I said to PD, "here's the deal. We need to locate a particular house. It's probably pretty close to here." I gave as full a description of Regina, Easton, and

Melly as I could, using as many cat terms as I could. Like pink hair meant nothing to them, but the fact that Melly always wore vanilla-scented perfume might help. I wished I knew more about Regina. Rufus added in as much as he could too. He said Regina smelled like stale pretzels, acne medicine, and some Cat word I didn't know. Ian watched the whole conversation with great interest while Oscar drove in really fast circles around the block.

Okay, said PD. *I know exactly where to start. Take me to the park that's by my house. That's where Queenie hangs out.*

"Where's the park?" I asked Ian. It was pretty useless asking a cat for street directions, since they told you how to get places by telling you how things smelled or how the light looked. Street signs meant nothing to them. Neither did streets or stop signs, for that matter, but I'd finally taught Meep to pay attention to those by appealing to her instincts of self-preservation.

Ian gave directions to Oscar and we arrived just a few minutes later. We all got out of the car and followed PD over to some picnic tables. It was a small park, but there was a BBQ grill, a slide, some swings, and a sandbox (i.e., a litter box, if you were a cat—I'd learned early on to never, ever play in one of those).

Hey, Queenie, said PD. *Got somebody for you to meet!*

An incredibly fat black cat with a tuft of white fur under her chin came waddling out of some bushes. *Purr Daddy! Been awhile. Where've you been, fishbreath?*

Queenie and PD brushed noses and sniffed butts. *I'd love to chat*, said PD, *but I'm here on business today*.

And I see you brought some friends, said Queenie. She sniffed Rufus and Meep, and then took a good look at me. *Well*, she said wonderingly. *What do we have here?*

"Hi," I said. "I'm Natalie. And this is Ian and Oscar."

Ian's mine, said PD, *so don't go getting any ideas, Queenie*.

Sure, sure, she said. *I remember him from when he used to come to the park when he was a little kitten. Still smells the same. Earthy and sweet. And don't get your tail in knots. I'm happier when I'm free.*

I'd never thought about it, but that is kind of what Ian smelled like. I wasn't sure if Queenie had meant it as a compliment or not, though. Meep's favorite smells were my gym shoes and three-week-old tuna cans. She was always squirreling them away under my bed.

PD and Rufus explained the situation to Queenie. I was glad to let them do it. I was honestly getting tired of telling the same depressing story over and over again. Each time I told it, I couldn't help but wonder if Melly was still okay. How desperate was Regina? What was she capable of doing? Would she really kill someone? I mean, she was psyching herself up with a cheesy mantra. Did she have the guts to actually do anything? I hoped she didn't.

Of course, she *had* nearly scratched my eyes out. And she hadn't even known then that I knew anything. She'd just known that I was the one who took Rufus. Would Melly tell her anything? I shook my head. I didn't want to think about it anymore. I joined Oscar and Ian, who were apparently discussing what they imagined cats talked about.

"I still can't believe it," said Ian. "Sorry, Nat. It's just really unreal. If you'd asked me, I wouldn't even have thought cats were intelligent enough to have a conversation with."

I leaned forward and whispered so our feline companions couldn't hear me. "Some of them really aren't. But then again, some of them are about as smart as your average middle schooler. It depends." At least he hadn't started calling me Cat Girl. That was something.

I'll put the word out. Just give me fifteen minutes, said Queenie. *I'll find out which house you need.* She darted off into the bushes, far faster than I would have thought she was capable of moving.

Quite a cat, that one, said Rufus. He sounded grudgingly impressed.

You know it, said PD. Then he went into a story that I wasn't about to repeat and most certainly didn't want to hear about Queenie and some dead animal they'd once found in the park. I grabbed Oscar and Ian by the hand and led them over to a picnic table so we could sit down and wait.

"Meep," I called, "why don't you come over here too?" Really, I didn't think she needed to hear stuff like that. I know I sure didn't.

Are you kidding? she called back. *I don't think so! I need to hang out with these cats more often!*

Great. There was no telling what kind of trouble she'd be getting into now. I probably wouldn't be able to keep her in the house. Who knew what she was going to be rolling herself around in?

"You really think that cat will be able to do it?" asked Oscar. He looked worried. It was about time. I felt like I'd been doing the worrying for both of us.

"Maybe," I said. "Cats are everywhere, you know. And they get around. Meep doesn't leave the house much, but she's gone over a mile away before without me even knowing about it until later. They're sneaky like that."

"Pebbles is—wait. Sorry, what did you say his name was again?"

"Um, Purr Daddy, or PD for short." I blushed a little, though I didn't know why. It's not like it was my idea to call him that.

"Right. PD is mostly an indoor cat, but my little brother lets him out sometimes. But I don't think he ever goes out of our yard."

PD was obviously paying attention to what we were talking about, since he started cat laughing.

Ian looked at him. "So, I'm guessing he doesn't agree with that assessment?"

"Not so much," I said. "Seriously, cats are pretty devious. I bet he gets out more than you know." After all, he knew right where to find Queenie.

Speaking of the devil, Queenie came sauntering back into view. *I've got some good news and some bad news,* she said. *What do you want first?*

TWENTY-SEVEN

FRIDAY, SEPTEMBER 11, 6:12 P.M.

"Never underestimate a cat. Actually, I take that back. Please, underestimate us all you want."
—QUEENIE

"The good news first, I guess," I said. Maybe it would have been better to start off with the bad, but I felt like I'd already had enough bad news to last me a lifetime. Ian and Oscar just looked back and forth from me to the cat.

Well, honey, I found the house you want. It actually isn't that far from here as the cat walks. You can get there in less than ten minutes in your car.

"That's great!" I turned to Oscar and Ian and hugged them both. "She found the house!" Oscar let out a huge cheer. Rufus started sharpening his claws on a picnic table.

"Did she say something about bad news too?" asked Ian. "I heard you say you wanted the good news."

Well, said Queenie, *I had Tom-Tom look in the windows — he's the one that reported in first with the location — and he said it doesn't look like there's anyone there. But he did smell a dog.*

Oh, that'll just be Fergie, said Rufus. *Totally harmless.*

225

"Just that it doesn't look like anyone's there. But that might be good. Maybe we can get in and scope things out before she gets home." I smiled, but I was worried. Where would she have taken Melly other than the house? Did she have more than one hiding spot?

Queenie gave me detailed directions—or rather, cat-level detailed directions. Ian and I deciphered them and we were off. Ten minutes later, just like Queenie promised, we pulled up outside a standard-issue North Shore suburban house in a nondescript subdivision. It could have been anyone's house: white siding with a red brick façade, bland front yard with close-cut grass, and evergreen bushes.

"You sure this is it?" asked Oscar after he turned off the car.

"That's what Queenie said." I shrugged.

"I just pictured it being more, I dunno, evil looking or something." Oscar looked disappointed.

"Well, she got it because she demanded it as part of her movie contract, right? That whole wanting-to-see-what-living-in-the-suburbs-was-like thing. So wouldn't it stand to reason that it'd look like an everyday house?"

"I guess so," said Oscar doubtfully. "It's just so *normal*."

It really was an exceptionally normal-looking place. There weren't even any flowers to give it personality. The backyard did have a tall privacy fence, though, which jibed with what that article had said. Not all houses had privacy fences around here. Quite a few people opted for the white picket fence thing or no fence at all.

Let me out, said Rufus. *I'll take a sniff.*

Me too, said PD. *I want in on the action.*

Me three! said Meep. Total follower.

"Okay," I said. "But don't go crazy. Come right back and tell me if you smell Fergie. That way we'll know it's really the right place. Then we need to plan our attack." I got out and opened the back door. The three cats all streaked out and made a beeline for the house. Meep went for the front door, while Rufus and PD each took a side.

Rufus came racing back mere moments later. He ran halfway across the yard and stopped. *It's the house*, he called. *I smell Fergie.* Then he was gone, back around the corner of the house.

"Rufus! Come back!" I half shouted. I didn't want to yell in case anyone was actually inside. Rufus, of course, didn't even respond. "Crap," I said to Oscar and Ian. "The kamikaze cat strikes again. What should we do?"

"Well, if no one is in there, maybe we should just, you know, break in?" Oscar made a motion like he was throwing a rock through a window or something. We all looked at each other and then at the house.

It looked quiet. Maybe too quiet?

"Okay," I said. "Let me think a minute." I put my hand over my eyes so I could concentrate, not that it really seemed to help. "How about this: Oscar, why don't you move the car down the street a bit? That way, if Regina comes back, hopefully, she won't notice it. And I'm going to call Viv one more time, you know, just in case." Just in case some crazy maniac kidnapper killed us all and our families needed to find the bodies. "Then I guess we should do it—break in."

I left Viv yet another message with all the details, including the address, while Oscar moved the car. Ian was kind of standing there watching everything. He looked lost. Why had I dragged him into this mess? If we survived, there was no way he was ever going to talk to me again. I just hoped the Cat Girl thing didn't get out. Maybe I could blackmail him with the SpongeBob underpants thing.

Oscar came back and the three of us joined Meep at the front door. There was no sign of either Rufus or PD anywhere.

I've been listening, said Meep, *but I haven't heard anything much. There are a couple of mice under those bushes. Other than that . . .* She looked hungrily in that direction, though I seriously doubted she'd ever caught a mouse in her life. She was all talk.

I tried the doorknob. Locked, of course. Ian cleared his throat. "Maybe we should try the back or the side? This is kind of exposed, don't you think?" He was looking up and down the street. Someone a few doors down was getting their mail.

"Good point." We went around the side of the house that Rufus had disappeared around. There were some windows and a gate to the backyard. We tried each window as we walked by, but none of them were open and the curtains were all closed. Happily, the gate actually was open. It didn't look like it had a lock at all. We opened it and quickly went in, shutting it behind us.

There was a patio and a small in-ground pool, but no sign of Rufus or PD or anyone else. Oscar went to a set of French doors and peeked inside. "The coast is clear," he said. Ian and I took a peek. It looked like a layout from a Pottery Barn catalog. You know the ones I mean, those perfectly arranged rooms that look like a human being has never set foot in them. Off to the left there was a kitchen and some signs of life: a bag of cheap dog food on the counter, an open box of cereal, and an empty milk jug.

I tried the door, but our luck had ended with the gate being unlocked. "What should we do?" I whispered.

Oscar didn't say anything. He just reached into my backpack and pulled out his dad's nunchucks. I'd forgotten he'd even stuck them in there. Before Ian and I even had time to get out of the way, he slammed the wooden ends into a pane of glass by the doorknob. *Crash.* One hit was all it took.

"Oscar!" I said.

"What? We had to get in, right?" He pulled his sleeve over his hand and brushed the glass away. If I didn't know better, I'd think he'd done that before.

"What if someone heard that?" I looked around, but nothing had changed anywhere.

"Who?" asked Oscar. "There's nobody here." He reached in, unlocked the door, and turned the knob. The door opened and he went in.

Two seconds later, Fergie came charging around the corner right at us, yapping her head off. Her pink fur was matted and had bits of gunk stuck in it, like she'd been used as a doggy mop.

"Shhhh! Fergie, shut up!" I said. The house seemed quiet other than Fergie, but I didn't want to take any chances. I picked her up and smoothed down the fur around her face. Poor thing, she smelled terrible. Regina definitely wasn't good with pets. And that says a lot about a person.

Fergie kept barking, but with less volume. She was looking at me like she desperately wanted me to understand something. Or maybe she just wanted to be fed. "Can you tell what she's saying?" I asked Meep.

I'm not very good at Dog, said Meep. *All I can get is that she's hungry and freaked out about someone seeing you? Being you? Smelling you? Sorry.*

"You don't speak Dog?" asked Ian. "Just Cat?"

"Yeah," I said. "Dogs just sound like dogs to me. Meep doesn't really get what she's saying either. Rufus can talk to her, but I don't know where he is, stupid cat." I put Fergie down and picked up the bag of dog food. The only bowl I found was one in the sink with old Cheerios stuck to it, so I just poured some food on the tile floor. Fergie dived right in. Ian rinsed out the Cheerios bowl and filled it with water for her too. See, *he* was good with pets.

"Well, I guess we should search the house," I said. If no one had come running after the breaking of the glass and

Fergie's loud welcome, then probably no one was here.

"Righty-o," said Oscar. "How about I take the upstairs?"

"Maybe we should stick together," I said. In movies, the characters always get picked off one by one when they separate. The house was actually kind of creepy, but maybe that was my mind playing tricks. If I weren't here looking for kidnap victims, it might seem like a nice place, even if everything was in shades of beige.

"Suit yourself," said Oscar. "We might as well start down here, then."

We left Fergie chowing down in the kitchen and walked the rest of the first floor. Besides the stuff we'd already seen, there was a dining room, an entry hall, a small office, and a bathroom. Everything was tastefully but blandly decorated. The only thing out of place was a ficus tree that had obviously died a slow, withering death.

Hey, said Meep. *I hear something upstairs.*

"Shhhh!" I told Oscar and Ian. "Meep hears something upstairs."

"Probably Rufus," said Oscar. "Or Ian's cat."

"Yeah, where is Pebbles?" asked Ian. "I haven't seen either one of them since they got out of the car."

"Is it Rufus or PD?" I asked Meep.

I'm not Talented, in case you've forgotten, said Meep. *I just hear something. I don't know what it is.*

I led the way to the stairs and we slowly climbed them. Oscar still had the nunchucks in his hand, and I was wishing

I'd brought something more useful than a cell phone. Maybe even the throwing stars. At the top of the landing, there were three closed doors. The hallway was carpeted in more beige and the walls were painted off white. The owners had left off the decorating up here. The walls were empty. It reminded me of a hospital.

"I don't think it could be Rufus," I whispered, "unless he's figured out how to open and close doors."

Ian opened the first door. It was a bedroom with piles of pink clothes and pink suitcases everywhere. We'd found Easton's stuff, but no Easton. The closet was empty except for a couple of pairs of shoes—non-pink and obviously larger than the ones Easton wore, so maybe they were Regina's.

We went to the next door and Oscar tried that one, leaping in with his nunchucks held in front of him after Ian opened the door. It was a bathroom. Makeup was spread out all over the counter, just like it had been in the dressing room at Wrigley. Regina was a total slob wherever she settled in, apparently.

We went back out into the hall and stood in front of the last door. We looked at each other. Then I grabbed the door handle and turned the knob.

TWENTY-EIGHT

"YOU WILL ALWAYS BE LUCKY IF YOU KNOW
HOW TO MAKE FRIENDS WITH STRANGE CATS."
—COLONIAL AMERICAN PROVERB

There were piles of non-pink clothes, an armoire, a chair, a random chain snaking across the floor, and a solitary mattress with a sheet crumpled on top of it. Meep must have been hearing things.

I took a step inside and was immediately knocked off my feet by someone or something shoving the door into me. I fell back against Ian, who had been right behind me, and we both toppled into Oscar. We all landed in a heap in the doorway, blocking whoever or whatever had knocked us over from escaping. Oscar's nunchucks whacked me in the head.

"Mmmrpphhmff!"

You should have listened to me, said Meep. *I told you I heard something up here.*

I quickly crawled to my feet and backed up so I could get a look at what we were up against. It wasn't Melly or Easton. Someone who looked like a sickly imitation of Victoria Well-

233

ing stood there with her eyes wide open and her hands tied behind her back. She had duct tape over her mouth, her hair had been chopped off in big, uneven lumps, and a dog chain around her ankle tied her to the leg of the solid wood armoire. And she was skinny. Like, anorexic skinny, not just movie star skinny. Well, even beyond normal anorexic movie star skinny. But her cheekbones and eyes were unmistakable.

"Victoria?" I said, totally confused. If this was Victoria, who was the other Victoria? Or Regina? Whoever.

"Oh my God!" shouted Oscar. "It is Victoria!" He obviously came to the same conclusion I did about this Victoria because he scrambled up, putting a foot in Ian's stomach on the way. "I'm your biggest fan!" he babbled to her, which was really a total lie, since I knew he'd have said the same thing to Ty in different circumstances. He grabbed her in a big hug. After just a moment too long, he dropped his arms from around her and stepped back to give her a good look. Or maybe it was to get farther away from the smell. I could smell her from the doorway. Regina obviously didn't consider hygiene or food to be important for her kidnap victims.

We had to find Melly. Soon.

"Victoria," he said, looking her up and down, "what on earth is going on?"

Smells pretty obvious to me, said Meep. *She had an accident. Or three.*

I motioned to Meep to shut up. At least no one else knew what she was saying. Victoria had definitely seen better days. She was wearing a pair of ragged gray sweatpants and a stained T-shirt. No shoes. She looked down at herself and then back up at him, her eyes still open as wide as they could go. "Mrrmmpphff!" she said.

"Oh!" said Oscar. He reached out and pulled the duct tape off in one quick motion before I could warn him to take it easy.

"Aaaaggh!" yelped Victoria, doubtless from losing a couple of layers of skin off her lips.

"There you go," he said. "Better?"

"Who *are* you?"

"I'm Oscar!" Before Oscar could hug her again, Ian stepped forward and ducked under Oscar's outstretched arms to go behind Victoria.

"Let's get her untied first, okay, Oscar?"

"Oh! Right! Sorry," said Oscar. "I'm just so excited to meet you. I mean, I was excited to meet you before, but apparently that wasn't even really you, so it doesn't count. And she was totally evil anyway, so it wasn't really all that exciting to meet *her*, if you know what I mean."

Victoria processed that. "You know about Regina?" she asked, rubbing her wrists once Ian had removed her bonds.

"Yes!" said Oscar before I could say anything at all. "We're here to rescue you!" Not exactly, but close enough, I guessed. I was even more worried about Melly now. Victoria looked scary. Like, you could knock her over with a feather. It was amazing she had managed to knock us over, which she'd probably accomplished only because we weren't expecting an attack. We'd make terrible BERM agents.

"I'm Nat," I said. "And you've met Oscar. This is Ian. Not to rush you or anything, but do you know where Regina is? And did she come by here with a girl named Melly? She kidnapped our friend today because we were on to her. Oh, and do you know where Easton West is?"

Victoria looked dazed. She sat down on the mattress, still rubbing her wrists. Her ankle was still chained, but it reached far enough for her to lie down on the mattress. I wondered how long she'd been tied up. How long had Regina been holding her? It had to have taken her a while to lose so much weight. Not that she was fat before or anything, but she had been one of the few starlets I'd have considered healthy. Or, at least, Regina as Victoria was healthy looking. I'm assuming that's how Victoria looked at one point. Most starlets looked like they were on the I-eat-only-one-meal-a-day plan. And why didn't Regina look like skin and bones when she looked like Victoria? She looked like Victoria was *supposed* to look. My head was seriously hurting. Personally, I think the BERM had it wrong. They'd classified Regina's Talent a B level? Seriously? She was obviously Talented enough to have been getting away with whatever she had been doing for ages.

"I don't know where Regina is. I thought you were her."

"That's why you jumped us?" asked Ian.

"Yes. Sorry about that. I was worried. When she left this

morning, she just sounded . . . well, desperate. I thought she was going to do something drastic. I thought . . . I thought she was finally going to kill me." Victoria rubbed at her ankle, which was raw and red where the chain was attached to her leg.

"Do you know where the key is to that?" Ian asked.

"Yeah, it's on the wall behind you." The key was hanging on a picture hanger in the far corner of the room, just out of Victoria's reach. That was evil. So close, but so far. Oscar grabbed the key.

"Oh, Victoria," said Oscar, unlocking the manacle around her ankle. He sat down by her and didn't even wrinkle his nose at the smell or the dirty clothes he had to push out of the way, which was more than I could say for myself. It was all I could do not to hold my nose. He put an arm around her and hugged her to his side. "We're here now. Everything is going to be okay."

"Oscar," I said. "We've got to find Melly. Regina had a reason to keep Victoria alive. If she's willing to get rid of a famous actress, what's stopping her from getting rid of Melly?" I couldn't think of a single thing other than maybe using her against me, and that worried me. She didn't even know how much I knew.

"Wait," said Victoria, "who is Melly again?"

I gave her the thousand-foot overview of the last week as quickly as possible, how it had all started with that video of Regina pretending to be Easton and ending with her kidnapping Melly. "So," I finished up, "do you have any idea at all where Regina could be keeping Easton or Melly? We thought she had Easton here."

"As far as I know, Easton is still here. I haven't heard her since Regina got mad that we were talking through the walls and moved her. I figured she was downstairs somewhere. Regina hasn't let me out of this room except to go to the bathroom since we got here." She picked up the chain and tossed it away from herself. "And not even much for that." Well, that explained the smell. Apparently, the bucket in the corner had been doing double duty.

"You poor, poor thing," said Oscar. "Everything is going to be okay. We're here now." He'd kept one arm around Victoria throughout the whole conversation, petting her arm. She leaned against him and started crying. For all his craziness, Oscar did know when to turn on the comfort when it was necessary. He'd been through tough stuff himself and knew how it was. I mean, coming out to your parents? Had to be one of the toughest things ever, and Oscar had made it look easy. I always wished I had the same level of confidence he had. Of course, I wasn't really good at the touchy-feely thing in general. I stood there, feeling like an unempathetic idiot.

Ian cleared his throat. "So, what next?" he asked me, like I had any clue at all.

Just then, I heard the pitter-patter of little cat feet coming up the stairs. A lot of little cat feet. PD and Rufus flew through the door, followed by an entire herd of cats I'd never seen before. Victoria screamed and even Ian backed up against a wall. It was like Revenge of the Cats or something.

"Where have you been?" I demanded. "And what's up with the cat army?"

I found some reinforcements, said PD.

Where is Easton? asked Rufus. He went up to Victoria and sniffed her. She shrank back against Oscar. What, was she afraid of cats?

The chatter of the cats was practically deafening.

"Everybody, shut up!" I yelled. They quieted down, and Victoria looked at me like I was the new messiah.

"Okay," I said, taking a deep breath. "Rufus, I don't know where Easton is. We haven't found her. PD . . ." I stopped. I didn't even know what to say about all of the cats. How had he found so many in such a short amount of time? There had to be, like, thirty of them. Maybe even more. The room was crawling with cats. What was I supposed to do with all of them?

Fergie said Easton isn't here, Rufus said. Fergie barked in agreement. She had followed the cats into the room. *She said she hasn't seen Easton since this morning. I'm very concerned.*

So was I, but I didn't want to freak him out more than he already was—or everyone else, since they were all looking at me like I knew what I was doing. "We just need to figure out our next move," I said.

You might want to figure that out elsewhere, said a black and white cat I didn't know. *You do know this house has an alarm system, right?*

Holy pants on fire. "Crap!" I yelled. "Everyone, out! We've got to get out of here! The police are probably on their way right now!" How long had we been standing here chatting? How long did it take for the police to respond to an alarm? I had too many questions and not enough answers. We didn't have time for the police and their inevitable questions.

"What?" said Oscar, jumping up and pulling Victoria to her feet. "What are you talking about?"

"Alarm system!" Now I remembered. We should have known. Oscar had said the house Victoria was staying in had an alarm system. It had been one of her demands. I really should have paid more attention to the Oscar Report. His addiction was useful—or would have been if I'd paid attention.

Ian was already halfway down the stairs. I followed him, along with a stream of cats. Oscar and Victoria brought up the rear. She stumbled into the wall a few times.

"Out the back," said Ian. "It'll be safer. We can cut through the neighbor's yard just in case." I followed him as he went out the back door, skidding a little on the broken glass. I looked back as Oscar slung Victoria over his shoulder so her bare feet wouldn't get cut. The cats poured out around us and Fergie brought up the rear.

"To the left," Oscar said. "I parked the car a few houses down in that direction!"

We exited out the gate and took off through a neighbor's backyard. Luckily, most of the houses didn't have monster privacy fences. We ran through three backyards, seriously surprising a guy taking out the trash, and ducked between some houses. Who knows what he thought was weirder, the herd of cats or Oscar carrying a barefoot Victoria over his shoulder. Probably the cats. There were just so many of them.

Ian crept to the corner and peered out. "The coast is clear," he said. I choked back some hysterical laughter. Had he really said that? Should I respond with "The crow flies at midnight" or something? Ian looked at me and grinned, like he knew what I was thinking. "Always wanted to say that," he said.

Oscar set Victoria down and pushed the button on Melly's key chain to unlock the car. "Let's make it quick," he said. "Who knows how long we've got."

He led the way and opened the passenger side door for Victoria to help her in. Ian and I climbed in the back seat and the cats started cramming in with us.

"Hold on a minute," I said. "Are all of you guys coming?" *Why not?* asked PD. *Who knows how much help we'll need?*

I was going to argue when Oscar said, "Hurry up! It's the police!" I looked out the window and saw a car pulling up in front of Regina's house. The last of the cats pushed in and I shut the door. There were cats *everywhere*. About ten or fifteen of them had oozed into the front seat and were draped on Victoria's lap and at her feet. There were even two fighting for space on Oscar's lap in the driver's seat. I had to tell one to get out from under Oscar's legs or we weren't going anywhere. Meep, Rufus, and PD were all perched on my lap, and I heard Fergie yip somewhere under the pile. I couldn't even see my feet for the cats covering them. If my mom and her allergies had been with us, she probably would have exploded.

"Slowly!" I said as Oscar started the car. "Don't make them suspicious." He nodded and pulled away from the curb at a reasonable speed, especially for Oscar.

I watched out of the corner of my eye as we drove past the police car. It was a cul-de-sac and we had no choice but to go by them. One officer was in the car and the other was walking up the front path. He didn't seem to be in a hurry. Oscar drove to the corner and came to a full and complete stop at the stop sign, another rarity for him.

I was about to breathe a sigh of relief when Ian yelled, "Go, go, go!" I looked out the back window at where he was looking. The guy who'd been taking out the trash had come out of his house and was jogging toward the police car and pointing in our direction.

Oscar floored it, and cats went flying in every direction.

TWENTY-NINE

FRIDAY, SEPTEMBER 11, 7:02 P.M.

"CATS DON'T ALWAYS LAND ON THEIR FEET.
SOMETIMES, THEY LAND ON THEIR CLAWS."
—NATALIE NG

For once, Oscar's crazy driving came in handy. That, and the fact that the police car was facing in the opposite direction. We were blocks away in no time with no sirens on our tail. My thighs, however, were not so lucky. Meep, Rufus, and PD had all instinctively dug in when Oscar took off.

"Whooo!" yelled Oscar. "Where to?"

"Just keep driving. Go toward the city, I guess," I said.

"Where in the city?" asked Ian, strapping on his seat belt while pushing cats out of the way. "Do you have any idea where we should go?"

"No," I said. "I have absolutely no idea."

"How about wherever they're filming?"

That seemed about as good of an idea as any I'd had. "Victoria," I asked, "Do you know if they'd still be filming at Wrigley this late? Or would they be done for the day? Or, hey, can you call Alan?"

"I don't know Alan's number," she said, "but he's got a reputation for working late."

"Wait," said Oscar. "But you worked with him on your last movie!"

"No," she said, "I met him when I auditioned for *Cheerleaders Don't Cry*. But Regina kidnapped me before I got a chance to work on it."

Holy crap. I was doing the math in my head, but Oscar beat me to it. "Regina took over your life that long ago? That, what, had to be, like, two years ago!"

"Over two and a half," said Victoria grimly.

Wow. I couldn't imagine. Two and a half *years*? How had Regina gotten away with it? It did explain why her acting sucked so bad in the last movie. She wasn't even in it. I wasn't going to go there, but Oscar couldn't resist.

"It's no wonder you were so terrible in *Cheerleaders*," he said. "It wasn't even you! How did Regina even talk herself into being in *Freddy's Day Off*?"

"Blackmail," said Victoria. "She's got something big on one of the producers."

Hollywood. Figures. "Well, Oscar," I said, "you're the movie expert, I guess. Do you think they're still at Wrigley or what?"

"I'm not sure," said Oscar, "but I know who to call." He dug around in his pocket for his phone. The car swerved back and forth in the lane and two people honked at us.

"Dude!" said Ian. "Case in point as to why Chicago is a hands-free cell-phone city."

"Fine, fine," said Oscar. "I'll do the Bluetooth thing through Melly's car." He turned for a moment and looked at me. "But no smart aleck comments from you, Nat, okay?"

"What? What about?" What'd I do? I hadn't said a word. "Who are you calling?"

He didn't answer me. He turned back around and got his phone connected with Melly's car about the same time that he pulled onto the highway headed toward the city. Then he dialed a number and we all listened to the phone ring.

I think I'm getting carsick, said a small gray cat near my feet. I didn't relay the information to anyone else. I just prayed the cat was wrong.

Someone answered Oscar's call. "Garrett. You may speak."

Garrett? Oh, yeah. The really pierced guy from our table at the cafeteria. The one who'd seemed interested in Oscar. Obviously, they'd both been attracted enough to exchange phone numbers. That was big. Oscar had sworn off dating after he'd broken up with he-who-shall-not-be-named, otherwise known as Darren. He was the guy who'd moved on to a pretty blond kid who didn't have even a quarter of the personality of Oscar, and who liked to flaunt said new boy in front of Oscar.

I didn't know why Oscar thought I'd have anything bad to say about it. Garrett had seemed nice enough, plus he was totally built and seriously pierced. Exactly the kind of guy Oscar ought to go parade in front of Darren, who was on the scrawny side. I'd never liked him. Not because he was scrawny or anything, but because he really hadn't been that nice to Oscar. And he had bad breath.

"Hey, Garrett. This is Oscar—"

"Oscar!" Garrett's voice warmed right up. Definitely attracted. "I'm glad you called! I wasn't sure if you would. Is everything okay with your crazy friend?"

"Um, yeah," said Oscar. "Actually, Nat's here. In the car. With me. Right now."

"Hey, Garrett," I said, for lack of anything better to say.

There was a pause. "Oh hi, Nat. I didn't mean—"

"Don't worry about it," said Oscar. "I mean, there's not time right now. It's an emergency. Do you know what the filming schedule is today? Are they still at Wrigley or what?"

"Yeah, actually, I'm here! I came out as soon as school let out. I signed up weeks ago. Right now I'm working my way through the craft services table. They opened it up for the extras after our part of the shoot was done." Wow. Oscar and Garrett were totally made for each other.

"Oh, so they're done shooting for the day?"

"Nah. They're just done with the outside stuff and the crowd scenes with the extras. They've moved inside."

"Great! That's perfect!" said Oscar. "Have you seen Victoria? Or Easton? Or Melly?"

"I saw Victoria a little while ago. Maybe about twenty minutes ago? The director was completely pissed because she showed up late or something. I heard some of the gaffers talking about it. She sounds like a total diva." He paused, and the only sound for a moment was the steady purring of a cat. I wasn't sure which one. It seemed really out of place, what with everything going on, but some cats purr when they're nervous. Garrett started talking again. "It's funny you should ask about Easton, though. I'm surprised you haven't heard."

"Heard what?" asked Oscar at the same time as Rufus. Fergie was even paying attention. She dug herself out from under the pile of cats by Ian's feet so she could hear better.

"She's in the hospital. They found her in her room at the York about half an hour ago. There was a suicide note and everything. Looks like she tried to OD. They haven't released any more details than that, but the blogs are all saying she did it because of the thing with her cat. I've been following the story online. Everyone's talking about it. And they still have no idea where the cat disappeared to yesterday morning."

I could hear the unspoken question in his voice. He obviously thought it was my fault.

"Wow, I can't believe she did it," said Oscar.

"Oscar!" I said.

"I don't mean Easton," said Oscar. "I mean Regina."

"Who's Regina?" asked Garrett.

"You'll find out soon enough," said Oscar grimly. "We're on our way to stop her now. Just start spreading the word, would you? Nat's the one who's going to save the day. None of this is her fault. It's going to stop tonight at Wrigley." He looked at me in the rearview mirror and nodded once decisively. "Thanks, Garrett. Talk to you soon. Call me if you see Victoria anywhere." Then he hung up and stepped on the gas.

I heard a whimper and looked down to see that Fergie had managed to climb up on my lap and was huddled into a miserable looking ball as close to Rufus as she could get. Rufus was licking her on the head. That said a lot about Easton, that her pets loved her so much. She must not be anything like Regina had pretended to be while she was her.

"I'm sure she'll be fine," I told them. "They'll take care of her at the hospital and we'll get you guys to her as soon as possible."

Ian reached over and scratched Fergie behind her ear. He looked at me and squeezed my hand and then went back to scratching the dog.

Oscar stomped on the gas and the car sped off even faster toward the city. If Regina had snuck off to drug Easton, what had she done with Melly?

THIRTY

FRIDAY, SEPTEMBER 11, 8:11 P.M.

"NO MATTER HOW MUCH CATS FIGHT,
THERE ALWAYS SEEMS TO BE PLENTY OF KITTENS."
—ANONYMOUS QUOTE, OFTEN ATTRIBUTED TO ABRAHAM LINCOLN
(BUT THE INTERNET THINKS ABRAHAM LINCOLN SAID EVERYTHING)

We made it into the city and all the way to Wrigleyville with the help of Melly's GPS. Someday, I was going to have to thank her dad for being anal and overprotective—if we got Melly out of this alive. The last couple of miles were the worst, after we got off the highway and things slowed to a crawl. When we got there, Oscar didn't even bother looking for a parking spot. He just drove right up onto the brick sidewalk off of Seminary Avenue and Clark Street and stopped the car by a statue of some guy with a baseball bat.

"Oscar," I said, "you can't just leave the car here! You'll get towed!"

He opened the door to get out. "Nat, it's now or never. There's no time. Go!"

I couldn't argue with that. The last thirty minutes driving and waiting had been miserable. If Regina was obviously willing to attempt to kill a famous blogger, what would she be willing to do to an unknown high-school student?

Victoria had told us everything that had happened to her on the ride in. I think she was happy to have a chance to talk to someone at all. Regina had kept her on a really tight leash. She'd been moved among basements and closets and everything in between. She'd even been stuck in the trunk of a car at one point. Regina had driven her everywhere, since she couldn't chance taking her on an airplane and going through security.

It had all started when Regina called her up out of the blue and pulled the whole "Hey, remember me?" thing and talked her into meeting for lunch. Victoria had only done it because she felt kind of guilty for how people, including her, had treated Regina back in high school, though she found out later Regina got her number not through her parents, like she'd claimed, but by calling her agent while impersonating a big time reporter.

Apparently, high school Regina had been seriously unpopular due to a combination of her crappy personality, an unfortunate bladder accident in the ninth grade, and bad hygiene. She'd kept her talent hidden well. Rumors of her criminal activities hadn't helped either. She had been caught stealing stuff from the locker rooms during games, and people had suspected her of some nasty pranks but could never prove it.

Oscar finally asked Victoria why she looked like hell and why Regina didn't. It turned out that Regina's Talent literally sucked some of the health out of you. She'd actually been feeding Victoria fattening fast food the whole time, but then stole the nutrients right back out of her. So Regina looked how Victoria *should* look, and Victoria looked like some kind of concentration camp victim. Her hands kept shaking and she gobbled down a granola bar I found in Melly's emergency stash like she hadn't seen food in a year.

She'd only recently butchered Victoria's hair. Regina had needed to change her voice when talking to Alan on the phone (while looking like Easton) and the hair in the bag had retained enough Victoria-ness for her to do that. It didn't last long, though, which was why Victoria's hair was so choppy. A few more days of it and she'd probably have wound up bald.

Even so, Victoria was ready to fight. She was out of the car and heading toward the stadium before Ian and I had even opened our doors. We, and a carload of cats, followed behind her. Two guys walking down the street stopped to stare at all of us.

"Cool," called one. "You guys got a trained cat show or something?"

"Um, yeah," I called back. "Jump, Meep, jump!" Meep shot me a look, but took a hop in the air and leapfrogged over PD.

"Awesome!" said the second guy. They both started to follow us. Well, it couldn't hurt. Maybe more witnesses would make things better. Regina would be less likely to do something desperate if people were watching. You'd think, anyway.

"This way," called out Oscar. "I think we can get in through this side." He led us over to a loading dock area off Seminary Avenue. There was a small moving truck there and someone had propped open a door with a crate.

"The back door is a good idea," I whispered to Ian. "I don't have a pass for you or Victoria, and there's no way we could sneak all these cats in past a guard anyway." I was still wearing my pass. For a moment I considered taking it off—why had I worn it all day?—but then I figured it might come in handy now that we were back at Wrigley. Not to go in the front door, though—that security guy from this afternoon certainly wouldn't buy our trained cat show story, and he probably remembered us anyway.

"Do we have any weapons?" Ian asked.

"I've got my nunchucks," said Oscar, waving them around. I saw the guys behind us pause and look at each other.

"Just part of the show," I called and smiled reassuringly. They nodded back and gave each other a high five. Who knows what they thought we were going to do with them.

You don't need any weapons, said Rufus. *Not when I've got these.* He stood on his hind legs and batted both his front paws in the air with his claws out. The two guys cheered as the other cats imitated him. We did look like a trained cat show.

"I think we're good," I said, gesturing to the cats. "Besides, the only other thing I've got in my bag is my phone."

"Okay," said Ian doubtfully, and followed Oscar and Victoria through the door and into a stark concrete block tunnel that was painted white. I brought up the rear.

"This way," said Oscar. "I bet they're by the locker room. I added Alan's Twitter to my feed." He held up his phone. "And he just posted something about how the room smells like Cheetos and funk."

Yeah, sounded like a locker room to me. We followed Oscar as he wound his way around. It was kind of amazing, actually. He had a great sense of direction, which was not something I was born with, especially not indoors. I had no idea where we were and then suddenly we were in the main concourse. Oscar ducked down behind a beer stand.

We heard the noise on the set before we saw it. Or rather, we heard the AD yelling at someone. Oscar peered around a corner of the beer stand. "Okay," he whispered. "They're here. I can see Ty and Alan, but I don't see Regina-Victoria or Melly anywhere." He turned around. "What should we do? Just run in kamikaze style and demand to see them?"

"Hey," said one of the guys, coming up behind me, "What gives? Is there a show or not?" I'd forgotten they were there. Apparently, they were pretty hard up for entertainment. Close up, though, I could smell the beer on them, so maybe that was why they'd been so willing to follow us. I mean, what, did they think random trained cat shows performed at Wrigley all the time?

"Shhh," I said to them. "They're shooting that Ty McKenzie–Victoria Welling movie up ahead."

"Cool!" said the brown haired one a little too loudly.

I shushed him again, and he put his index finger up to his mouth and swayed just a tiny bit. "Victoria's hot," he whispered back. "You guys know her? Can you hook me up?"

I glanced at the real Victoria. She turned around to face the guy directly with a somewhat hopeful look. He looked right at her with no sign of recognition. Ouch. That was rough.

"Dude," said Ian, "I heard that Victoria loves it when guys mob her. If you see her, you totally should."

I poked him. "What are you doing?" I asked. I smiled apologetically at Victoria. Way to rub it in.

Ian leaned over to whisper in my ear. "If they see someone that looks like Victoria, it'll be Regina, right?"

"Oh!" I turned to the guys. "Yeah, she loves it. Like, full-on hugging and everything! She totally gets off on it."

"Really?" said the one with the glasses. "That rocks!" He wobbled, then turned around back the way we'd come. "I'm gonna go get the rest of the guys over at the Cubby Bear. They gotta get in on this!"

"Good idea!" said the hard up one with the brown hair. They both ran back the way we'd come, glasses guy bouncing off the wall a few times. I'd be amazed if we saw them again, but maybe they had a better sense of direction than I did.

"Anyway," said Oscar, "what should we do now? Nat?"

I avoided answering the question by creeping to the edge of the beer stand and taking a look at the set. A small crowd of movie people was standing outside two open white metal doors, along with a bunch of equipment.

"That's the locker room?" I would never have guessed it.

"Yeah, that's the entrance to it, anyway," said Oscar.

"How do you even know that? I don't see a sign," I said. And it was right in the middle of the first floor concourse. Near a condiment station. I mean, ketchup and Cubs?

"Hey, just because I'm gay doesn't mean I can't watch baseball," said Oscar. Then he grinned. "It's bonding time with my dad. We've done the ballpark tour a couple of times and everything. I just made him promise not to expect me to remember a player's RBI and he made me promise not to tell him which players had cute butts."

"Huh," said Ian.

"For the record," said Oscar, "the first baseman is kinda hot. And the locker room really does smell like Cheetos."

It looked like they were getting ready to film inside the locker room. Everyone's attention outside the locker room was focused inward, and while I was watching, I saw Ty and Alan step inside.

"Well, I don't think we should storm the castle or anything." I said, deciding as I said it. "Not when we don't know where Regina is. Besides, if they recognize me, they probably won't even listen before they call the cops. I'm not exactly their favorite person. I'm just lucky Alan didn't pay any attention to me earlier today. He had eyes only for Melly." I looked back at everyone to see if they agreed. Ian and Oscar were nodding. "Do you think Victoria—sorry, Regina—would be in a scene in the locker room?"

"*I'd* like to be in that scene," said Oscar.

Ian snorted. "Focus, Oscar," he said. He was learning fast. Oscar just grinned.

"I've read the script," said Victoria. "Regina made me run lines with her. She's not in the locker room scene, just the stuff in the stands and the buying tickets and things like that."

"So, she's probably not in there." I said. "Which means she's hopefully maybe in her dressing room?"

"Or hiding out in the stands or something," said Ian. "Maybe we should spread out and look. Meet back here in, like, ten minutes? Or raise the alarm if we see her?"

I couldn't think of anything better, so I nodded. "I'll check out the dressing room, since I know where it is and it's more private."

"I'll take Victoria," said Oscar. He grabbed Victoria by the hand. "The real Victoria. We'll do the stands. I'll find Garrett too, and he can help."

"Ian, they don't know what you look like, unless they remember you from the cafeteria scene. So you're probably still on their good side. You want to try and see if you can get a peek into the locker room, just in case?"

Ian saluted me. "Aye, aye, Captain," he said.

"What about the cats?" asked Victoria.

Oh. Good question. A whole herd of cats was kind of noticeable. "Um," I looked down at Rufus and Meep, who were sitting on my feet. "Why don't you guys park it right here and try and stay out of sight?"

I don't like it, said Rufus.

Me either, said Meep. *What if you need us?* She held up a paw and stuck her claws out.

"Well, if someone needs you, we'll just yell 'Cats!' okay?" I looked at Oscar and Ian. They nodded. Meep still looked doubtful, so I figured I'd try and butter them up a little. "Since you all have such excellent hearing and sense of direction, I'm sure you'll be able to find whoever has called for you. So it'll be like you're on call, okay?"

Acceptable, said Rufus. *But whoever finds her had better save her for me.* He let out a small growl from the back of his throat.

♥

I managed to get to the area where I'd found the storage closet/dressing room without running into anyone other than a blue-shirted Wrigley employee with a broom. She took a glance at my lanyard and pass and didn't say anything. Good thing I'd left it on.

I didn't see anyone around, but I thought I heard footsteps. I ducked behind a bunch of equipment and some racks of clothing. I went to peek around the corner, managed to trip over an electrical cord, and fell into one of the racks. The whole thing fell on top of me with a huge crash.

"Crapola!" I said, batting away a shirt. I heard some more footsteps and a door being slammed. I flung clothes off left and right, stood up, and looked down the hall.

"Nat! Oh my God, get me out of here!" Melly was

running to me, her eyes wide and her hair completely disheveled.

"Melly!" I threw off the last shirt and ran to meet her. I swallowed her up in a huge hug. "I was so worried about you! Are you okay? Did she do anything to you?"

"No, I'm fine. I just want to get out of here. Let's go!"

"Okay," I said. "This way. Oscar and the cats are over this way." I grabbed her hand and tried to pull her down the tunnel back the way I had come.

"The cats? Tiddlywinks is here?"

I laughed. "Don't let Rufus hear you call him that!" I pulled her a few more steps. She seemed so sluggish and confused. I wondered if Regina had slipped her something. Maybe one of Rufus's pills. Would cat medicine work on a person? "I'll explain later. It's total craziness. You won't believe what we've been through. Just follow me. Ian's even here, if you can believe it!"

Melly finally showed some life. "We don't have time to mess around with all that," she said firmly. "We've got to get out of here! Victoria will be back any minute. Just follow me!" Melly tried to pull me in the opposite direction.

"Oh, yeah," I said, not budging. "I forgot you don't know the latest! Victoria's not the problem. It's Regina we need to watch out for."

Melly dropped my hand and stepped back, her nose wrinkled in confusion. "What are you talking about?"

"It's a *really* long story and I'll tell you all about it, I promise. But let's get back to everyone else first." I reached for her hand, but she stepped even farther back down the hall. I don't know why she wanted to go that way. She didn't know her way around Wrigley any better than I did. "You can even meet Victoria. The *real* Victoria. She's with Oscar. And Easton's okay too. She's just in the hospital. Now that you're safe, it's all good. We can let the BERM take care of Regina."

Melly stopped retreating and put her hands on her hips. "I did not come this far for you to screw everything up for me." She stepped forward and shoved me. I fell back against a wall and cracked my head on the concrete.

Frick on a stick. It wasn't Melly. Couldn't be. Melly would have known about Rufus. And Melly would never leave Oscar behind or slam me into a wall, for that matter. It had to be Regina.

"Regina—" was all I managed to choke out before she had her hands on my throat and pushed me back against the wall.

"I heard you coming," she said. "I thought I could get you out of the way once and for all, but here you are telling me you've brought the BERM into this." Flecks of spittle hit me in the face, she was leaning so close to me.

I pushed, but she wasn't moving. I couldn't get a sound out because I couldn't breathe. I was starting to see sparkly flashes of light when I heard Meep say, *What do you think you're doing to my Natalie?*

I had never been so glad to have Meep completely disregard my instructions before in my entire life. She let out a throat-rattling battle cry. I caught a glimpse from the corner of my eye of her launching herself at Regina with the obvious intention of doing great bodily harm. Regina screamed and her grip on my neck loosened. I pushed at her as hard as I could and she fell back.

"Go, Meep," I yelled. "Get help! Cats!" Meep took one last swipe at Regina's leg and darted off down the hall faster than I had ever seen her move, still yowling.

Regina punched me right in the face and pulled back her hand to do it again, but I caught it, barely. She sneered at me, which was a look I'd never seen on Melly's face before. Then I felt something almost like a pull deep down inside me, kind of around the general vicinity of my stomach. A warm burning feeling spread upward through my torso.

"This won't hurt a bit," she snarled. That was a total lie. I felt like someone was twisting my insides into knots and squeezing parts of me that weren't meant to be squeezed. I blinked back tears as I watched her face transform into mine. The clothes she was wearing seemed to shimmer for a moment and then—*blink*—they matched mine.

I stumbled. She took advantage of my momentary weakness by grabbing me around the throat again and pushing me against the wall. I managed to get my hands around her throat at the last minute and did my best to push her off. We struggled back and forth, but she definitely had the upper hand. I felt really weak, like she'd sucked a year of my life away.

That's when the brigade arrived with Meep in the lead. They must have already been on their way after hearing Meep's battle cry. Oscar had even managed to find Garrett, apparently.

"Nat!" yelled Ian. "Wait . . . Nat?"

I grunted, but Regina copied me and grunted too. I couldn't get a word out. Oscar and Ian looked at each other, then Oscar grabbed Regina and Ian grabbed me and they pulled, but Regina wasn't letting go, so I didn't let go either.

For the love of kittens, said Rufus. *You humans can't do anything right.* He squirmed between Oscar's legs and sunk his teeth into Regina's leg. Meep, PD, and the rest of the cats followed him and swarmed Regina. Oscar was pushed out of the way by the furry tide. Regina was forced to let go of me when a couple of calicos and a Maine Coon jumped on her arms and held on with their claws. I fell back against Ian.

The hall wasn't that big, and now it was completely packed full of people and cats yowling their heads off. Cat war cries were echoing around us. You could barely see Regina for the cats, though you could hear her cussing up a storm—in my voice. Oscar was on the opposite side of her, watching the mayhem and holding Victoria back with one hand. She looked like she wanted to join in. She'd grabbed a baseball bat from somewhere and was holding it over her head like a war club, though she looked like she would keel over from the effort.

"Are you okay?" asked Ian. That was when I noticed I was leaning back against his chest. We were both breathing hard.

"Yeah," I said, wondering how long I could stay there before it got weird. There was no telling if I'd ever be in this spot again. Well, hopefully never again in exactly this spot, not in these circumstances. "I'm okay now. She was pretending to be Melly and she caught me by surprise." That's when it hit me. "Oh no, where is Melly?" I took a step toward the cat pileup. "Guys, hey guys!" I yelled. "Back off! I need to ask Regina a question."

The cats reluctantly pulled back to reveal a very scratched and bloody Regina kneeling on the floor, who still looked like me. It was surreal. They surrounded her, practically piled up on top of each other. She dragged herself onto all fours and stared up at me with utter hate in her eyes.

Told you, said one calico to another. *Tastes like chicken.*

Looking at Regina, I realized I needed to get a haircut, and that I should never ever sneer. It was definitely not a good look for me. Of course, neither was the ripped shirt with my raggedy old bra showing. I hoped Ian wasn't looking.

Even completely torn up and surrounded by cats, Regina wasn't ready to give up. Rufus parked himself directly in front of her, no more than an inch away from her face.

"Regina, where is Melly?" I asked.

She just bared her teeth at me. I made another mental note to never do that in public. It was beyond creepy looking at her looking like me and yet so evil.

I was about to question her again, maybe this time with some prodding from Rufus, when Jason, the AD, came running up behind Oscar, followed by Alan and a bunch of other people from the set. One guy had a handheld camera and it looked like he was still recording.

"What in hell is going on?" asked Alan. He looked first at me, then down at Regina, then back at me again. Both of our hats had been knocked off. "You again?" he said, but slowly, like he was confused. "There are two of you? Did you come here to attack Victoria again?" He turned to Jason. "Call the police, would you?"

"Wait a minute," said the real Victoria and pointed at Regina with the bat. "That's who you need to have arrested."

Alan stepped forward to get a good look at Victoria. Her butchered hair was standing up all over the place, she had no makeup on, and she'd probably lost at least twenty-five pounds, but she was definitely and unmistakably Victoria Welling. That is, unless you were an inebriated horndog fan. "Victoria?" he said. "What happened to you? Just what is going on here?"

Regina must have realized at that point that the jig was up. She shrieked and dived at Victoria. "You ruined my life!" she howled. Even the cats were taken by surprise.

Regina didn't so much grab Victoria as land on her. They fell into the pile of clothing and a few of the cats, who screeched and fled. I watched as Regina transformed into Victoria—or how Victoria would look, if she didn't look like death warmed over—and the real Victoria passed out. All of the wounds Regina had gotten from the cats were gone, but she was still in my clothing. Apparently, she could control her wardrobe. Class B Talent my skinny butt. Those BERM paper pushers were idiots.

"What the—" said Alan and Jason together. Then Alan turned to the camera guy. "Are you getting this?"

"You bet I am," said the guy. Movie people. Not even remotely fazed by the craziness. I mean, did they think this was all special effects or something?

Regina stood up. Oscar and I each took a step toward her and she held up a hand. "One step closer and I'll kill her," she said. She reached down and pulled Victoria up by her armpits.

"With what?" I asked. She didn't have anything other than her hands, and even though she was strong, I didn't think she was that strong. And she definitely wasn't hiding anything in her shirt other than a too-exact copy of my ratty bra.

"She's already weak," said Regina. "If I pull from her one more time, it'll kill her." She started backing up, dragging Victoria along with her.

"Wait a minute here," said Alan. He turned to me. "Would someone mind telling me what's going on?"

"You've been working with a fake Victoria," I said. "That's really Regina Fedorka. Her Talent is to be able to transform into anyone she touches. And she's got the real Victoria right there." I left out the part about her being about to kill the real Victoria, since he hopefully got that from Regina. But maybe not. He took a step toward Regina like he was planning on being the hero of this story.

"I wouldn't do that," I said. "She did it once to me—that pulling thing—and I think she's telling the truth. I think she could kill Victoria." Anyone looking at Victoria could see it was possible. She looked practically translucent, she was so pale. She hadn't even come to yet.

"And you can bet I will," said Regina. She kept backing up, and Oscar had to step out of her way. "She's outlived her usefulness anyway. And this acting thing isn't as much fun as I'd imagined it would be."

"Explains a lot," I heard one of the movie guys say to another one. "Her acting sucks."

Regina heard him too. She sneered in his direction, but kept dragging Victoria along the hall with her.

"What should we do?" asked Oscar. "The cats?"

Rufus and PD began following Regina. "Call off the cats," she told me. "I mean it, Cat Girl. I don't know what kind of control you've got over them, but call them off now."

"Stand down, guys," I said.

I can be very, very fast, said Meep.

"I know you can," I said, "but I don't think it would take her long to kill Victoria. We can't chance it."

"Are you talking to the *cat*?" asked Alan, master of the obvious.

I ignored him. Regina was dragging Victoria backward. If Victoria had been a healthy weight and conscious, maybe that would have slowed Regina down more. As it was, Regina was progressing pretty steadily. If I remembered

265

right, that way was one of the main concourse areas that led to a big ramp and then the gates. If we let her get away, I had no idea how we'd ever find her again. She'd probably ditch Victoria, but then she could just grab anyone on the street and change her face. She could be anyone and we'd never know.

That was not a comforting thought.

"Rufus," I whispered as softly as I could and trying not to move my lips, since I knew with his cat hearing, he'd pick up on it anyway, "You all get ready. I'm going to see if I can get her talking to delay her."

Okay, he said, *but I still think I could have her by the throat before she knew what hit her.*

"Regina," I called out, "I just want to know one thing."

She laughed a brittle dry laugh. "Find your friend on your own time," she said.

"No, that's not it," I said, though Melly's location was topmost in my mind. I took a couple of slow steps in her direction. She kept walking and dragging, but didn't say anything. Some of the cats crept forward a little too.

"Why'd you do it? I mean Easton. Why'd you kidnap her too? Didn't you have enough on your plate keeping Victoria locked up?"

Regina laughed again, but it was about the most humorless sound I'd ever heard. "That stupid blogger. She was going to ruin the whole thing with her big mouth. Would you believe she actually found my house? She broke in with her credit card, of all things. I caught her talking to Victoria. I wasn't about to let her ruin everything, just like I'm not going to let you ruin everything either. You can stop right where you are."

I stopped midstep and put my foot back down. Frick on a stick. She'd figured me out.

Hey, said PD, *I smell beer.*

"It's a ballpark," I whispered back. Beer smell came with the territory.

Yeah, continued PD, *but I also smell unwashed guys.*

Ah. The drunk dudes who'd gone to find their friends. They'd actually made it back into Wrigley. I cleared my throat and cupped my hands around my mouth. "And next up, we have an AMAZING, death-defying trick featuring not one, not two, but five cats and a ring of fire! With our special guest star, Victoria Welling! Everyone give a nice round of applause to welcome our special guest!" I motioned to everyone standing behind me and started clapping.

Ian picked up on it first and started clapping like crazy and wolf whistling. Then Oscar joined in, elbowing Garrett so he'd start clapping too. After a moment, even Alan and Jason and the movie guys were clapping and stomping their feet. Regina stopped and stared at us.

"I don't know what—" she started to say when a crowd of guys rounded the corner behind her and shouted when they saw us. There were at least ten of them.

"We made it!" shouted the blond guy.

"Welcome to the show!" I shouted back. "Why don't you give our special guest a big Chicago welcome!"

They whooped, took one look at Regina-Victoria, and descended on her with open arms.

THIRTY-ONE

FRIDAY, SEPTEMBER 11, 8:41 P.M.

"IN A FIGHT, ALWAYS BET ON THE CAT."
—PD

The guys didn't even notice the real Victoria, whom Regina was separated from in the first two seconds after they mobbed her. Oscar ran to Victoria and caught her as she slumped to the floor.

"Okay," I said to anyone who was listening. "We've got to grab her, like a bunch of us at once, I think. So if she weakens one person by pulling from them, everyone else will still be okay. Are you ready?" I caught a nod from Ian and one from Alan, who still looked very confused, but I didn't wait for any more. I didn't want to give Regina a chance to get over her surprise.

I ran forward and spotted Regina's flailing arm in the middle of the guys. I grabbed her hand and pulled. Ian came up beside me and grabbed her wrist. Alan and Garrett wiggled through and shouldered their way between two guys in Cubs baseball caps to grab her other arm and her shoulder. We all pulled and extracted her from her fans.

"Guys, guys! Great job! A Chicago welcome I'm sure she'll never forget!" I shouted. "Next show in ten minutes! And free refreshments! Go wait in the bleacher section!"

They ran off in the direction of the field, cheering and completely oblivious. As soon as they were gone, a ring of cats surrounded Regina.

If she makes a single move, said Rufus, *we're taking her out.*

"Agreed," I told him. Then I leaned over to stare Regina in the face. "You try anything," I said, "anything at all, and I'll let Tiddlywinks eat your liver for dinner. And trust me, he really wants to."

She glared at me. Alan waved a few more movie guys over and told them to get something to tie her up with so we wouldn't have to hold her any longer. They came back with some rope (where they found it, I really don't know, but I guess that's why they were on staff) and tied up Regina. She still hadn't said a word.

"Well," said Alan, looking at me. "I guess I owe you an apology."

"I'm not worried about that right now," I said. "I just really want to know where my friend Melly is."

"Nat?"

I nearly fell over, I turned around so fast. Melly—the real Melly—stood in the door of a supply closet with her hand to her head. I whooped and ran to her to grab her up in a hug. Oscar managed to clap his hands without dropping Victoria.

270

"Don't you ever do that again," I said.

"Do what?" she asked. She looked like she didn't even know which way was up.

"Go off with the bad guy. Your life is much more important than your acting career. Seriously, woman, dead girls can't act."

"Okay, okay," she said. "You can yell at me later. Right now, can I just get something to eat?"

I was with her on that one. After what Regina had done, that pulling thing or whatever she called it, I was starving. I also couldn't remember the last time I'd eaten today in between the running around, breaking into houses, and saving people.

"Excuse me," said Alan, "but what are we supposed to do with her?" He pointed to Regina, who looked like she wanted to bite his finger off.

Honestly, I really didn't care what he did with her. but he was looking at me like I should have the answers.

You could let me have her, said Rufus.

That was actually pretty tempting. I was seriously considering it when my phone rang. I answered it. "Nat!" screamed Viv in my ear. "Where are you? I'm at the house you told me about and there's broken glass, but nothing else. Where are you?"

"Here," I said, and handed my phone to Alan. "This is Viv. She's my sister and she's with the BERM. Why don't you guys talk about it? We're going to go eat." Let someone else deal with the drama for a while. Stick a fork in me. I was done.

And we left, a stream of cats following us. Rufus, of course, stayed behind to guard Regina, who still looked like Victoria. I wondered if we'd ever know what she really looked like.

♥

Meep led us to the craft services table. Apparently, tuna sandwiches were on the menu, so she had no trouble finding it. Melly had wanted to go get real food at a restaurant, but there was no way we could get into any place with all of the cats. Ian called his dad to tell him what was going on, and his dad told him how to get into his office (after some moments of stunned silence) so we could have somewhere private to recuperate in.

Oscar woke Victoria up by waving some fruit juice under her nose. She grabbed it and drank it down before her eyes even opened. The boys just kept passing food to Melly, Victoria, and me. I had no idea how Victoria had done it for so long. After just one touch from Regina, I was absolutely starving. I'd never been so hungry in my life.

Melly was ultra-relieved to find out that Easton had survived. While we had been zooming around the suburbs breaking into a house and herding cats, Melly had been living her own nightmare. Her first clue that a walk-on role in the movie may not have been worth it was when Regina pulled a knife on her to get her out of Wrigley. Then seeing

Easton West out cold and trussed up in the trunk of a rental car had *really* brought it home.

Regina forced Melly to drive her to the York, where they got Easton upstairs after Regina-as-Victoria made some kind of excuse about Easton suffering from a massive hangover from partying too hard. Since Easton (a.k.a. Regina) wasn't on the hotel staff's good side anyway, they'd taken that at face value. Melly had even tried to give the concierge a clue, but Regina had given her a sharp poke in the side that shut her up. Upstairs, Melly had been absolutely horrified and helpless to see Regina pump Easton full of some kind of drug and write out a suicide note.

The only good thing about Melly being there was that Easton would probably be dead otherwise. She'd pretended she had to go to the bathroom while Regina was writing the note, plugged the sink, and turned the water on. It had taken a little while, but water had seeped out into the hall and down through the floor into the room below. That was how the hotel had found Easton. I had to give it to Melly. I don't think I would have thought of doing something like that. Or I'd have tried the bathtub and it would have taken so long to overflow it would have been too late, or so loud that Regina would have caught me.

Garrett followed us to craft services and listened to the whole story with wide eyes as he sat right next to Oscar. He even asked if he could hold the nunchuks, but what I think he really wanted to hold was Oscar's hand.

Alan found us after a while and said Viv was on her way with a whole contingent of BERM guys. Too little too late, if you asked me, but at least I didn't have to worry about it anymore. He had us tell him everything that had happened, starting from the beginning. He kept shaking his head like he didn't believe us, and he made me demonstrate the whole cat thing.

So I had PD sniff him, and he told me Alan had eaten an Italian beef for lunch and that he had a smelly foot fungus, but I left that last part out. I figured Alan probably already knew that and if he didn't, I didn't want to be the one to tell him.

After we'd eaten pretty much everything left on the craft services table that was edible (seriously, tofu dogs?), we went looking for Melly's phone and my dad's video camera. Regina had pocketed both of them, but Alan's guys had patted her down and she didn't have either one on her. We finally found my dad's camera smashed up in a trash can. Melly's phone wound up being really easy to find because it started ringing while we were searching the dressing room.

It was her dad and it was apparently his fourth attempt at reaching her. He was not pleased. Melly tried to explain to him what was going on, but she only got as far as "kidnapped," and he told her to stay put because he was on his way, and hung up.

"I guess I ought to call my parents too, huh?" asked Oscar. They probably weren't freaked like Melly's dad since they were used to Oscar wandering in late on Friday nights, but still. This was pretty big. "Are you going to call your parents, Nat?"

I thought about it. Really, I did. For about two seconds. "Viv's already on her way. I'll wait and see what she says." Delay the inevitable as long as possible.

Mr. Zinsz, Melly's dad, arrived in record time. He must have floored it the entire way. Viv or the BERM people had contacted the cops, and they were swarming all over the place, interviewing extras and the drunk guys and whatnot, so we didn't even know Mr. Z had arrived until there was a huge commotion at one of the entrances. We were on our way to get Oscar's phone out of Melly's car when we heard Mr. Z shouting and ran the rest of the way down to check it out. We had left all the animals hanging out in the office except Meep, who'd decided I wasn't to be trusted on my own anymore and was trotting along beside me. It was kind of sweet, for Meep.

"Melly!" That was Mr. Z. "That's my daughter!" He looked like he was about to haul off and hit the cop who was trying to stop him. "You let me in right now or I'm going to sue the department for everything they've got!" Even thirty yards away, we could see that his face was bright red.

"Whoa," said Oscar, slowing down. "Mr. Z's gone postal."

"Yeah," said Garrett. "He's gonna get tased."

"Dad!" yelled Melly and ran on. Oscar, Ian, Garrett, and I hung back a little. Good thing Victoria had stayed in the office with Alan to recuperate. Mr. Z was okay, but he was pretty overprotective and it often seemed like he thought we were a bad influence on Melly. Maybe it was the way he unfailingly said something about the purple streaks in my hair or the green in Oscar's. It was kinda like he was joking, but kind of not at the same time. And really, going, "Hey, what's that in your hair, mold?" every time he saw us wasn't all that funny anyway.

The police saw Melly coming and let her dad in. He grabbed her in a huge hug. He was still crushing her ribs when Oscar and I walked up.

"Hey, Mr. Z," I said.

He let Melly go, but kept a hand on her shoulder. "Whose fault is this?" His glare was clearly focused on both me and Oscar equally. Ian kind of ducked behind us. I didn't blame him. Mr. Z is a big guy with a round head and he always wore a perfectly tailored suit. He's kind of imposing. Like a villain in a James Bond movie.

"I don't know that it's anybody's fault, exactly," I said. "Things just kind of got out of hand."

"Things always get out of hand with you two, don't they?" He pulled Melly to him.

That wasn't fair. It's not like we'd ever gotten Melly kidnapped before. And it's not like any of this was *my* idea. She was the one talking about responsibility and all of that, and it wasn't my fault she went along with Regina in the beginning, though she still redeemed herself in the end by, hey, *saving*

Easton's life. I raised my eyebrows at Melly a little, hoping she would notice but Mr. Z wouldn't. Wasn't she going to say anything to defend us?

"Dad," she finally said, "it's not their fault. We were all—"

But that was as far as she got before Viv and her brigade arrived. Viv swept in and crushed me in a huge hug. Then she hugged Oscar too. She was going to hug Melly, but Mr. Z still had his arm wrapped tight around Melly's shoulder. He didn't look like he was ever going to let go.

"I'm so glad you guys are okay!" Viv's normally perfect hair was messy and even her shirt was untucked. "You were supposed to wait to hear back from me!"

"We couldn't get in touch with you," I said.

"And the clock was ticking," said Oscar.

"Yeah, Dad," said Melly. "If they'd waited any longer, who knows what would have happened to me. Regina tried to kill Easton West. I know. I was with her. She made me watch."

"Who is Easton West? Wait," said her dad. "I don't care. We're going home. You can tell me the rest of the story there."

"Wait a minute, sir," said Viv. "I'm afraid we've got to take a statement from your daughter first. As you're obviously aware, some serious crimes have been committed."

"And who the hell are you?" asked Mr. Z, taking a step toward Viv and dragging Melly along with him like a rag doll.

Wow. Mr. Z was seriously off the deep end. One of Viv's coworkers, a largish guy in a dark blue suit and serious sideburns, stepped forward warningly. I mean, hello. Other than Viv, they all exuded "secret government agency." Not that they were secret, exactly. Most people knew the BERM existed, but hardly anyone knew exactly what they did. Other than what Viv had let slip during dinner conversations, I didn't really know what they did either. What was Mr. Z thinking?

Viv held up a hand. "I'm Natalie's sister. But I'm also an agent with the Bureau of Extrasensory Regulation and Management. And I think maybe you need to calm down a little." She didn't flinch.

Woof. Go, Viv!

Mr. Z went from red to purple.

That was when Mr. Sideburns intervened. He swept forward, murmured some words to Mr. Z and then led him and Melly off somewhere into the stadium. Four more agents split off from the pack and each one took one of us by the arm. Before I knew it, I was settled into someone's Wrigley office being officially debriefed. Meep was there and Viv popped in every now and then, but I had no idea where anyone else was. I felt kind of like a criminal or like I was in a bad spy movie. All that was missing was a bright overhead light shining in my face. I got the feeling they'd have used one if one were available, but the lights at Wrigley were normal ballpark fare.

I was pretty fed up. I felt like I had explained everything at least three times by the time Viv finally came back in. "I am so done here," I said to her, ignoring the agent who had been annoying me with all the questions. His name was Frank and he had the personality of a sponge. "Where is everyone else?"

"Oscar and Melly are just about done," she said. "And all those cats are waiting for you. Where in the world did you find them all anyway?"

I ignored the question about the cats. I'd already gone over that with Frank. Repeatedly. "And Victoria? Regina? What's going on with them?"

"They've taken Victoria to the hospital for observation." She looked sidelong at Frank. "And Regina has been taken to the BERM headquarters for her interrogation."

Interrogation? They should be taking her there for a beating. But that probably wasn't legal.

When they finally let me out of the room, I ran into Ian in the hallway. He was leaning against the wall, looking about as worn out as I felt.

"Hey," he said. "They let me out a little early since I didn't really have much to say. Oscar and Melly are still talking and Oscar's parents got here a little while ago. How are you holding up?"

I'm fine, said Meep sarcastically. *Thanks for asking.* I ignored her. She was just miffed because the goons hadn't asked her any questions.

"I feel like Jason Bourne," I said, "but without all the muscles—or the mad skills."

He laughed. "My dad got here a little while ago too. He can't wait to meet you."

I didn't know what to say to that. Was that a good thing? Or a "he can't wait to meet you because he's heard you're such a sideshow freak" kind of thing? Instead of replying, I started off to where the craft services table was.

"Hold on. You don't want to go that way."

"Why not? I need to check on the cats." I was worried they were going to start using the outfield as a litter box or that Rufus might have led them in a rebellion.

"Pebbles helped me move the cats. They're all waiting down by my dad's car. If you go that way, there's a bunch of TV and newspaper reporters. I think Alan called them."

"Oh!" I stopped. "Thanks. That's the last place I want to be. I just want to go home." That wasn't entirely true. Viv had told me she'd called home and explained everything, but I wasn't exactly anxious to face the music. After all, I was the suspended-got-arrested-caused-total-chaos child. I couldn't even imagine the talking-to I was going to get when I got home. They'd finally notice me all right—but not the kind of notice I was necessarily hoping for.

"Your chariot awaits." He took my arm and led me off down the hall. "You know," he said, "it's really weird, actually talking to Pebbles and having him listen."

"You have no idea," I said. Thank heavens he couldn't hear what PD was probably saying back.

THIRTY-TWO

"HOW YOU BEHAVE TOWARDS CATS HERE BELOW
DETERMINES YOUR STATUS IN HEAVEN."
—ROBERT A. HEINLEIN

The plan was for Ian and me to take all the cats home in his
dad's car since that way, they could tell me where to drop
them off in the neighborhood. Ian's dad was going to take the
train home. He was on the phone when Ian brought me by
for introductions, so I got off easy with a wave and a smile.

I climbed into the car, and Meep, Rufus, Fergie, and PD
climbed in to sit on my feet. The rest of the cats were piled in
the back, wedging themselves into a space that should have
been much too small to fit them all. That was a cat Talent I
wish I had sometimes. Since Easton was still in the hospital, Rufus and Fergie were coming home with me—mostly
because Rufus had refused to go off with any of the BERM
guys, saying they hadn't proven their trustworthiness yet. I
took that as a compliment, though I had the sneaking suspi-
cion that they'd refused to let him guard Regina and he was
just pissed at them.

Ian pulled out of the parking lot and started home. "Well," he said after a few minutes, "that was crazy."

He always has been a master of understatement, said PD.

I laughed.

Ian looked at me sideways out of the corner of his eye. "Did Pebbles say something?"

PD laughed his cat laugh. *He's always going to wonder now, isn't he? This could be fun.*

"He just said you had a talent for understatement, that's all." I winked at PD. "PD likes you a lot," I said. "You don't have to worry about anything. You might want to stop calling him Pebbles, though."

"Yeah," said Ian. "PD. Sorry, man."

No problem, said PD. *Pebbles was your mom's fault anyway.*

Huh. Now that my secret was out, was I going to have to translate for people all the time? That could get annoying.

"You know," I said, "you really don't have to tell anybody at school. About the whole talking to cats thing."

"You don't want anybody to know? Why not? It's cool." He sounded surprised.

Cool? In what universe? "Yeah . . . I mean, like what about Jonas Smith?"

"Frog Boy?"

"Exactly," I said. I couldn't help but wince a little.

"Well, you're not Jonas Smith. He doesn't bathe, you know. And he, like, *sniffs* people's hair. He'd be weird even if he didn't kiss frogs or whatever it is he does."

I've been telling you, said Meep. *It won't be that bad. And cats are way better than frogs. Frogs are dinner.*

That reminded me, once again, of why I was not one of those people who kissed their cats on the nose.

♥

We dropped off all the neighborhood cats back on various streets surrounding Regina's house. A few people walking their dogs gave us strange looks as we stopped and let a cat out, but no one said anything. Of course, that could have been because we just drove off as fast as we could. Then Ian drove over to my house. All the lights were on, so Mom and Dad were definitely home and awake. Ian parked and turned off the car.

"Do you want me to come in with you?"

"No!" I opened the door. "I mean, no, thanks. I probably need to, um, explain a few things to them." It would be best if he didn't meet my mom seconds before she was about to tear into me. Actually, it would be best if he never met my mom at all.

I climbed out, and Meep, Fergie, and Rufus followed me. "Thanks for the ride. And . . . you know, everything." Like not telling me I was a freak. And trying to save me from a crazy lunatic. All that stuff.

"Sure." He leaned over the passenger seat and smiled up at me. "You know," said Ian, "that was one heck of a first date. Maybe next time we can try it without the psycho killer, you think?"

Yeah, PD yelled from somewhere around Ian's ankles. *And maybe next time there'll be kissing!*

Meep and Rufus snickered as I turned red. I waved at Ian as he drove off, glad once again that no one else could understand cats.

But did he say "next time"?

I opened the door and was immediately assaulted by Emmy. She must have been waiting right there, probably watching through the window.

"Look at your eye!" She shrieked, right in my ear. "It's purple!" Then she grabbed me in a huge hug and practically crushed my ribs. She was getting strong, but then again, she hadn't given me a hug since she was about six. She wasn't much of a hugger and neither was I. She pulled back, looked at me again, and then hauled off and hit me in the arm. "Don't you ever do that again!" she said.

"Do what?" I shut the door behind me after all the animals had made it in. I wished she hadn't mentioned my eye. I had been able to ignore the throbbing until she reminded me. Regina had a mean right hook.

Emmy gaped at me. "You could have *died*," she wailed. Then she burst into tears and ran off down the hall. What the hell?

"Natalie? Is that you?" my mother called from her office.

Who else would it be? "Yeah," I said. Viv said she had already explained, so I just dived in. "It's me. And Rufus—the other cat—is here, just to warn you. And a dog. You ought to stay clear unless you have a mask." Was it too much to hope that she wouldn't leave her office?

No such luck. Mom and Dad both arrived at the same time. They stopped in the entryway. They were backlit by the light from the hall and I couldn't tell whether they were sad or mad or furious or what. Rufus and Meep sat down in front of me and we all stared back. Fergie had already passed out asleep in a corner. She was snoring little doggy snores.

"See, it all started with Oscar and this video—" I began. Then they both ran at me. I flinched. Not that they'd ever been into corporal punishment or anything, but I'd never been in so much trouble before. I imagined if they ever wanted to take it up, now would be the time.

Then they both grabbed me and squeezed, just like Emmy had, except without the tears. Rufus and Meep scattered to keep from getting stepped on. Then Mom stood back, took me by the shoulders, and took a good look at me.

"Look at your eye! Dennis, look at her eye!"

I needed a mirror. Just how bad exactly did my eye look? Ian hadn't said anything about it. Neither had Viv. Maybe it was getting worse, the way bruises do sometimes. I'd gotten a glimpse of it in the car window and it hadn't looked *that* bad.

"I'm sorry," I started again.

"Natalie," said Dad, "just stop." Even though he had on his striped pajamas, he looked serious.

I shut up.

Mom pointed to the couch. I sat. Meep and Rufus joined

me, but Meep especially looked ready to run. She knew how Mom could be. I had the feeling I was going to be grounded for the next few years. Maybe until I was out of college. Could they do that? Knowing Mom, if she could, she would.

"First off," said Mom, "you should have come to us right away."

I opened my mouth to say something, but she wasn't done yet.

"Sneaking around like that—smuggling a cat into the house, getting suspended—getting arrested!" Rufus sank down a little and hid his head behind my ankle. *Finally* something scared him. "What were you thinking?"

"I—"

"*Allison,*" said Dad. He gave Mom a let-me-do-the-talking look, which was very rare. He put a hand on my shoulder. "Natalie, your mom is just worried about you. I've been worried too. I wondered what you were up to when I first smelled the new cat in the house."

"You knew about Rufus?"

"He was kind of hard to miss," said Dad. "Especially at first."

Rufus raised his head. He looked a little put out, but Dad was right. I couldn't believe he hadn't said anything. What had I been thinking, trying to sneak Rufus past the supersniffer?

"But why—"

"Because I trust you," said Dad. He looked at Mom, who had her lips pursed like she'd just sucked on a lime. "We *both* do."

He elbowed mom and she very pointedly did not look at him but she did allow herself a small nod. "Of course we do," she said. Someone should tell her she's not a very good liar. I didn't need to be Viv to see right through her.

"And I knew you and Genevieve had everything under control when I heard you at the police station."

"Wait. What? What are you talking about?" I looked from Dad to Mom and back again. Mom looked a little peeved, but she held her tongue. "You were there?"

Holy tuna cakes, said Meep to Rufus. *Dad's been holding out on us. I knew he was sneakier than he looked. He's got the sniffer of a bloodhound, you know.*

"I got there late," he said, "but I was there on the other side of the window. I heard the whole story. I thought it was a great opportunity for both you and your sister to prove yourselves to the BERM."

"What?" It was a good thing I was already sitting down. My head swam a little.

"Especially you, Natalie," he continued. "I've been telling the bureau chief for years that we need to re-examine our priorities. The BERM has always seen the potential in Talents like Genevieve's and in people like Regina, but they've completely disregarded the potential of Talents like yours."

"Stupid ones," I said automatically.

Hey, said Meep, *I told you to stop that.*

"Never say that, Natalie," said Mom. "Your Talent isn't stupid."

I looked at her. Who was she kidding?

"Granted," she said, "it doesn't seem as useful as some at first glance."

Dad held up a hand at her and she stopped talking. He truly was wearing the pants in the family tonight. "*All* Talents have a purpose," he said. "And I'd say that you proved that to the BERM with your actions over the last week."

"We just hope that next time, you'll think about letting me in on what's going on so I don't have to hear about it secondhand," said Mom. She gave Dad the elbow this time, and it was his turn to nod.

Let's hope there's not a next time, said Meep.

You said it, said Rufus. *I really don't think my fur can stand it.*

I couldn't help it. I laughed. Hysterically. "Sorry," I spit out between giggles, "I just . . . I don't even know what to think about this. You guys trust me? And Dad thinks I'm the new BERM poster child for the Talented? But I'm your screwup daughter!" I started hiccupping.

"Language!" said Mom. "What do you mean our 'screw-up daughter'?"

"Emmy . . . ," I said. "Viv . . . you're always going on and on about them." *Hiccup.* Horny toads on a stick. Of course I'd be hiccupping now.

Mom actually put her arm around my shoulder. "Natalie, if I don't spend as much time haranguing you as your sisters, it's because you don't need to be coddled and encouraged like they do. You've always been comfortable doing your own thing and succeeding on your own."

Meep snorted. So did Rufus. Comfortable? Me? Succeeding? I hiccupped again. I didn't know what to say.

They both hugged me again. "Why don't you go get cleaned up and get some sleep," said Dad. "It's getting late. We can talk more tomorrow. I'll get some ice for your eye, okay?"

Mom sneezed. "Just take the pink cat along with you, would you?"

I wandered off in the direction of the bathroom, Meep and Rufus trailing behind me. Apparently, I was in a parallel universe and no one had thought to tell me.

THIrTY-THree

"never try to out-stubborn a cat."
—robert a. HeINLeIN

I woke up to Emmy screaming in my ear. "You're in the paper!" She dropped a section of the *Chicago Tribune* right on top of my face. I pulled it off and wiped the sleep out of my eyes, wincing when I touched my black eye. Considering how it had looked before I went to bed, it was probably deep purple by now. Meep, still asleep, rolled off my pillow and fell into Rufus.

Cretin, mumbled Rufus, and swished his tail right into my nose. Note to self: never have more than one cat at a time.

"Just look!" Emmy shouted right in my ear again. "You're on the front page!"

"What are you screaming about?" I shoved both cats off the bed and sat up. The paper fell onto the floor. Emmy huffed, picked it up, and stuck it in my face again. I took it.

She was right. There was last year's school picture (with the unfortunately large pimple right next to my nose, making me look like I had three nostrils) front and center. "'Cat Girl' saves celebrities" was the headline.

Oh no.

I read the article. Everything was there. *Everything.*

"Oh my God," I said. I threw the paper on the floor where Meep pounced on it and shredded a couple of pages before Emmy could get it from her. Good kitty.

"Isn't it awesome?" Emmy was dancing around my room, dangling strips of the shredded newspaper in front of Meep and Rufus. They batted at it and flip-flopped themselves end over end all over the room. Cats may sleep a lot, but they can wake up awfully fast when they want to.

"Awesome? Are you kidding? I'm going to have to move." There was no way I could go back to school. School? Heck, I needed to move out of state! I wondered if Auntie Esther would take me in? She lived in California. Maybe that would be far enough away.

"It's on the Internet too," said Emmy with a wicked glint in her eye, completely ignoring my misery. "And I heard Viv say something about the story being nationally syndicated or something. She's here, you know. Downstairs."

Oy. Maybe California wasn't far enough away. Well, there was always the family we had in China, even though I only knew, like, four words in Chinese.

"Mom said to come out when you're ready." She smiled sweetly at me and twirled out the door. Evil, evil girl. She'd gotten over her upset over my near-death experience pretty quickly.

Poodle farts on a stick. I flopped back on my bed and pulled my pillow down over my face. Maybe I could just stay in my room. Mom was a supergenius. She could home school me.

Oh, get up, said Meep. *Go face the tuna. So your secret's out. You're a hero. Get over it.*

"You wouldn't understand," I said. Not that the article had been bad, exactly, but my life was over. I was Cat Girl now. There was no going back. I wondered if Frog Boy had room at his lunch table.

I pulled on a pair of jeans and a T-shirt from the floor, giving them the sniff test. I needed clean laundry bad, but I'd worry about it after breakfast. I stumbled out the door and down the hall to the living room.

Viv was on the couch, but so were a bunch of guys. Mostly all in suits. One of them was Alan. They all stood up as I came into the room, except for Viv. Mom and Dad came in from the kitchen. Mom looked at my hair and cleared her throat, but didn't say anything. Maybe I should have brushed it—and maybe Emmy could have *told* me we had visitors. I put up my hand to comb my fingers through it but then decided that was a little too obvious, so I stopped. Then I figured that looked spastic and I was going to turn it into a greeting, but I wound up just kind of standing in the doorway with my hand in the air.

"Um," I said.

"Natalie," said Dad, "you've met Alan Leonard already, I believe."

I wanted to say, "Yeah, Dad, he's the guy who got me arrested," but I resisted. Instead, I gave Alan a little wave, which gave me an excuse to lower my hand.

"And this is Mr. Whaley, the *mayor* of Chicago," said Mom, motioning at a stocky older guy with slicked-back black hair and gray sideburns. Crap. I *really* should have brushed my hair. And my teeth. No wonder Emmy had been smiling her evil smile. I bet she was doing her chameleon thing right now and hiding out somewhere in the room. First she goes all huggy on me last night, and now this. At least things were back to normal . . . I guess.

"Nice to meet you," I said. I didn't wave this time.

Dad introduced the rest of them. There was a guy from the *Tribune*, another from the *Daily Herald*, a BERM dude who worked with Viv (not Frank the sponge, but the one who had talked to Mr. Z), and a guy from the *Jerry King Show*. Holy mother of TV shows. No amount of hair brushing would have made a difference, not for this crowd. Maybe a makeover.

"Young lady," said the mayor, "I just want to shake your hand. You've really done Chicagoland proud." He stepped forward and held out his hand. I took it. He pumped my hand up and down a few times while Mom beamed at me.

Alan stood up. "Everyone in the crew would like to invite you and your friends onto the set today while we're filming the big parade sequence. We've cleared it with your parents."

He patted me on the back. "And I personally wanted to thank you, but also apologize."

"Um, sure," I said. I had the nagging feeling I was still asleep and dreaming. Mom said it was okay to go on set? Though I guess it wasn't a school day, so maybe that was why.

He should be apologizing to me too, said Rufus. *Tell him I want tuna.*

"Oooh! Did he say something?" asked Jerry King.

"Yeah, he, um, wants some tuna."

"That's just amazing!"

A cat wanting tuna? That wasn't amazing. That was *normal*.

Each of the guys in turn came over and either shook my hand or patted me on the back and told me how incredible I was. The TV show guy actually wanted me to come on his show, along with Rufus, Easton, and Victoria. Easton, apparently, was okay, just weak. They'd pumped her stomach in time to prevent any permanent damage, though she still needed time to recover. The doctors had thought her ravings about being kidnapped were side effects of the drugs she'd almost overdosed on. They'd actually bought the whole "I'm going to kill myself because of my cat" thing.

"What about Regina?" I asked the BERM guy when everyone finally sat down again. He looked pretty much exactly what I expected an agent to look like: close-cropped hair, button-down shirt, and kind of a square jaw. Thankfully, I'd lucked into Frank last night. He had been annoying, but not as scary as this guy would have been.

"Don't worry about her," he said. "We have things under control. The BERM is evaluating her status right now."

Rufus snorted. *You should have let us finish her off. Then you really wouldn't need to worry about her. I watch the news. She'll be out in no time, just you wait and see.*

Everyone looked at me like they wanted me to translate what Rufus had said. "He said . . . thanks. And he's sure she's in good hands."

Rufus rolled his eyes at me, but didn't say anything else. He wasn't stupid.

But what he said worried me. They were evaluating her status? What did that mean? Were they evaluating her as in they were going to deport her butt to Siberia? Or were they evaluating her as having a Talent they could exploit? They were a governmental agency. I wasn't sure I trusted them. But maybe I just watched too much TV. Besides, Dad and Viv were very pro BERM and I did trust them. Well, Dad, anyway.

♥

The mayor had arranged for us to have a police escort and everything, which was good since a lot of streets were closed. I'd actually never been to the Von Steuben German Day Parade, but from the size of the crowd, it was a pretty big deal. Either that, or people had gotten wind that the movie was going to be filming. Maybe both. Emmy had been waving to people as we drove by, which had driven Viv absolutely nuts. They had argued about it the whole time. Maybe Mom had been right. I was definitely less annoying than they were sometimes. Dad had finally told them both to calm down.

"Cat Girl!" yelled Oscar. He and Melly had converged on me as soon as I had exited our car. I cringed and looked around to see if anyone had heard him. I couldn't help it. He grabbed me in a huge full-body Oscar hug and nearly squashed Rufus against my chest. I hadn't wanted to take Rufus with me (thank goodness Meep had decided she'd had enough adventure to last her a lifetime), but he'd insisted that he wanted to experience one of our "quaint cultural ceremonies" and then he'd guilted me with the fact that Easton always took him to everything. Cats could lay on the guilt like you wouldn't believe. The only person I knew who was better at it was my grandmother. My *nai nai* could even get my dad to eat his broccoli, and he hated it. He said it smelled like farts.

"Oops, sorry, little furry dude," Oscar said. "Didn't see you there."

I am going to ignore that, said Rufus. *This time. But tell him not to call me that again or the claws are coming out.*

"Your eye!" said Melly. "It's —"

"Yeah, I know," I said. "Purple." At least the throbbing had died down to a dull ache overnight, but ibuprofen was my best friend today.

"And blue!" said Oscar. "I think I see some green in there too. You're in Technicolor!"

Melly reached out a finger to touch the edge of my eye.

It was pretty spectacular, if I said so myself. Regina packed quite a wallop. But it was the bump on the back of my head that hurt the worst.

"Your dad let you come?" I asked. The last time I'd seen Mr. Z, he'd seemed like he wasn't going to let Melly out of his sight until she was eighteen.

"Yeah," said Melly. "Sorry about that last night. He's over in the stands, along with Oscar's parents. Everybody's here. Dad was okay, mostly, after he calmed down. But I'm grounded."

"Grounded?" That's nice. Get kidnapped, get grounded. "Then why did he let you come?"

"We can talk about that later," said Oscar. "Right now, we've got to get you to makeup!"

Emmy made as if she was going to follow us, but Viv held her back. Viv was definitely getting a better than normal Christmas present from me this year. And another battery charger for her phone.

I held on tight to Rufus with one arm as Melly pulled me with the other. Oscar followed behind. We passed some floats, including one that looked like a boat. Lots of people were lining up in groups, most of them in some kind of weird German outfit. Lederhosen? Or is that a Swiss thing? Maybe I should have worn something more festive. I'd changed out of my smelly T-shirt into a nicer, cleaner one (and brushed both my hair and my teeth), but I still had on my jeans.

Melly led us to a white trailer down an alley and opened

the door without even knocking. Claire Ryan was sitting in a chair with a makeup lady fussing over her. Another chair was open and Melly pushed me down into it.

"Hey, Hannah, I've got another one for you. Hi, Claire, how are you doing?" said Melly, like hobnobbing with actresses and makeup artists was something she did every day.

Claire nodded. "I'm good." Then she stood up and fluffed her hair after peering at herself in the mirror. "Looks nice, Hannah, thanks," she said to the makeup lady. "Break a leg today," she said to Melly, and left the trailer.

"What was that about?" I set Rufus down on the makeup table. "Break a leg? And why do I need makeup?"

"You haven't heard yet?" Oscar plopped himself down and lounged in the chair Claire had left. It was a normal-sized chair, but somehow he found a way to stretch out and curl up at the same time. Nobody could get comfortable like Oscar.

"Heard what? I haven't heard anything. But I did meet the mayor this morning. And Jerry King." The news didn't have the reaction I expected. They both just nodded. Geez, how much had I missed last night?

"Alan's letting me audition for the movie! Victoria isn't going to be able to do it because of, you know. . . ."

"Because she looks like hell on a cracker," said Oscar. "Regina should sign up as a Weight Watchers counselor — or maybe that would be dictator."

"They're going to have to reshoot all of the scenes Regina was in. Claire's going to be auditioning for the Molly part

298

too, so even if I don't get it, I've got a chance at Claire's current part!" Melly was literally jumping up and down. "Even my dad is psyched! He said maybe all those acting lessons are paying off after all. Alan totally schmoozed him too."

"Wow," I said. Just, wow. I guess she is getting used to hobnobbing with famous people. I bet her "grounding" wouldn't last long. Her dad may be anal, but he totally dotes on Melly and spoils her rotten.

"Hold still," said Hannah. She globbed a bunch of concealer around my eye. "That's quite a shiner you've got."

You should see the other guy, said Rufus. *Oh, wait, you barely even touched her. . . .*

"Shut up," I said.

"Excuse me?" asked Hannah. She raised her eyebrows at me, causing them to disappear beneath her shaggy bangs.

"Sorry, I was talking to Rufus," I said.

"I heard about that cat thing you do," she said. She bent down to stare into Rufus's face. He held his ground and stared right back at her. "Can you have him tell me something?"

Oh, this was going to get real old. Fast.

Rufus curled his lip up on one side so his canine tooth showed. *You can tell her I have nothing to say to someone who stinks of grease. That woman eats entirely too many french fries.*

"Um," I said, "he's not feeling real talkative right now."

And she should lay off of the hairspray. I know about the ozone layer. She's probably responsible for the hole over the Antarctic. He cat laughed.

"He's just thirsty," I said. "Probably a fur ball coming along. I'll get him some water in a minute."

Rufus totally humphed at me, but he sat down and shut up. Hannah kept working on my face while Melly and Oscar told me everything that I'd missed. Mostly, I realized that they were the ones who had spilled everything to whoever would listen, which included a bunch of reporters (Alan had been the one to call them last night; probably figured it would be good for his movie), not just the Trib. The story was *everywhere*, as was my last year's school picture.

"Yeah," said Oscar, "sorry about that. I tried to give them a better picture, but they were in a hurry. They got it from the paper's archive from when you won that math competition last year."

I took back all the good things I've ever said about math.

The picture was only the icing on the cake, though. Oscar and Melly had told *everything*. Alan, I understood — he had a business to promote and he didn't know me. But my friends? So much for pinkie swears. So much for trust. "How could you guys do this to me?"

"What?" asked Oscar. He raised his eyebrows and looked at Melly like they were completely innocent.

"You totally outed me!" I batted Hannah's hand away and swiveled the chair to face the two people who were always supposed to have my back.

"What do you mean?" asked Melly.

I just silently looked from one to the other with my

eyebrows raised. They were both doing their best to look blameless. Finally, Melly had the decency to look down.

"What's the one thing that I've always kept hidden? That I asked you both to never tell anyone, ever? The one thing you *swore* you'd never reveal?"

"Yeah, but—" said Oscar.

"But what?" I stood up and Oscar straightened in his chair. "Oscar, I would never have done this to you."

"That's not fair," he said. "This is completely different."

"Nat," said Melly, "it was going to come out anyway. I mean, Alan saw everything. He even got part of it on camera. Even Ian knows."

"Ian isn't going to say anything. He promised me last night. Like you guys promised me." I picked up Rufus around the middle and he hung from my arm like a furry pink purse. "I gotta go," I said. I opened the door and then stopped to turn back to Melly. "Just because you want to be famous," I said, "doesn't mean I want to." I let the door slam shut behind me. Hopefully Hannah had mostly finished before I'd waved her off. An eye that was half covered up would be worse than one that wasn't covered at all.

Well, said Rufus, *that was enjoyable. How do you treat your enemies?*

"Shut up," I said. "They had no right to talk to anyone about it. They're my *friends*. And Viv could have made Alan keep it quiet."

Sure, sure, said Rufus. *Certainly the BERM would have bribed dozens and dozens of media hungry movie people to keep them quiet.*

"Whatever." I knew he was right, but that didn't make it okay that they'd told.

By the way, in case you hadn't noticed, I am not a fashion accessory. Perhaps you could carry me with a little more dignity?

I ignored him and kept walking. I finally found my family chatting with Alan by a parade float.

"Can we go?" I asked my dad.

"Go?"

"Home," I said. Duh. Why was I here anyway? So Alan could show me off to the media?

"Oh, you can't go!" said Alan. He put an arm around my shoulders and started walking. I shifted Rufus so he wouldn't get squished. "I've got a special spot for you in the reviewing stands! Right next to the mayor! It'll be the perfect spot— you'll be able to see your friend Melly as she auditions. I'm going to be taping the whole route and the parade master has kindly allowed us to put our float in the parade so I can get some good shots. We're even having a whole 'Twist and Shout' moment! Of course, we'll be doing the real close-up shots later on with extras as the crowd, but this will allow us to get some usable footage of the whole parade, just like John Hughes did! Except we have permission."

He's a talker, isn't he? I shifted Rufus so that his butt fit into my elbow and he wasn't dangling quite so much. He did look pretty silly being carried like a purse. People were staring at us.

302

"Did he say something?"

"No," I said. I refused to translate anything else. I wished Rufus would shut up so people would stop asking.

"Well, you can tell him that Easton is going to be in the stands as well! She insisted that the hospital let her out in time for the parade so she could meet you."

You are not going home, said Rufus firmly. He poked me with a claw. *You'll just have to stick it out. I want my person.*

My whole family was following along behind us. "We'll all be there, Natalie," said Mom. Emmy squinted at me like she was daring me to ruin Rufus's day. Even Dad looked like he wanted to stay. So much for being on my side.

"Fine," I told Rufus. "Whatever." At least I'd be getting rid of the root of all furry evil. But as soon as this parade was over? I was out of here, even if I had to take the train home by myself. Nothing good could come of this.

"Great, great," said Alan. "And here we go!" He stopped in front of a set of bleachers. It was filling up with people. As promised, the mayor was right in the center and Easton was sitting in front of him. And so was Victoria. She'd been cleaned up, but she still looked like something had run her over. Her hair had been clipped short all the way around to get rid of the spots where Regina had cut chunks away.

As soon as Rufus caught sight of Easton, he used me as a springboard and flung himself into the bleachers. He narrowly missed some guy's head, but then squirreled his way up the rest of the rows to throw himself in Easton's lap.

"Tiddlywinks!" she shrieked, making everyone who hadn't already freaked out jump. "My baby!" She gathered him up and gave him a huge hug and then started making kissy faces with him. Gross. Maybe I should tell her what he does with that mouth.

"You must be Natalie!" Easton called out to me after she finished kissing on Rufus. "Get up here, my little poppet!"

Everyone who'd been staring at her turned to stare at me. Then the whispering and pointing started. I thought about turning around and leaving, but Alan and my family were right behind me, so I kept climbing instead. I sat down between Easton and Victoria, where Easton was patting the bleachers. Well, now I knew how a fish in a fishbowl felt.

"Good to see you again," said Victoria. "Easton, meet my savior."

Savior? Sheesh. "Hey, Victoria," I said. "You look, um, better. I didn't expect to see you here. And hi, Easton. As you can tell, Ru–um, Tiddlywinks is glad to see you."

Rufus had mentioned before he didn't want to tell her about the name thing. He didn't want her to think he didn't like the name she'd given him. It was kind of sweet, for Rufus.

It felt really weird to be sitting there between two celebrities and down one row from the mayor and chatting like it was normal. Not to mention all the people staring at me. You'd think they'd be staring at Victoria instead. Or at Easton.

"The doctors didn't want to let me out but I made them," said Victoria. "I've been cooped up for two and a half years.

304

It's just so good to be outside. Besides, I wanted to say thank you again." She gave me a shoulder squeeze. I nodded, not really sure what to say.

Easton looked a little pale herself, but that could have been all the pink she had on. She even had on her trademark high heels, which I would never have attempted in bleachers. Or after being in the hospital. Actually, never at all. I was purely a Converse or combat boots kind of girl.

"There was no way I was going to miss this chance to meet you either. Tell me *everything*," said Easton. She put Rufus on her lap, grabbed my face in her hands, and kissed both of my cheeks. I had the distinct feeling that I was now covered in pink lipstick.

"I'm sure you've already heard pretty much everything," I said. "It was all in the paper." I looked out at the crowd, glad to have something to focus on besides my weird situation. The people around me had gone back to doing whatever they were doing, but I still felt like someone was watching me. Maybe Rufus did too. His hackles were up. Or maybe that was because Easton apparently liked to pet him the wrong way. Strangely enough, he didn't seem to mind.

"No," said Easton. "*Not that*." She turned to Rufus. "Tiddlywinkums, tell Momma everything!"

Great. There went my rule about not translating anymore today.

THIrTY-FOUr

"IF YOU WANT TO KNOW THE CHaracter OF a Man,
FIND OUT WHAT HIS CAT THINKS OF HIM."
—anonYMOUS

Awhile later, I was saved from Rufus rehashing his early
days (apparently, he had a lot to say on Easton's choice of
men during those years) by the arrival of Ian. Victoria wel-
comed him with a hug and invited him to sit between us. I
think she was as happy to see him as I was. We'd both had
enough of Rufus and Easton.

There were really no limits to what Rufus wanted to tell
Easton and no limits to what Easton wanted to know about.
One thing I could say about her: she really, really loved her
cat. It was kind of disturbing. Maybe that whole suicide
scheme that Regina had dreamed up wasn't as far-fetched as
I'd thought it was. The only fly in her day was that we hadn't
brought Fergie with us too. Poor dog, she was still at home
sleeping. Those little fluffy mutts didn't have much stamina.

"Hey, Ian," I said, wishing I'd given him a hug like Victoria had. But it would have been kind of weird with my family

sitting on the next row up near the mayor. And I wasn't completely sure we were in the okay-to-hug stage. Honestly, I had no idea what stage we were in at all. Yesterday had been one heck of a first date. More like a first disaster.

"Hi, Nat." He smiled at me and then gave Rufus a pat.

"Oooohhh, cute," said Easton. "And who are you?" She looked like she wanted to eat him up. Geez, back off, cougar woman!

"This is Ian," I said. "My—" I sputtered to a stop. "My, um, friend." Frick on a stick. That was lame.

"Ian helped Nat and Oscar save me from Regina. They all go to the same high school," said Victoria. At least Victoria hadn't manhandled him when she hugged him. Easton was looking at him like she wanted to take a bite out of him.

"Yeah," said Ian. "Nat's my trig partner in crime." He leaned into me and bumped shoulders.

Trig partner? Was I back to that? Had I ever been beyond that?

Easton quizzed Ian while I sat there like an idiot trying to think of something to say. Trig partner? *Really?*

Then the parade finally got going. I hadn't been so excited to see a parade start since I was a kid, though it was more like relief. Had Ian been staring at Easton's cleavage? I couldn't tell for sure. But then, probably everyone was staring at her cleavage. Her shirt was cut practically to her belly button. At least she wasn't rocking one of those split-down-the-middle hospital gowns. I got the distinct feeling it wouldn't bother her at all to have all her bits on display.

The first part of the parade was a bunch of official-looking people walking. I clapped along with everyone else in the stands. They had a big banner, but other than that, nothing interesting unless, I guess, you were German American. The next bit was better, with some floats and some people in funny German outfits dancing. I didn't see Melly or Ty or any of the other actors yet, though there was a camera stationed at the far right corner of the stands filming the whole thing.

Then I heard the unmistakable Wonder Woman theme song. That could only be Viv's phone. Who else on this planet would have that as their ringtone? I couldn't believe she'd forgotten to turn her phone to vibrate. I twisted around to glare at her. She looked embarrassed, but she still took the call. From the look on Mom's face, it was obvious Viv was going to be hearing about this faux pas later.

Viv went pale and pocketed her phone. She whispered something to Mom and Dad, then they all got up and started clambering down the bleachers, stopping to gather up Oscar's parents and Melly's dad (who hadn't even bothered to say hello to me earlier). Viv stopped at our row and stepped over a few people—and on one of them. She bent down and whispered in my ear, with her elbow in Ian's face.

"Regina's escaped. They think she's after you and probably Victoria too. There's a good chance she's heading this way or maybe even already here, since she knew the shooting schedule. We all need to go. *Right now.*"

"What? Escaped? How?" What good were the professionals if they let the bad guy escape?

"What's going on?" asked Victoria. She looked like she was on full alert.

Viv sighed. Quietly, so that Victoria could hear too, she said, "Regina's escaped custody. Based on the record of her initial testing in the system, we believed her power was restricted to mimicking only females. So she was being guarded by all male guards. But apparently her Talent isn't limited in the way we thought. She managed to knock out her guard during a shift change by touching him and then she basically walked out of the building using his ID. They believe she's headed this way. They found a day trader from the Chicago Mercantile Exchange passed out on the street, and a jogger as well, not too far from here. We don't currently know who she looks like for sure, but she's got a gun."

"Great," I said. Total frick on a stick.

"I'm sure everything will be fine. There are tons of agents out looking for her and the police have been notified as well. But my superiors think it would be best if I got all of you somewhere safe."

Fine my foot. I should have listened to that feeling of impending doom I'd passed off as paranoia. "And where would that be?" I asked. "She could be anyone, anywhere, anytime." I looked down at the street. Suddenly, everyone looked threatening. Even the women dressed in the old-fashioned German dresses that were dancing by in the parade. Was the one with the red hair staring at me with an evil glint in her eye?

"I'm sure they'll catch her," said Viv. "It's just a matter of time."

"Yeah, right," said Victoria. "I kept thinking someone would stop her and save me. If it hadn't been for Nat, I'd still be trapped. Or dead." She was glancing up and down the street frantically and all around us like Regina could pop out of anywhere—which was true.

Easton finally caught on completely to what we were talking about. "Ack!" She fumbled in her little pink clutch, nearly dropping Rufus. She pulled out a taser, which was practically too big to even fit in her tiny purse to begin with, and started waving it around. It was, of course, bright pink. With sparkles. Ian grabbed it before she could shock one of us or some random unsuspecting person in the bleachers below us.

"Let's go," said Viv. She grabbed my arm. "We can talk about all of this later when we're in a secure location, okay?"

Poodle farts. On a stick. I could only imagine one of two scenarios here: (a) they would try to catch Regina and fail miserably (because, seriously, how are they going to catch someone who can look like someone else and knows that they are looking for her?), and we would have to go into hiding or protective custody or whatever for the rest of our lives, or (b) they would try to catch her and fail miserably, and we would refuse to go into hiding and wake up one morning to

Regina standing over our beds with a waffle iron in her hand. Not that she even needed a weapon when she could touch you, steal your identity, and drain your life away.

Neither of those options sounded good to me at all. There was only one way to recapture Regina. There was only one person who could pick her out of a crowd no matter what she looked like.

Me. With the help of Rufus's nose.

THIRTY-FIVE

"when trouble strikes, you want a cat at your back.
barring that, a human will do."
—rufus brutus the third

Viv was herding Easton and Victoria down the bleachers when she noticed I wasn't following behind her.

"Come on, Nat," she said, looking up at me in the bleachers. "Let's go." She looked at me intently, like she was afraid I was going to do exactly what I was planning to do. I'd have to be careful with what I said. If I lied, she'd know.

I looked her square in the eye. "I'll be right behind you." She paused a moment, then nodded and kept going.

"Hey, Easton," I said. "I'll take Ruf—Tiddlywinks for you." I held out my hands and put on an innocent face. "You ought to be careful in those heels, especially what with recovering from your ordeal and everything."

"Oh, you're too sweet," she said. She handed Rufus over to me. "I wouldn't trust Tiddlywinks to just anyone, you know."

"I'll take good care of him," I said. Rufus looked at me curiously, but I waved Easton on ahead of me. She followed behind Viv. I stayed a few steps back and followed behind as well, like I'd said I would, but when I got to the bottom of the bleachers and they went left, I headed right instead and ducked behind a group of parade watchers. I found a big-bellied guy who was paying close attention to the parade (the current float had some pretty blonde girls dressed in some kind of native German folk costumes that had low, square-cut necklines) and made sure he was between me and Viv. If I was lucky, she wouldn't notice I was gone for a while.

So, what's up? I'm sure you didn't bring me down here to get a closer look at the parade.

"Nope," I said. "I need your help, Rufus. Do you remember what Regina smells like?"

Remember? Her stench is burned into my brain. Why? What are you thinking?

"We can get Regina if you help me. It's the only way. You know it and I know it."

"And I know it, too," said Ian.

I jumped about a foot in the air and almost elbowed the big guy in the gut. "What are you doing here?"

"I saw you give your sister the slip and figured you were up to something. Which you obviously are."

"Well, go back," I said. "It's too dangerous. She's got a gun and who knows what else she's picked up on the way here?"

"Exactly," he said. "You can't do this by yourself."

She won't be by herself, stupid. I'll be with her, said Rufus.

Maybe Ian was starting to pick up a little Cat. "*And* you need someone with you who's taller than knee height. I don't care if he does have claws. Besides, I've got this." He held up Easton's pink taser.

A little old woman with overly permed hair gave us a slightly terrified look. I put my hand on Ian's and brought it down. I took the taser from him and jammed it in my pocket.

"Thanks," I said. "I hadn't thought about a weapon. Do you know how to use it?"

"Not sure. I think you point and shoot it like a gun. I've only seen one on some reality TV show when they shocked some celebrities for fun."

Just leave it to me, said Rufus. *You'll probably hurt yourselves. I'll take care of her.*

"You know," said Ian, "we *could* enlist the help of one of the agents." He motioned back toward the bleachers where a sunglass-wearing, solidly built guy in a suit had appeared and was monitoring the crowd. He had BERM written all over him. Not literally, but it might as well have been. He couldn't be any more obvious unless he was wearing a T-shirt with the BERM logo on it.

"Are you kidding me? If Regina sees him with us, she'll know something's up for sure."

"True enough. But that's another reason why I'm perfect to help you out," said Ian. "Regina won't think it's suspicious at all if I'm with you."

Why? Because she's seen us together before? Because he's my age? Because . . . ?

"Okay," I said. "But whatever we do, we should hurry. Once Viv figures out we're gone, she'll be back and she'll probably have reinforcements."

Ian grabbed the hand that wasn't hanging on to Rufus and pulled me past the big guy. We slipped through the crowd along the parade route in the opposite direction Viv and everyone else had gone. I hoped he couldn't tell that my hand was all sweaty. And I hoped no one was paying any attention to the huge bulge in my right pocket. Easton's taser felt big enough to take out an elephant.

"If Regina's already here and paying attention, we'll just look like boyfriend and girlfriend getting away from the family," he whispered.

Oh. "Right. Very not suspicious." Except for the fact that, as love-struck teens, we apparently needed a cat chaperone. But maybe she wouldn't notice Rufus.

What was I thinking? Of course she'd notice Rufus. He was *pink*. I'd boosted him up and he was draped around my shoulders like some kind of living scarf now, but he was still bright pink.

"And we won't get separated this way." He squeezed my hand.

Was it just me, or was he justifying the hand holding a little too much?

"I noticed something yesterday," I said. "I think she can't

change when she's touching more than one person. Or being touched. Whatever. Like when all the guys grabbed her? She just stayed as Victoria and didn't try to turn."

"Interesting," he said.

Who cares? said Rufus. *Just use that stun gun thing on her and make her beg. Then let me at her when she's down.*

"Hey," said Ian. "Isn't that Melly and Oscar on that float?"

It was the float I'd seen Alan standing by earlier. Strangely enough for a German Day parade float, it had American flags on it. It paused in front of the stands, and the camera crew looked like they were on full alert. Oscar was dressed in some odd lederhosen kind of thing and a Peter Pan-style hat with a feather and everything. He was in the back of the float, along with a bunch of other similarly dressed people. But Melly was center stage, right next to Ty. Or rather, center float.

Ty grabbed a microphone and started lip-syncing to "Twist and Shout." He grabbed Melly around the waist and danced with her. She sang along with him, or at least mouthed the words. It was hard to tell. All of the other people on the float, including Oscar, were clapping and swaying. About halfway through the song, Alan made a motion with his hand and Melly jumped down from the float. Some of the movie crew helped Claire up and she took Melly's place. I guessed it must be part of the audition thing Melly had told me about. Maybe they were filming the audition and would decide between the two later? It wasn't like they could reschedule German Day for a filming delay, so they seemed to be making the best of it.

The crowd was singing and dancing along with the people on the float, pretty much just like I remembered from the *Ferris Bueller* movie, except not so choreographed. It was like a giant party.

I think I smell her, yowled Rufus over the noise, right into my ear.

I squeezed Ian's hand. He looked at me and I nodded and motioned with my chin toward Rufus. Ian raised an eyebrow, then nodded back.

"Where?" I asked Rufus. He had his claws firmly embedded in my shoulders. With the number of times I'd been clawed this week, I was probably going to be scarred for life.

I don't know yet, he growled. *There are a lot of people here, in case you hadn't noticed, and many of them smell decidedly unwashed. I'll let you know.*

I put my right hand in my pocket on the taser and scanned the crowd. Melly had moved off to the side and was holding her hands up and swaying with the music. She looked absolutely ecstatic. I saw Alan nudge one camera guy and point to her. The camera guy swiveled his camera away from the center of the float and pointed it at Melly. I bet Claire wouldn't like that.

Someone else didn't seem to like it either. A skinny girl with dishwater blonde hair was staring at Melly with this look on her face like she'd eaten something foul. There wasn't anything particularly ugly about her, but she just looked *mean*. Her mouth was curled in a familiar snarl. It *had* to be Regina. No matter what body she was in, she had the same evil look.

"Is that her?" I asked Rufus. "Can you tell?"

He took a look and sniffed the air. *I can't tell for sure. The smell is coming from that way, definitely, but there are a lot of smells coming from that way. And the horse that passed by earlier had some bad grain.*

"It has to be her," I said to Ian. "Who else would be looking at Melly like that?"

"Maybe she's just jealous?"

I groaned. What a guy thing to say. "Sorry," he said. "You're probably right. But are you sure enough about it to stun her with the taser before she does anything?"

Well, when he put it that way. I watched the girl for a few minutes. She hadn't made a move on Melly or anything. She was just glaring at her. It's not like it was a crime to glower at someone.

"Rufus?"

Still can't tell, he said. *You'll have to get me closer.*

"Closer," I said to Ian. He nodded and stepped forward to squeeze between two older women dancing to "Twist and Shout." I followed behind him as he pulled on my hand. I got an elbow in my ear from one overly enthusiastic dancer. Rufus swiped at her. Luckily she didn't notice.

"Keep it together, Rufus," I said.

You try picking out one person's smell in this mess, said Rufus. *And I'm going to have a headache for days. It's loud.*

"Sorry," I said.

We snaked between gyrating dancers and old people with walkers and some parade security people until we were about five feet away from Melly and the mystery girl. She still hadn't done anything, and Melly was still dancing and singing, oblivious to everything but the camera. Good thing the camera guy was positioned kind of behind and to the left of the mystery girl, or else she'd be ruining the shot with the sour expression on her face.

"Okay, Rufus," I whispered. "I think this is as close as we can get. What do you think?"

Before he could take a good sniff, the girl looked up and saw us. Her lip pulled back even further. She was practically baring her teeth at us. It had to be Regina. Who else would hate me on sight? Other than old people who just hate teenagers. She glanced at Melly, then back at me, and gave me the most wicked grin I've ever seen. She put her hand in her pocket and stepped toward Melly.

I fumbled getting the taser out of my pocket, but managed to point it at her. I dropped Ian's hand so I could put both hands on the taser to aim it. Rufus dug his claws into my shoulder, steadying himself.

"Gun!" yelled a woman next to me, and at first I thought she was talking about the taser. It was vaguely gun shaped, though I'd never seen a gun that was anywhere near so pink.

But it was Regina she was pointing at. She'd pulled a real gun out of her pocket. I couldn't tell who she was bringing it up to point at. Was she trying to shoot Melly? Me? Rufus?

People screamed and panicked, but with the crowd plus camera crew everywhere, there wasn't anywhere to go. Melly stopped dancing and looked around, confused. One guy shoved in between me and Regina, screaming his head off, leaving a hole in the crowd.

Shoot her! Rufus howled.

I pulled the trigger.

Nothing happened.

"It must have a safety!" Ian shouted at me, but there was no time to look for one. I had no idea what a safety looked like. I barely knew what a *trigger* looked like.

I took Rufus, still yowling, from around my neck and pitched him as hard as I could in the general direction of Regina. "I'm sorry, Rufus!" I shouted, and followed behind him. He landed on her forearm as the gun went off, but Regina stayed standing, barely. I couldn't tell where the bullet had gone, but no one dropped, so that was a good sign. People scattered in every direction, except for Melly, who froze where she was.

Ian had leaped at the same time I did, but I reached Regina first. I didn't see Rufus. Had she shot him? Oh, no. Maybe I should have thrown the stupid taser instead. What was I thinking? Well, I guess I'd been thinking "ticking furry time bomb with claws." It had worked once before, after all.

Then Rufus shrieked and I saw him climbing up the back of her leg. *The gun*, he yowled. *Get the gun!*

Regina raised the gun and pointed it at me. Before she could pull the trigger, I whacked her square across the face with the taser so hard that I heard it crack. The taser, that is. I wouldn't have minded if it were her face. She stumbled, but she didn't drop the gun. I threw the taser down and grabbed for her gun instead. I pushed so that it was pointed straight up in the air. We danced around like that as Ian tried to help and Rufus kept climbing until he was up to the back of her neck. He hauled himself over her shoulder and bit her right on the nose.

If she hadn't hated cats before, I was pretty sure she did now.

"I'm going to kill you and then your stupid cat," she yelled at me from behind the wall of wailing fur that was Rufus. She shook her head and his grip on her nose loosened, but he was still firmly attached with his claws to her shoulder. A crow bar couldn't pry him off this time.

"Not if I have anything to do about it," I said grimly, and kept working at wrestling the gun away from her.

Then she surprised me by just letting it go. I stumbled back, juggling the gun, and almost lost it. She grabbed Rufus by the neck and pulled him off, losing some skin and strips of her shirt in the process. She threw him on the ground and kicked him toward the sidewalk. People were still stampeding by, except for the camera guy, who seemed completely blasé about the whole thing and was still filming.

I didn't have time to see if Rufus was okay, though, because she grabbed my arm, and at first I thought she was going for the gun again. But then I felt that familiar pull. She was trying to drain me of energy! Or maybe she was just trying to change her look long enough to confuse things. Either way, I could feel my knees starting to buckle.

"Ian," I yelled, "Touch me! Or grab her! Or both!" I hoped he remembered what I'd said. I wasn't sure if it was better for him to be touching her or me. Or if it would work at all. Maybe she'd just been surprised by the guys at the ballpark and my bright idea was going to get us both killed.

Regina was kind of swinging me around, making it hard to stay on my feet and probably harder for Ian to grab us. He finally wrapped us both in a huge bear hug. The feeling I was being pulled apart from the inside out immediately stopped.

"Don't let go!" I yelled and dropped the gun to grab her myself.

That was when Oscar took a running leap from atop the float and landed on top of all of us.

THIRTY-SIX

MONDAY, SEPTEMBER 14, 7:32 A.M.

"I'VE HEARD IT SAID THAT CATS ARE DEVIOUS, EVIL, AND MEAN. WHY ARGUE?
WE ALSO HAVE MANY OTHER GOOD QUALITIES."
—RUFUS BRUTUS THE THIRD

I kept insisting it was Oscar who had saved the day with his flying leap, but that didn't stop everyone from wanting to talk to me. Mom and Dad hadn't let me out of their sight on Sunday as we made the rounds of the BERM offices and the mayor's office, and we were even interviewed on one of the local news channels. I really hadn't wanted to do the interview, but so many reporters were hounding us and surrounding our house that Dad finally agreed to one interview to get them off our backs. Principal Johnson had even given us a call after the interview had aired. He had actually apologized for doubting me in the whole cafeteria fiasco, not to mention the ancient-history dustup with my biology teacher. Mom, of course, had grabbed the phone from me and had given him a talking to about ever allowing crazy movie people around the students of Shermer High again.

323

She'd also given a piece of her mind to Viv, not to mention the BERM higher-ups, including Dad. The pants in the family had definitely gone back on Mom.

Regina was in BERM custody again under constant watch by no fewer than three agents at a time in a maximum-security facility. She was in a cell by herself with no body contact allowed. If she somehow managed to escape again, I didn't want to be the guy in charge. Mom was ready to seriously go medieval on the BERM if they let Regina break out again.

When I arrived at school on Monday, it was surreal. Oscar and Melly were waiting for me in our usual spot. But this time, it wasn't like we were an island of freakishness that everyone else just flowed around on their way into the building. It was more like we were the main stage at Lollapalooza.

There was a lot of "Hey, Cat Girl" going on, but also a bunch of "Tase her, dude!" and high fives for all of us. A couple of seniors tried to get Oscar to duplicate his flying tackle, but Garrett came along at exactly the right time and managed to talk him out of it. Finally, Principal Johnson himself came out and told us to get to class so that everyone would disperse. We went inside to one last round of applause.

"Well," I said. "I gotta go to trig. I guess I'll see you later?"

"Sure!" said Oscar. Melly gave me a hug and nodded, then they both left. Things were still a little weird among the three of us. We hadn't had a chance to really talk since I'd blown up at them in the makeup trailer. They'd been interviewed all over the place on Sunday too, but I'd seen them and their families only in passing in the BERM building.

Or since Alan had turned over the camera guy's tape of the parade to the local CBS station, as if the newspaper article and interview hadn't been bad enough. The clip was even on YouTube (and somehow, I kind of suspected Oscar might have put it up there himself). I was officially famous. We all were. It kind of made Oscar and Melly talking to the press on Friday a bit less important. I was still mad about it, but Emmy had summed it up. "The cat's out of the bag now," she'd said last night. "You might as well get used to it."

At least no one had meowed at me so far.

I pushed open the door to trigonometry and the room went silent. Then Shackerman from his spot in the back of the room called out, "Hey, Ian. Here's your girlfriend! *Meee-yoooow-ow!*"

I froze.

Ian stood up. "Hey, Shackerman, you just wish you *had* a girlfriend. Or that she was half as kick-ass as Nat."

"Yeah, watch out, Shack," said Sarah Yung from the front row. "Or maybe Cat Girl will scratch your eyes out." She laughed and then meowed at Shackerman. He hissed back and clawed in her direction like a cat.

I ran.

♥

The thing about school is, there's really nowhere to run to. The hallways were still pretty full of kids making their way to class, the classrooms were obviously full, and even the bathrooms were busy. Shoot, girls' bathrooms were pretty much always busy. That left the cafeteria or the library, and I really didn't want to set foot on the site of my last huge school humiliation, so I headed straight to the library.

It was empty, thankfully. Half the lights hadn't even been turned on yet. I sat down in one of the study cubicles in a dark corner and put my head down on my crossed arms. I had to admit that I'd had hope this morning that maybe it wouldn't be so bad. Then all the kids outside had been all "you go, girl" and slapping me on the back. But I should have known better. After all, this was high school. Let the nightmare and the meowing begin.

"Hey," said Ian.

I didn't lift my head. "How did you find me?" I said into my sleeve.

"I was right behind you. Didn't you hear me calling you?"

"No." Great. I bet that was a nice scene going down the hallway. Yet another thing to live down. "Sorry."

I heard the scrape of a chair as he pulled one over from the next cube and sat down. I could just make out the toe of his right shoe. He'd drawn a smiley face with X's for eyes on it.

"So, what're you doing?"

"Nothing," I said. Which was true. This was pretty much as nothing as it gets.

"This isn't the Nat I know," he said. "The Nat I know totally kicks butt. She takes out body-stealing kidnappers and breaks into houses." He put his hand on my shoulder. It felt warm even though my shirt.

"I knew this was going to happen," I said. I felt like I was back in kindergarten with that kid getting everyone to meow at me and the teachers just standing by not doing anything.

"What?"

"The whole Cat Girl thing. The meowing." I hitched my shoulders up and let them fall again, but his hand stayed where it was. I was *not* going to cry. Not in front of Ian.

"Shackerman? Shackerman is a douche biscuit with a brain the size of a peanut. He's only scraping by in trig because he cheats like a madman."

"You know it won't be just Shackerman." And even if he was an idiot, he was a popular one. Parties at his house always wound up with half the school there and the cops being called. They were legendary. Last year, he'd been voted most likely to take over a small Caribbean island nation.

"Nat. Look at me." He squeezed my shoulder.

I squished my eyes shut tight for a second, then picked up my head and looked at Ian. He had his head cocked to the side like a curious puppy.

"Do you really care what people like Shackerman think of you? I mean, *Shackerman*? Does anyone even know what his first name is?"

I couldn't help it. I laughed. Then I hiccupped. So much for being cool. But cool really wasn't me. And I really and truly had no clue what Shackerman's first name was.

"That's better." He took his hand from my shoulder and put it under my chin instead. "Do you think Shackerman would have the balls to throw a cat at someone who'd pulled a gun?"

I laughed again. "He'd probably pee himself."

He smiled, then turned serious on me. "Nat, there will always be people out there who'll have something crappy to say. You know, not everyone appreciates my stellar sense of humor—or my style." He ran his free hand through his hair, giving it even more of an I-just-woke-up look. "I figure, why let someone else ruin my day? That's what I've got parents for."

"Does Shackerman by any chance have a cat?"

"I believe he does." He gave me a wicked grin. "Now *that* is the Nat I know and love." He went red as he realized what he'd said, and so did I.

I cleared my throat. "Well, I guess we'd better get back to class before Mr. Beck sends out a search squad." We both stood up, but neither of us took a step toward the door.

"You know, if we count Saturday, we've been on two dates now." Ian was still a little red.

"Both with a psycho killer," I said. "Sorry about that. Though I don't know that I'd count the parade as a date. More like a train wreck."

"Still . . ." He cupped my chin again. "*If* we count that and, you know, you grant me a little leeway with the definition of a date and we count *this* . . ."

"The library?" Did my voice actually squeak? And how

had I never noticed before that the library was actually kind of romantic, in a dusty kind of way? Or maybe it was that only half of the lights were on.

"Sure," he said. "Isn't there some kind of rule about third dates and kissing?"

I didn't know if there was one or not, but I nodded. I didn't think I could actually say anything coherent.

He lowered his head to mine until his lips were only an inch away. "So," he said, "what do you think? Is this a date?"

I could feel his breath tickling my lips. To heck with being timid. I reached up with both hands and pulled his face down that final inch. His lips were softer than I expected and he tasted like cinnamon and orange juice. My knees went a little liquid as his tongue just barely touched my lower lip.

"Wow," he whispered, pulling back. "Cat Girl can kiss."

EASTON WEST'S BLOG

Tuesday, September 15, 3:45 P.M.: Hellooooo poppets! Am I glad to be back! And the real me too! If you weren't following the news, I apologize for the purely uninspired and blatantly FALSE blog posts (which I've deleted now) you've found here . . . but it wasn't me! It was just someone who looked like me, not that all of you lovelies out there in cyberspace can see me as I sit here typing diligently away. (Or can you? I forget how my webcam works. . . .)

Yes, dear readers, I was a victim of Regina Fedorka, along with the lovely Victoria Welling (who isn't actually looking so lovely right now, but you can't blame her for that—she's been a kidnappee for over two YEARS).

And if it weren't for one plucky young lady named Natalie "Cat Girl" Ng and her intrepid band of friends, there's a very good chance I'd be a ghost right now! And not just me! My beloved Tiddlywinks too!

Besides saving my life (with the help of my Tiddlywinks, I might add—my brave furry boy!), Cat Girl has done the impossible!

I always knew that my furry baby was special. With Cat Girl's help, I've been able to really sit down and talk with him, and he's got a lot to say! So stay tuned. I might be having an extended stay here in Chicagoland so I can get to know Tiddlywinks even better.

And you, dear readers, will of course be the first to find out! ♥

AUTHOR'S NOTE

Ferris Bueller's Day Off, written and directed by John Hughes, was released in 1986. Starring Matthew Broderick as Ferris, as well as Alan Ruck, Mia Sara, and Jennifer Grey, it has been called one of the best 100 films of all time by *Total Film* magazine and the number one teen film of all time by *Empire* magazine.

Hughes, who died in 2009, went to high school in Northbrook, Illinois, and he often returned to that locale in his films, though he either left the actual town name unreferenced or called it "Shermer." (Shermerville was the original name of Northbrook.) I don't think he would mind that I borrowed the name for Natalie's high school.

The movie was filmed in 1985 primarily in the Chicago area, including scenes at two local high schools (New Trier High School and Glenbrook North High School) and many of Chicago's most famous landmarks. Many students served as extras on the film and it has a huge following even today, so many years later.

Hughes once said, "Chicago is what I am. A lot of *Ferris* is sort of my love letter to the city."

While I lived in the Chicago area for only a few years, I enjoyed my time there and I really loved exploring Ferris